OVER
THE
RAINBOW

OVER THE RAINBOW

Tales of Fantasy and Imagination

This volume first published in
Great Britain in 1983 by

Octopus Books Limited
59 Grosvenor Street
London W1

This edition first published in 1984

All rights reserved

Arrangement and illustrations © 1983 Hennerwood Publications Limited

ISBN 0 7064 2159 0

Printed in the United States of America
by Halliday Lithograph

CONTENTS

The Truth About Pyecraft   H.G. Wells   9

Warriors in the Mist   Ursula Le Guin   22
from *A Wizard of Earthsea*

The Cats, the Cow, and the Burglar   E. Nesbit   37
from *The Phoenix and the Carpet*

Doctor Dolittle's Reward   Hugh Lofting   61
from *The Story of Doctor Dolittle*

The White-haired Children   Ruth Ainsworth   69

Harriet's Hairloom   Joan Aiken   89

The Way Out   Mary Norton   107
from *The Borrowers Afloat*

Riddles in the Dark   J.R.R. Tolkien   125
from *The Hobbit*

The Phantom Tollbooth   Norton Juster   148
from *The Phantom Tollbooth*

Rip Van Winkle   Washington Irving   168

The Lion and the Unicorn   Lewis Carroll   188
from *Through the Looking-Glass*

The Wind on the Moon   Eric Linklater   198
from *The Wind on the Moon*

By Caldron Pool   C.S. Lewis   214
from *The Last Battle*

CONTENTS

A Ring of Stones   Alan Garner   231
from *The Weirdstone of Brisingamen*

Particle Goes Green   Helen Cresswell   250

Escape to the Emerald City   L. Frank Baum   271
from *The Marvellous Land of Oz*

Acknowledgements   287

The Truth About Pyecraft

H. G. Wells

e sits not a dozen yards away. If I glance over my shoulder I can see him. And if I catch his eye—and usually I catch his eye—it meets me with an expression—

It is mainly an imploring look—and yet with suspicion in it.

Confound his suspicion! If I wanted to tell on him I should have told long ago. I don't tell and I don't tell, and he ought to feel at his ease. As if anything so gross and fat as he could feel at ease! Who would believe me if I did tell?

Poor old Pyecraft! Great, uneasy jelly of substance! The fattest clubman in London.

He sits at one of the little club tables in the huge bay by the fire, stuffing. What is he stuffing? I glance judiciously and catch him biting at the round of hot buttered teacake, with his eyes on me. Confound him!—with his eyes on me!

That settles it, Pyecraft! Since you will be abject, since you will behave as though I was not a man of honour, here, right under your embedded eyes, I write the thing down—the plain truth about Pyecraft. The man I helped, the man I shielded, and who has requited me by making my club unendurable, absolutely unendurable, with his liquid appeal, with the perpetual 'don't tell' of his looks.

And, besides, why does he keep on eternally eating?

Well, here goes for the truth, the whole truth, and nothing but the truth!

Pyecraft—I made the acquaintance of Pyecraft in this very smoking-room. I was a young, nervous new member, and he saw it. I was sitting all alone, wishing I knew more of the members, and suddenly he came, a great rolling front of chins and abdomina, towards me, and grunted and sat down in a chair close by me and wheezed for a space, and scraped for a space with a match and lit a cigar, and then addressed me. I forget what he said—something about the matches not lighting properly, and afterwards as he talked he kept stopping the waiters one by one as they went by, and telling them about the matches in that thin, fluty voice he has. But, anyhow, it was in some such way we began our talking.

He talked about various things and came round to games. And thence to my figure and complexion. 'You ought to be a good cricketer,' he said. I suppose I am slender, slender to what some people would call lean, and I suppose I am rather dark, still—I am not ashamed of having a Hindu great-grandmother, but, for all that, I don't want casual strangers to see through me at a glance to her. So that I was set against Pyecraft from the beginning.

But he only talked about me in order to get to himself.

'I expect,' he said, 'you take no more exercise than I do, and you probably eat no less.' (Like all excessively obese people he fancied he ate nothing). 'Yet'—and he smiled an oblique smile—'we differ.'

And then he began to talk about his fatness and his fatness; and all he did for his fatness and all he was going to do for his fatness; what people had advised him to do for his fatness and what he had heard of people doing for fatness similar to his. 'A priori,' he said, 'one would think a question of nutrition could be answered by dietary and a question of assimilation by drugs.' It was stifling. It was dumpling talk. It made me feel swelled to hear him.

One stands that sort of thing once in a way at a club, but a time came when I fancied I was standing too much. He took to me altogether too conspicuously. I could never go into the smoking-room but he would come wallowing towards me, and sometimes he came and gormandized round and about me while I had my lunch. He seemed at times almost to be clinging to me. He was a bore, but not so fearful a bore as to be limited to me; and from the first there was something in his manner—almost as though he knew, almost as though he penetrated to the fact that I might—that there was a remote, exceptional chance in me that no one else presented.

'I'd give anything to get it down,' he would say—'anything,' and peer at me over his vast cheeks and pant.

Poor old Pyecraft! He has just gonged, no doubt to order another buttered teacake!

He came to the actual thing one day. 'Our Pharmacopoeia,' he said, 'our Western Pharmacopoeia, is anything but the last word of medical science. In the East, I've been told—'

He stopped and stared at me. It was like being at an aquarium.

I was quite suddenly angry with him. 'Look here,' I said, 'who told you about my great-grandmother's recipes?'

'Well,' he fenced.

'Every time we've met for a week,' I said, 'and we've met pretty often—you've given me a broad hint or so about that little secret of mine.'

'Well,' he said, 'now the cat's out of the bag, I'll admit, yes, it is so. I had it—'

'From Pattison?'

'Indirectly,' he said, which I believe was lying, 'yes.'

'Pattison,' I said, 'took that stuff at his own risk.'

He pursed his mouth and bowed.

'My great-grandmother's recipes,' I said, 'are queer things to handle. My father was near making me promise—'

'He didn't?'

'No. But he warned me. He himself used one—once.'

'Ah! ... But do you think—? Suppose—suppose there did happen to be one—'

'The things are curious documents,' I said. 'Even the smell of 'em. . . . No!'

But after going so far Pyecraft was resolved I should go farther. I was always a little afraid if I tried his patience too much he would fall on me suddenly and smother me. I own I was weak. But I was also annoyed with Pyecraft. I had got to that state of feeling for him that disposed me to say, 'Well, take the risk!' The little affair of Pattison to which I have alluded was a different matter altogether. What it was doesn't concern us now, but I knew, anyhow, that the particular recipe I used then was safe. The rest I didn't know so much about, and, on the whole, I was inclined to doubt their safety pretty completely.

Yet even if Pyecraft got poisoned—

I must confess the poisoning of Pyecraft struck me as an immense undertaking.

That evening I took that queer, odd-scented sandalwood box out of my safe and turned the rustling skins over. The gentleman who wrote the recipes for my great-grandmother evidently had a weakness for skins of a miscellaneous origin, and his hand-writing was cramped to the last degree. Some of the things are quite unreadable to me—though my family, with its Indian Civil Service associations, had kept up a knowledge of Hindustani from generation to generation—and none are absolutely plain sailing. But I found the one that I knew was there soon enough, and sat on the floor by my safe for some time looking at it.

'Look here,' said I to Pyecraft next day, and snatched the slip away from his eager grasp.

'So far as I can make it out, this is a recipe for Loss of Weight. ('Ah!' said Pyecraft.) I'm not absolutely sure, but I think it's that. And if you take my advice you'll leave it alone. Because, you know—I blacken my blood in your interest, Pyecraft—my ancestors on that side were, so far as I can gather, a jolly queer lot. See?'

'Let me try it,' said Pyecraft.

I leant back in my chair. My imagination made one mighty effort and fell flat within me. 'What in heaven's name, Pyecraft,' I asked, 'do you think you'll look like when you get thin?'

He was impervious to reason. I made him promise never to say a word to me about his disgusting fatness again whatever happened—never, and then I handed him that little piece of skin.

'It's nasty stuff,' I said.

'No matter,' he said, and took it.

He goggled at it. 'But, but—' he said.

He had just discovered that it wasn't English.

'To the best of my ability,' I said, 'I will do you a translation.'

I did my best. After that we didn't speak for a fortnight. Whenever he approached me I frowned and motioned him away, and he respected our compact, but at the end of the fortnight he was as fat as ever. And then he got a word in.

'I must speak,' he said. 'It isn't fair. There's something wrong. It's done me no good. You're not doing your great-grandmother justice.'

'Where's the recipe?'

He produced it gingerly from his pocket-book.

I ran my eye over the items. 'Was the egg addled?' I asked.

'No. Ought it to have been?'

'That,' I said, 'goes without saying in all my poor

dear great-grandmother's recipes. When condition or quality is not specified you must get the worst. She was drastic or nothing.... And there's one or two possible alternatives to some of these other things. You got fresh rattlesnake venom?'

'I got rattlesnake from Jamrach's. It cost—it cost—'

'That's your affair, anyhow. This last item—'

'I know a man who—'

'Yes. H'm. Well, I'll write the alternatives down. So far as I know the language, the spelling of this recipe is particularly atrocious. By-the-bye, dog here probably means pariah dog.'

For a month after that I saw Pyecraft constantly at the club and as fat and anxious as ever. He kept our treaty, but at times he broke the spirit of it by shaking his head despondently. Then one day in the cloak-room he said, 'Your great-grandmother—'

'Not a word against her,' I said: and he held his peace.

I could have fancied he had desisted, and I saw him one day talking to three new members about his fat-ness as though he was in search of other recipes. And then, quite unexpectedly, his telegram came.

'Mr Formalyn!' bawled a page-boy under my nose and I took the telegram and opened it at once.

'For heaven's sake come—Pyecraft.'

'H'm,' said I, and to tell the truth I was so pleased at the rehabilitation of my great-grandmother's repu-tation this evidently promised that I made a most excellent lunch.

I got Pyecraft's address from the hall porter. Pyecraft inhabited the upper half of a house in Bloomsbury, and I went there as soon as I had done my coffee and Trappistine. I did not wait to finish my cigar.

'Mr Pyecraft?' said I, at the front door.

They believed he was ill; he hadn't been out for two days.

'He expects me,' said I, and they sent me up.

I rang the bell at the lattice-door upon the landing.

'He shouldn't have tried it, anyhow,' I said to myself. 'A man who eats like a pig ought to look like a pig.'

An obviously worthy woman, with an anxious face and a carelessly placed cap, came and surveyed me through the lattice.

I gave my name and she opened his door for me in a dubious fashion.

'Well?' said I, as we stood together inside Pyecraft's piece of the landing.

"E said you was to come in if you came,' she said, and regarded me, making no motion to show me anywhere. And then, confidentially, "'E's locked in, sir.'

'Locked in?'

'Locked himself in yesterday morning and 'asn't let anyone in since, sir. And ever and again swearing. Oh, my!'

I stared at the door she indicated by her glances. 'In there?' I said.

'Yes, sir.'

'What's up?'

She shook her head sadly. "E keeps on calling for vittles, sir. 'Eavy vittles 'e wants. I get 'im what I can. Pork 'e's 'ad, sooit puddin', sossiges, noo bread. Everything like that. Left outside, if you please, and me go away. 'E's eatin', sir, somethink awful.'

There came a piping bawl from inside the door: 'That Formalyn?'

'That you, Pyecraft?' I shouted, and went and banged the door.

'Tell her to go away.'

I did.

Then I could hear a curious pattering upon the door, almost like someone feeling for the handle in the dark, and Pyecraft's familiar grunts.

'It's all right,' I said, 'she's gone.'

But for a long time the door didn't open.

I heard the key turn. Then Pyecraft's voice said, 'Come in.'

I turned the handle and opened the door. Naturally I expected to see Pyecraft.

Well, you know, he wasn't there!

I never had such a shock in my life. There was his sitting-room in a state of untidy disorder. Plates and dishes among the books and writing things, and several chairs overturned, but Pyecraft—

'It's all right, o' man; shut the door,' he said, and then I discovered him.

There he was right up close to the cornice in the corner by the door, as though someone had glued him to the ceiling. His face was anxious and angry. He panted and gesticulated. 'Shut the door,' he said. 'If that woman gets hold of it—'

I shut the door, and went and stood away from him and stared.

'If anything gives way and you tumble down,' I said, 'you'll break your neck, Pyecraft.'

'I wish I could,' he wheezed.

'A man of your age and weight getting up to kiddish gymnastics—'

'Don't,' he said, and looked agonized. 'Your damned great-grandmother—'

'Be careful,' I warned him.

'I'll tell you,' he said, and gesticulated.

'How the deuce,' said I, 'are you holding on up there?'

And then abruptly I realized that he was not holding on at all, that he was floating up there—just as a gas-filled bladder might have floated in the same position. He began a struggle to thrust himself away from the ceiling and to clamber down the wall to me. 'It's that prescription,' he panted, as he did so. 'Your great-gran—'

'No!' I cried.

He took hold of a framed engraving rather carelessly
as he spoke and it gave way, and he flew back to the
ceiling again, while the picture smashed on to the sofa.
Bump he went against the ceiling, and I knew then
why he was all over white on the more salient curves
and angles of his person. He tried again more carefully, coming down by way of the mantel.

It was really a most extraordinary spectacle, that
great, fat, apoplectic-looking man upside down and
trying to get from the ceiling to the floor. 'That prescription,' he said. 'Too successful.'

'How?'

'Loss of weight, almost complete.'

And then, of course, I understood.

'By jove, Pyecraft,' said I, 'what you wanted was a
cure for fatness! But you always called it weight. You
would call it weight.'

Somehow I was extremely delighted. I quite liked
Pyecraft for the time. 'Let me help you!' I said, and

took his hand and pulled him down. He kicked about, trying to get foothold somewhere. It was very like holding a flag on a windy day.

'That table,' he said, pointing, 'is solid mahogany and very heavy. If you can put me under that—'

I did, and there he wallowed about like a captive balloon, while I stood on his hearthrug and talked to him.

I lit a cigar. 'Tell me,' I said, 'what happened?'

'I took it,' he said.

'How did it taste?'

'Oh, beastly!'

I should fancy they all did. Whether one regards the ingredients or the probable compound or the possible results, almost all my great-grandmother's remedies appear to me at least to be extraordinarily uninviting. For my own part—

'I took a little sip first.'

'Yes?'

'And as I felt lighter and better after an hour, I decided to take the draught.'

'My dear Pyecraft!'

'I held my nose,' he explained. 'And then I kept on getting lighter and lighter—and helpless, you know.'

He gave way suddenly to a burst of passion. 'What the goodness am I to do?' he said.

'There's one thing pretty evident,' I said, 'that you mustn't do. If you go out of doors you'll go up and up.' I waved an arm ·upward. 'They'd have to send Santos-Dumont after you to bring you down again.'

'I suppose it will wear off?'

I shook my head. 'I don't think you can count on that,' I said.

And then there was another burst of passion, and he kicked out at adjacent chairs and banged the floor. He behaved just as I should have expected a great, fat, self-indulgent man to behave under trying circumstances—that is to say, very badly. He spoke of me and of my great-grandmother with an utter want of discretion.

'I never asked you to take the stuff,' I said.

And generously disregarding the insults he was putting upon me, I sat down in his armchair and began to talk to him in a sober, friendly fashion.

I pointed out to him that this was a trouble he had brought upon himself, and that it had almost an air of poetical justice. He had eaten too much. This he disputed, and for a time we argued the point.

He became noisy and violent, so I desisted from this aspect of his lesson. 'And then,' said I, 'you committed the sin of euphemism. You called it, not Fat, which is just and inglorious, but Weight. You—'

He interrupted to say that he recognized all that. What was he to do?

I suggested he should adapt himself to his new conditions. So we came to the really sensible part of the business. I suggested that it would not be difficult for him to learn to walk about on the ceiling with his hands—

'I can't sleep,' he said.

But that was no great difficulty. It was quite possible, I pointed out, to make a shake-up under a wire mattress, fasten the under things on with tapes, and have a blanket, sheet, and coverlid to button at the side. He would have to confide in his housekeeper, I said; and after some squabbling he agreed to that. (Afterwards it was quite delightful to see the beautifully matter-of-fact way with which the good lady took all these amazing inversions.) He could have a library ladder in his room, and all his meals could be laid on the top of his book-case. We also hit on an ingenious device by which he could get to the floor whenever he wanted, which was simply to put the British Encyclopaedia (tenth edition) on the top of his open shelves. He just pulled out a couple of volumes and held on, and down he came. And we agreed there must be iron staples along the skirting, so that he could cling to those whenever he wanted to get about the room on the lower level.

As we got on with the thing I found myself almost keenly interested. It was I who called in the house-keeper and broke matters to her, and it was I chiefly who fixed up the inverted bed. In fact, I spent two whole days at his flat. I am a handy, interfering sort of man with a screwdriver, and I made all sorts of ingeni-ous adaptations for him—ran a wire to bring his bells within reach, turned all his electric lights up instead of down, and so on. The whole affair was extremely curious and interesting to me, and it was delightful to think of Pyecraft like some great, fat blow-fly, crawling about on his ceiling and clambering round the lintel of his doors from one room to another, and never, never, never coming to the club any more. . . .

Then, you know, my fatal ingenuity got the better of me. I was sitting by his fire drinking his whisky, and he was up in his favourite corner by the cornice, tack-ing a Turkey carpet to the ceiling, when the idea struck me. 'By jove, Pyecraft!' I said, 'all this is totally un-necessary.'

And before I could calculate the complete conse-quences of my notion I blurted it out. 'Lead under-clothing,' said I, and the mischief was done.

Pyecraft received the thing almost in tears. 'To be right ways up again—' he said.

I gave him the whole secret before I saw where it would take me. 'Buy sheet lead,' I said, 'stamp it into discs. Sew 'em all over your underclothes until you have enough. Have lead-soled boots, carry a bag of solid lead, and the thing is done! Instead of being a prisoner here you may go abroad again, Pyecraft! you may travel—'

A still happier idea came to me. 'You need never fear a shipwreck. All you need do is just slip off some or all of your clothes, take the necessary amount of luggage in your hand, and float up in the air—'

In his emotion he dropped the tack-hammer within an ace of my head. 'By jove!' he said, 'I shall be able to come back to the club again.'

The thing pulled me up short. 'By jove!' I said, faintly. 'Yes. Of course—you will.'

He did. He does. There he sits behind me now stuffing—as I live!—a third go of buttered teacake. And no one in the whole world knows—except his housekeeper and me—that he weighs practically nothing; that he is a mere boring mass of assimilatory matters, mere clouds in clothing, niente, nefas, and most inconsiderable of men. There he sits watching until I have done this writing. Then, if he can, he will waylay me. He will come billowing up to me....

He will tell me over again all about it, how it feels, how it doesn't feel, how he sometimes hopes it is passing off a little. And always somewhere in that fat, abundant discourse he will say, 'The secret's keeping, eh? If anyone knew of it—I should be so ashamed.... Makes a fellow look such a fool, you know. Crawling about on a ceiling and all that....'

And now to elude Pyecraft, occupying, as he does, an admirable strategic position between me and the door.

WARRIORS IN THE MIST

Ursula Le Guin

he island of Gont, a single mountain that lifts its peak a mile above the storm-racked Northeast Sea, is a land famous for wizards. From the towns in its high valleys and the ports on its dark narrow bays many a Gontishman has gone forth to serve the Lords of the Archipelago in their cities as wizard or mage, or, looking for adventure, to wander working magic from isle to isle of all Earthsea.

Of these some say the greatest, and surely the greatest voyager, was the man called Sparrowhawk, who in his day became both dragonlord and Archmage. His life is told of in the *Deed of Ged* and in many songs, but this is a tale of the time before his fame, before the songs were made.

He was born in a lonely village called Ten Alders, high on the mountain at the head of the Northward Vale. Below the village the pastures and ploughlands of the Vale slope downward level below level towards the sea, and other towns lie on the bends of the River Ar; above the village only forest rises ridge behind ridge to the stone and snow of the heights.

The name he bore as a child, Duny, was given him by his mother, and that and his life were all she could give him, for she died before he was a year old. His father, the bronzesmith of the village, was a grim unspeaking man, and since Duny's six brothers were older than he by many years and went one by one from home to farm the land or sail the sea or work as smith in other towns of the Northward Vale, there was no one to bring the child up in tenderness.

He grew wild, a thriving weed, a tall, quick boy, loud and proud and full of temper. With the few other children of the village he herded goats on the steep meadows above the river-springs; and when he was strong enough to push and pull the long bellows-sleeves, his father made him work as smith's boy, at a high cost in blows and whippings.

There was not much work to be got out of Duny. He was always off and away; roaming deep in the forest, swimming in the pools of the River Ar that like all Gontish rivers ran very quick and cold, or climbing by cliff and scarp to the heights above the forest, from which he could see the sea, that broad northern ocean where, past Perregal, no islands are.

A sister of his dead mother lived in the village. She had done what was needful for him as a baby, but she had business of her own and once he could look after himself at all she paid no more heed to him. But one day when the boy was seven years old, untaught and knowing nothing of the arts and powers that are in the world, he heard his aunt crying out words to a goat which had jumped up on to the thatch of a hut and would not come down: but it came jumping when she cried a certain rhyme to it.

Next day herding the longhaired goats on the meadows of High Fall, Duny shouted to them the words he had heard, not knowing their use or meaning or what kind of words they were:

> Noth hierth malk man
> hiolk han merth han!

He yelled the rhyme aloud, and the goats came to him. They came very quickly, all of them together, not making any sound. They looked at him out of the dark slot in their yellow eyes.

Duny laughed and shouted it out again, the rhyme that gave him power over the goats. They came closer, crowding and pushing round him.

All at once he felt afraid of their thick, ridged horns and their strange eyes and their strange silence. He tried to get free of them and to run away. The goats ran with him keeping in a knot around him, and so they came charging down into the village at last, all the goats going huddled together as if a rope were pulled tight round them, and the boy in the midst of them weeping and bellowing. Villagers ran from their houses to swear at the goats and laugh at the boy. Among them came the boy's aunt, who did not laugh. She said a word to the goats, and the beasts began to bleat and browse and wander, freed from the spell.

'Come with me,' she said to Duny.

She took him into her hut where she lived alone. She let no child enter there usually, and the children feared the place.

It was low and dusky, windowless, fragrant with herbs that hung drying from the crosspole of the roof, mint and moly and thyme, yarrow and rushwash and paramal, kingsfoil, clovenfoot, tansy and bay. There his aunt sat crosslegged by the firepit, and looking sidelong at the boy through the tangles of her black hair she asked him what he had said to the goats, and if he knew what the rhyme was. When she found that he knew nothing, and yet had spellbound the goats to come to him and follow him, then she saw that he must have in him the makings of power.

As her sister's son he had been nothing to her, but now she looked at him with a new eye. She praised him, and told him she might teach him rhymes he would like better, such as the word that makes a snail look out of its shell, or the name that calls a falcon down from the sky.

'Aye, teach me that name!' he said, being clear over the fright the goats had given him; and puffed up with her praise of his cleverness.

The witch said to him, 'You will not ever tell that word to the other children, if I teach it to you.'

'I promise.'

She smiled at his ready ignorance. 'Well and good. But I will bind your promise. Your tongue will be stilled until I choose to unbind it, and even then, though you can speak, you will not be able to speak the word I teach you where another person can hear it. We must keep the secrets of our craft.'

'Good,' said the boy, for he had no wish to tell the secret to his playmates, liking to know and do what they knew not and could not.

He sat still while his aunt bound back her uncombed hair, and knotted the belt of her dress, and again sat cross-legged throwing handfuls of leaves into the firepit, so that a smoke spread and filled the darkness of the hut. She began to sing. Her voice changed sometimes to low or high as if another voice sang through her, and the singing went on and on until the boy did not know if he waked or slept, and all the while the witch's old black dog that never barked sat by him with eyes red from the smoke. Then the witch spoke to Duny in a tongue he did not understand, and made him say with her certain rhymes and words until the enchantment came on him and held him still.

'Speak!' she said to test the spell.

The boy could not speak, but he laughed.

Then his aunt was a little afraid of his strength, for this was as strong a spell as she knew how to weave: she had tried not only to gain control of his speech and silence, but to bind him at the same time to her service in the craft of sorcery. Yet even as the spell bound him, he had laughed. She said nothing. She threw clear

water on the fire till the smoke cleared away, and gave the boy water to drink, and when the air was clear and he could speak again she taught him the true name of the falcon, to which the falcon must come.

This was Duny's first step on the way he was to follow all his life, the way of magery, the way that led him at last to hunt a shadow over land and sea to the lightless coasts of death's kingdom. But in those first steps along the way, it seemed a broad, bright road.

When he found that the wild falcons stooped down to him from the wind when he summoned them by name, lighting with a thunder of wings on his wrist like the hunting-birds of a prince, then he hungered to know more such names and came to his aunt begging to learn the name of the sparrowhawk and the osprey and the eagle. To earn the words of power he did all the witch asked of him and learned of her all she taught, though not all of it was pleasant to do or know.

There is a saying on Gont, *Weak as woman's magic*, and there is another saying, *Wicked as woman's magic*. Now the witch of Ten Alders was no black sorceress, nor did she ever meddle with the high arts of traffic with Old Powers; but being an ignorant woman among ignorant folk, she often used her crafts to foolish and dubious ends. She knew nothing of the Balance and the Pattern which the true wizard knows and serves, and which keep him from using his spells unless real need demands. She had a spell for every circumstance, and was forever weaving charms. Much of her lore was mere rubbish and humbug, nor did she know the true spells from the false. She knew many curses, and was better at causing sickness, perhaps, than at curing it. Like any village witch she could brew up a love-potion, but there were other, uglier brews she made to serve men's jealousy and hate. Such practices, however, she kept from her young prentice, and as far as she was able she taught him honest craft.

At first all his pleasure in the art-magic was, child-like, the power it gave him over bird and beast, and the knowledge of these. And indeed that pleasure stayed with him all his life. Seeing him in the high pastures often with a bird of prey about him, the other children called him Sparrowhawk, and so he came by the name that he kept in later life as his use-name, when his true-name was not known.

As the witch kept talking of the glory and the riches and the great power over men that a sorcerer could gain, he set himself to learn more useful lore. He was very quick at it. The witch praised him and the children of the village began to fear him, and he himself was sure that very soon he would become great among men. So he went on from word to word and from spell to spell with the witch till he was twelve years old and had learned from her a great part of what she knew: not much, but enough for the witchwife of a small village, and more than enough for a boy of twelve. She had taught him all her lore in herbals and healing, and all she knew of the crafts of finding, binding, mending, unsealing and revealing. What she knew of chanters' tales and the great Deeds she had sung to him, and all the words of the True Speech that she had learned from the sorcerer that taught her, she taught again to Duny. And from weather-workers and wandering jugglers who went from town to town of the Northward Vale and the East Forest he had learned various tricks and pleasantries, spells of illusion. It was with one of these light spells that he first proved the great power that was in him.

*

In those days the Kargad Empire was strong. Those are four great lands that lie between the Northern and the Eastern Reaches: Karego-At, Atuan, Hur-at-Hur, Atnini. The tongue they speak there is not like any spoken in the Archipelago or the other Reaches, and they are a savage people, white-skinned, yellow-haired, and fierce, liking the sight of blood and the

smell of burning towns. Last year they had attacked
the Torikles and the strong island Torheven, raiding in
great force in fleets of red-sailed ships. News of this
came north to Gont, but the Lords of Gont were busy
with their piracy and paid small heed to the woes of
other lands. Then Spevy fell to the Kargs and was
looted and laid waste, its people taken as slaves, so
that even now it is an isle of ruins. In lust of conquest
the Kargs sailed next to Gont, coming in a host, thirty
great longships, to East Port. They fought through that
town, took it, burned it; leaving their ships under
guard at the mouth of the River Ar they went up the
Vale wrecking and looting, slaughtering cattle and
men. As they went they split into bands, and each of
these bands plundered where it chose. Fugitives
brought warning to the villages of the heights. Soon
the people of Ten Alders saw smoke darken the eastern sky, and that night those who climbed the High
Fall looked down on the Vale all hazed and red-
streaked with fires where fields ready for harvest had
been set ablaze, and orchards burned, the fruit roast-
ing on the blazing boughs, and barns and farmhouses
smouldered in ruin.

Some of the villagers fled up the ravines and hid in
the forest, and some made ready to fight for their lives,
and some did neither but stood about lamenting. The
witch was one who fled, hiding alone in a cave up on
the Kapperding Scarp and sealing the cave-mouth
with spells. Duny's father the bronze-smith was one
who stayed, for he would not leave his smelting-pit
and forge where he had worked for fifty years. All that
night he laboured beating up what ready metal he had
there into spearpoints, and others worked with him
binding these to the handles of hoes and rakes, there
being no time to make sockets and shaft them properly. There had been no weapons in the village but
hunting bows and short knives, for the mountain folk
of Gont are not warlike; it is not warriors they are

famous for, but goat-thieves, sea-pirates, and wizards.

With sunrise came a thick white fog, as on many autumn mornings in the heights of the island. Among their huts and houses down the straggling street of Ten Alders the villagers stood waiting with their hunting bows and new-forged spears, not knowing whether the Kargs might be far off or very near, all silent, all peering into the fog that hid shapes and distances and dangers from their eyes.

With them was Duny. He had worked all night at the forge-bellows, pushing and pulling the two long sleeves of goathide that fed the fire with a blast of air. Now his arms so ached and trembled from that work that he could not hold out the spear he had chosen. He did not see how he could fight or be of any good to himself or the villagers. It rankled at his heart that he should die, spitted on a Kargish lance, while still a boy: that he should go into the dark land without ever having known his own name, his true name as a man. He looked down at his thin arms, wet with cold fog-dew, and raged at his weakness, for he knew his strength. There was power in him, if he knew how to use it, and he sought among all the spells he knew for some device that might give him and his companions an advantage, or at least a chance. But need alone is not enough to set power free: there must be knowledge.

The fog was thinning now under the heat of the sun that shone bare above on the peak in a bright sky. As the mists moved and parted in great drifts and smoky wisps, the villagers saw a band of warriors coming up the mountain. They were armoured with bronze helmets and greaves and breast-plates of heavy leather and shields of wood and bronze, and armed with swords and the long Kargish lance. Winding up along the steep bank of the Ar they came in a plumed, clanking, straggling line, near enough already that

their white faces could be seen, and the words of their jargon heard as they shouted to one another. In this band of the invading horde there were about a hundred men, which is not many; but in the village were only eighteen men and boys.

Now need called knowledge out: Duny, seeing the fog blow and thin across the path before the Kargs, saw a spell that might avail him. An old weather-worker of the Vale, seeking to win the boy as prentice, had taught him several charms. One of these tricks was called fogweaving, a binding-spell that gathers the mists together for a while in one place; with it one skilled in illusion can shape the mist into fair ghostly seemings, which last a little and fade away. The boy had no such skill, but his intent was different, and he had the strength to turn the spell to his own ends. Rapidly and aloud he named the places and the boundaries of the village, and then spoke the fogweaving charm, but in among its words he enlaced the words of a spell of concealment, and last he cried the word that set the magic going.

Even as he did so his father coming up behind him struck him hard on the side of the head knocking him right down. 'Be still fool! keep your blattering mouth shut, and hide if you can't fight!'

Duny got to his feet. He could hear the Kargs now at the end of the village, as near as the great yew-tree by the tanner's yard. Their voices were clear, and the clink and creak of their harness and arms, but they could not be seen. The fog had closed and thickened all over the village, greying the light, blurring the world till a man could hardly see his own hands before him.

'I've hidden us all,' Duny said, sullenly, for his head hurt from his father's blow, and the working of the doubled incantation had drained his strength. 'I'll keep up this fog as long as I can. Get the others to lead them up to High Fall.'

The smith stared at his son who stood wraithlike in that weird, dank mist. It took him a minute to see Duny's meaning, but when he did he ran at once, noiselessly, knowing every fence and corner of the village, to find the others and tell them what to do. Now through the grey fog bloomed a blur of red, as the Kargs set fire to the thatch of a house. Still they did not come up into the village, but waited at the lower end till the mist should lift and lay bare their loot and prey.

The tanner, whose house it was that burned, sent a couple of boys skipping right under the Kargs' noses, taunting and yelling and vanishing again like smoke into smoke. Meantime the older men, creeping behind fences and running from house to house, came close on the other side and sent a volley of arrows and spears at the warriors, who stood all in a bunch. One Karg fell writhing with a spear, still warm from its forging, right through his body. Others were arrow-bitten, and all enraged. They charged forward then to hew down their puny attackers, but they found only the fog about them, full of voices. They followed the voices, stabbing ahead into the mist with their great, plumed, bloodstained lances. Up the length of the street they came shouting, and never knew they had run right through the village, as the empty huts and houses loomed and disappeared again in the writhing grey fog. The villagers ran scattering, most of them keeping well ahead since they knew the ground; but some, boys or old men were slow. The Kargs stumbling on them drove their lances or hacked with their swords, yelling their war-cry, the names of the White God-brothers of Atuan:

'Wuluah! Atwah!'

Some of the band stopped when they felt the land grow rough underfoot, but others pressed right on, seeking the phantom village, following dim wavering shapes that fled just out of reach before them. All the mist had come alive with these fleeing forms, dodging, flickering, fading on every side. One group of the Kargs chased the wraiths straight to the High Fall, the cliff's edge above the springs of Ar, and the shapes they pursued ran out on to the air and there vanished in thinning mist, while the pursuers fell screaming through fog and sudden sunlight a hundred feet sheer to the shallow pools among the rocks. And those that came behind and did not fall stood at the cliff's edge, listening.

Now dread came into the Kargs' hearts and they began to seek one another, not the villagers, in the uncanny mist. They gathered on the hillside, and yet always there were wraiths and ghost-shapes among them, and other shapes that ran and stabbed from behind with spear or knife and vanished again. The Kargs began to run, all of them, downhill, stumbling, silent, until all at once they ran out from the grey blind mist and saw the river and the ravines below the village all bare and bright in morning sunlight. Then they stopped, gathering together, and looked back. A wall of wavering, writhing grey lay blank across the path, hiding all that lay behind it. Out from it burst two or three stragglers, lunging and stumbling along, their long lances rocking on their shoulders. Not one Karg looked back more than that once. All went down, in haste, away from the enchanted place.

Farther down the Northward Vale those warriors got their fill of fighting. The towns of East Forest, from Ovark to the coast, had gathered their men and sent them against the invaders of Gont. Band after band they came down from the hills, and that day and the next the Kargs were harried back down to the beaches above East Port, where they found their ships burnt; so they fought with their backs to the sea till every man of them was killed, and the sands of Armouth were brown with blood until the tide came in.

But on that morning in Ten Alders village and up on the High Fall, the dank grey fog had clung a while, and then suddenly it blew and drifted and melted away. This man and that stood up in the windy brightness of the morning, and looked about him wondering. Here lay a dead Karg with yellow hair long, loose, and bloody; there lay the village tanner, killed in battle like a king.

Down in the village the house that had been set afire still blazed. They ran to put the fire out, since their battle had been won. In the street, near the great yew, they found Duny the bronze-smith's son standing by himself, bearing no hurt, but speechless and stupid

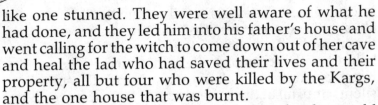

like one stunned. They were well aware of what he had done, and they led him into his father's house and went calling for the witch to come down out of her cave and heal the lad who had saved their lives and their property, all but four who were killed by the Kargs, and the one house that was burnt.

No weapon-hurt had come to the boy, but he would not speak nor eat nor sleep; he seemed not to hear what was said to him, not to see those who came to see him. There was none in those parts wizard enough to cure what ailed him. His aunt said. 'He has overspent his power,' but she had no art to help him.

While he lay thus dark and dumb, the story of the lad who wove the fog and scared off Kargish swordsmen with a mess of shadows was told all down the Northward Vale, and in the East Forest, and high on the mountain and over the mountain even in the Great Port of Gont. So it happened that on the fifth day after the slaughter at Armouth a stranger came into Ten Alders village, a man neither young nor old, who came cloaked and bareheaded lightly carrying a great staff of oak that was as tall as himself. He did not come up the course of the Ar like most people, but down, out of the forests of the higher mountainside. The village goodwives saw well that he was a wizard, and when he told them that he was a healall, they brought him straight to the smith's house. Sending away all but the boy's father and aunt the stranger stooped above the cot where Duny lay staring into the dark, and did no more than lay his hand on the boy's forehead and touch his lips once.

Duny sat up slowly looking about him. In a little while he spoke, and strength and hunger began to come back into him. They gave him a little to drink and eat, and he lay back again, always watching the stranger with dark wondering eyes.

The bronze-smith said to that stranger, 'You are no common man.'

'Nor will this boy be a common man,' the other answered. 'The tale of his deed with the fog has come to Re Albi, which is my home. I have come here to give him his name, if as they say he has not yet made his passage into manhood.'

The witch whispered to the smith, 'Brother, this must surely be the Mage of Re Albi, Ogion the Silent, that one who tamed the earthquake—'

'Sir,' said the bronze-smith who would not let a great name daunt him, 'my son will be thirteen this month coming, but we thought to hold his Passage at the feast of Sun-return this winter.'

'Let him be named as soon as may be,' said the mage, 'for he needs his name. I have other business now, but I will come back here for the day you choose. If you see fit I will take him with me when I go thereafter. And if he prove apt I will keep him as prentice, or see to it that he is schooled as fits his gifts. For to keep dark the mind of the mageborn, that is a dangerous thing.'

Very gently Ogion spoke, but with certainty, and even the hardheaded smith assented to all he said.

On the day the boy was thirteen years old, a day in the early splendour of autumn while still the bright leaves are on the trees, Ogion returned to the village from his rovings over Gont Mountain, and the ceremony of Passage was held. The witch took from the boy his name Duny, the name his mother had given him as a baby. Nameless and naked he walked into the cold springs of the Ar where it rises among rocks under the high cliffs. As he entered the water clouds crossed the sun's face and great shadows slid and mingled over the water of the pool about him. He crossed to the far bank, shuddering with cold but walking slow and erect as he should through that icy, living water. As he came to the bank Ogion, waiting, reached out his hand and clasping the boy's arm whispered to him his true name: Ged.

Thus was he given his name by one very wise in the uses of power.

The feasting was far from over, and all the villagers were making merry with plenty to eat and beer to drink and a chanter from down the Vale singing the *Deed of the Dragonlords*, when the mage spoke in his quiet voice to Ged: 'Come, lad. Bid your people farewell and leave them feasting.'

Ged fetched what he had to carry, which was the good bronze knife his father had forged for him, and a leather coat the tanner's widow had cut down to his size, and an alder-stick his aunt had becharmed for him: that was all he owned besides his shirt and breeches. He said farewell to them, all the people he knew in all the world, and looked about once at the village that straggled and huddled there under the cliffs, over the river-springs. Then he set off with his new master through the steep slanting forests of the mountain isle, through the leaves and shadows of bright autumn.

THE CATS, THE COW, AND THE BURGLAR

E. Nesbit

yril, Anthea (nicknamed Panther), Robert and Jane find a magic carpet in their nursery. Wrapped inside it is a strange egg which hatches into the Phoenix, whose ancient powers transform the children's lives. One evening after tea, the Phoenix offers to entertain them—with quite extraordinary results ...

'This is mere trifling,' said the Phoenix. 'Come, decide what I shall fetch for you. I can get you anything you like.'

But of course they couldn't decide. Many things were suggested—a rocking-horse, jewelled chessmen, an elephant, a bicycle, a motor-car, books with pictures, musical instruments, and many other things. But a musical instrument is agreeable only to the player, unless he has learned to play it really well; books are not sociable, bicycles cannot be ridden without going out of doors, and the same is true of motor-cars and elephants. Only two people can play chess at once with one set of chessmen (and anyway it's very much too much like lessons for a game), and only one can ride on a rocking-horse. Suddenly, in the midst of the discussion, the Phoenix spread its wings and fluttered to the floor, and from there it spoke.

'I gather,' it said, 'from the carpet, that it wants you

to let it go to its old home, where it was born and brought up, and it will return within the hour laden with a number of the most beautiful and delightful products of its native land.'

'What *is* its native land?'

'I didn't gather. But since you can't agree, and time is passing, and the tea-things are not washed down—I mean washed up—'

'I votes we do,' said Robert. 'It'll stop all this jaw, anyway. And it's not bad to have surprises. Perhaps it's a Turkey carpet, and it might bring us Turkish delight.'

'Or a Turkish patrol,' said Robert.

'Or a Turkish bath,' said Anthea.

'Or a Turkish towel,' said Jane.

'Nonsense,' Robert urged, 'it said beautiful and delightful, and towels and baths aren't *that*, however good they may be for you. Let it go. I suppose it won't give us the slip,' he added, pushing back his chair and standing up.

'Hush!' said the Phoenix; 'how can you? Don't trample on its feelings just because it's only a carpet.'

'But how can it do it—unless one of us is on it to do the wishing?' asked Robert. He spoke with a rising hope that it *might* be necessary for one to go—and why not Robert? But the Phoenix quickly threw cold water on his new-born dream.

'Why, you just write your wish on a paper, and pin it on the carpet.'

So a leaf was torn from Anthea's arithmetic book, and on it Cyril wrote in large round-hand the following:

We wish you to go to your dear native home, and bring back the most beautiful and delightful productions of it you can—and not to be gone long, please.

> *Signed*   CYRIL.
> ROBERT.
> ANTHEA.
> JANE.

Then the paper was laid on the carpet.

'Writing down, please,' said the Phoenix; 'the carpet can't read a paper whose back is turned to it, any more than you can.

It was pinned fast, and the table and chairs having been moved, the carpet simply and suddenly vanished, rather like a patch of water on a hearth under a fierce fire. The edges got smaller and smaller, and then it disappeared from sight.

'It may take it some time to collect the beautiful and delightful things,' said the Phoenix. 'I should wash up—I mean wash down.'

So they did. There was plenty of hot water left in the kettle, and every one helped—even the Phoenix, who took up cups by their handles with its clever claws and dipped them in the hot water, and then stood them on the table ready for Anthea to dry them. But the bird was rather slow, because, as it said, though it was not above any sort of honest work, messing about with dishwater was not exactly what it had been brought up to. Everything was nicely washed up, and dried, and put in its proper place, and the dish-cloth washed and hung on the edge of the copper to dry, and the tea-cloth was hung on the line that goes across the scullery. (If you are a duchess's child, or a king's, or a person of high social position's child, you will perhaps not know the difference between a dish-cloth and a tea-cloth; but in that case your nurse has been better instructed than you, and she will tell you all about it.) And just as eight hands and one pair of claws were being dried on the roller-towel behind the scullery door there came a strange sound from the other side of the kitchen wall—the side where the nursery was. It was a very strange sound, indeed—most odd, and unlike any other sounds the children had ever heard. At least, they had heard sounds as much like it as a toy engine's whistle is like a steam siren's.

'The carpet's come back,' said Robert; and the others felt that he was right.

'But what has it brought with it?' asked Jane. 'It sounds like Leviathan, that great beast—'

'It couldn't have been made in India, and have brought elephants? Even baby ones would be rather awful in that room,' said Cyril. 'I vote we take it in turns to squint through the keyhole.'

They did—in the order of their ages. The Phoenix, being the eldest by some thousands of years, was entitled to the first peep. But—

'Excuse me,' it said, ruffling its golden feathers and sneezing softly; 'looking through keyholes always gives me a cold in my golden eyes.'

So Cyril looked.

'I see something grey moving,' said he.

'It's a zoological garden of some sort, I bet,' said Robert, when he had taken his turn. And the soft rustling, bustling, ruffling, scuffling, shuffling, fluffling noise went on inside.

'I can't see anything,' said Anthea, 'my eye tickles so.'

Then Jane's turn came, and she put her eye to the keyhole.

'It's a giant kitty-cat,' she said; 'and it's asleep all over the floor.'

'Giant cats are tigers—father said so.

'No, he didn't. He said tigers were giant cats. It's not at all the same thing.'

'It's no use sending the carpet to fetch precious things for you if you're afraid to look at them when they come,' said the Phoenix, sensibly. And Cyril, being the eldest, said—

'Come on,' and turned the handle.

The gas had been left full on after tea, and everything in the room could be plainly seen by the ten eyes at the door. At least, not everything, for though the carpet was there it was invisible, because it was completely covered by the 199 beautiful objects which it had brought from its birthplace.

'My hat!' Cyril remarked. 'I never thought about its being a *Persian* carpet.'

Yet it was now plain that it was so, for the beautiful objects which it had brought back were cats—Persian cats, grey Persian cats, and there were, as I have said, 199 of them, and they were sitting on the carpet as close as they could get to each other. But the moment the children entered the room the cats rose and stretched, and spread and overflowed from the carpet to the floor, and in an instant the floor was a sea of moving, mewing pussishness, and the children with one accord climbed to the table, and gathered up their legs, and the people next door knocked on the wall—and, indeed, no wonder, for the mews were Persian and piercing.

'This is pretty poor sport,' said Cyril. 'What's the matter with the bounders?'

'I imagine that they are hungry,' said the Phoenix. 'If you were to feed them—'

'We haven't anything to feed them with,' said Anthea in despair, and she stroked the nearest Persian back. 'Oh, pussies, do be quiet—we can't hear ourselves think.'

She had to shout this entreaty, for the mews were growing deafening, 'and it would take pounds' and pounds' worth of cat's-meat.'

'Let's ask the carpet to take them away,' said Robert. But the girls said 'No.'

'They are so soft and pussy,' said Jane.

'And valuable,' said Anthea, hastily. 'We can sell them for lots and lots of money.'

'Why not send the carpet to get food for them?' suggested the Phoenix, and its golden voice became harsh and cracked with the effort it had to make to be heard above the increasing fierceness of the Persian mews.

So it was written that the carpet should bring food for 199 Persian cats, and the paper was pinned to the carpet as before.

The carpet seemed to gather itself together, and the cats dropped off it, as raindrops do from your mackintosh when you shake it. And the carpet disappeared.

Unless you have had 199 well-grown Persian cats in one small room, all hungry, and all saying so in unmistakable mews, you can form but a poor idea of the noise that now deafened the children and the Phoenix. The cats did not seem to have been at all properly brought up. They seemed to have no idea of its being a mistake in manners to ask for meals in a strange house—let alone to howl for them—and they mewed, and they mewed, and they mewed, and they mewed, till the children poked their fingers into their ears and waited in silent agony, wondering why the whole of Camden Town did not come knocking at the door to ask what was the matter, and only hoping that the food for the cats would come before the neighbours did—and before all the secret of the carpet and the Phoenix had to be given away beyond recall to an indignant neighbourhood.

The cats mewed and mewed and twisted their Persian forms in and out and unfolded their Persian tails, and the children and the Phoenix huddled together on the table.

The Phoenix, Robert noticed suddenly, was trembling.

'So many cats,' it said, 'and they might not know I was the Phoenix. These accidents happen so quickly. It quite un-mans me.'

This was a danger of which the children had not thought.

'Creep in,' cried Robert, opening his jacket.

And the Phoenix crept in—only just in time, for green eyes had glared, pink noses had sniffed, white whiskers had twitched, and as Robert buttoned his

coat he disappeared to the waist in a wave of eager
grey Persian fur. And on the instant the good carpet
slapped itself down on the floor. And it was covered
with rats—398 of them, I believe, two for each
cat.

'How horrible!' cried Anthea. 'Oh, take them away!'

'Take yourself away,' said the Phoenix, 'and me.'

'I wish we'd never had a carpet,' said Anthea, in
tears.

They hustled and crowded out of the door, and shut
it, and locked it. Cyril, with great presence of mind, lit
a candle and turned off the gas at the main.

'The rats'll have a better chance in the dark,' he said.

The mewing had ceased. Every one listened in
breathless silence. We all know that cats eat rats—it is
one of the first things we read in our little brown
reading books; but all those cats eating all those rats
—it wouldn't bear thinking of.

Suddenly Robert sniffed, in the silence of the dark
kitchen, where the only candle was burning all on one
side, because of the draught.

'What a funny scent!' he said.

And as he spoke, a lantern flashed its light through
the window of the kitchen, a face peered in, and a
voice said—

'What's all this row about? You let me in.'

It was the voice of the police!

Robert tip-toed to the window, and spoke through
the pane that had been a little cracked since Cyril
accidentally knocked it with a walking-stick when he
was playing at balancing it on his nose. (It was after
they had been to a circus.)

'What do you mean?' he said. 'There's no row. You
listen; everything's as quiet as quiet.'

And indeed it was.

The strange sweet scent grew stronger, and the
Phoenix put out its beak.

The policeman hesitated.

'They're *musk*-rats,' said the Phoenix. 'I suppose some cats eat them—but never Persian ones. What a mistake for a well-informed carpet to make! Oh, what a night we're having!'

'Do go away,' said Robert, nervously. 'We're just going to bed—that's our bedroom candle; there isn't any row. Everything's as quiet as a mouse.'

A wild chorus of mews drowned his words, and with the mews were mingled the shrieks of the musk-rats. What had happened? Had the cats tasted them before deciding that they disliked the flavour?

'I'm a-coming in,' said the policeman. 'You've got a cat shut up there.'

'A cat,' said Cyril. 'Oh, my only aunt! *A* cat!'

'Come in, then,' said Robert. 'It's your own look out. I advise you not. Wait a shake, and I'll undo the side gate.'

He undid the side gate, and the policeman, very cautiously, came in.

And there in the kitchen, by the light of one candle, with the mewing and the screaming going on like a dozen steam sirens, twenty waiting motor-cars, and half a hundred squeaking pumps, four agitated voices shouted to the policeman four mixed and wholly different explanations of the very mixed events of the evening.

Did you ever try to explain the simplest thing to a policeman?

*

The nursery was full of Persian cats and musk-rats that had been brought there by the wishing carpet. The cats were mewing and the musk-rats were squeaking so that you could hardly hear yourself speak. In the kitchen were the four children, one candle, a concealed Phoenix, and a very visible policeman.

'Now then, look here,' said the policeman, very loudly, and he pointed his lantern at each child in turn, 'what's the meaning of this here yelling and caterwaul-

ing? I tell you you've got a cat here, and some one's a
ill-treating of it. What do you mean by it, eh?'

It was five to one, counting the Phoenix; but the
policeman, who was one, was of unusually fine size,
and the five, including the Phoenix, were small. The
mews and the squeaks grew softer, and in the com-
parative silence, Cyril said—

'It's true. There are a few cats here. But we've not
hurt them. It's quite the opposite. We've just fed
them.'

'It don't sound like it,' said the policeman grimly.

'I daresay they're not *real* cats,' said Jane madly,
'perhaps they're only dream-cats.'

'I'll dream-cat you, my lady,' was the brief response
of the force.

'If you understood anything except people who do
murders and stealings and naughty things like that,
I'd tell you all about it,' said Robert; 'but I'm certain
you don't. You're not meant to shove your oar into
people's private cat-keepings. You're only supposed
to interfere when people shout 'murder' and 'stop
thief' in the street. So there!'

The policeman assured them that he should see
about that; and at this point the Phoenix, who had
been making itself small on the pot-shelf under the
dresser, among the saucepan lids and the fish-kettle,
walked on tip-toed claws in a noiseless and modest
manner, and left the room unnoticed by any one.

'Oh, don't be so horrid,' Anthea was saying, gently
and earnestly. 'We *love* cats—dear pussy-soft things.
We wouldn't hurt them for worlds. Would we,
Pussy?'

And Jane answered that of course they wouldn't.
And still the policeman seemed unmoved by their
eloquence.

'Now, look here,' he said, 'I'm a-going to see what's
in that room beyond there, and—'

His voice was drowned in a wild burst of mewing

and squeaking. And as soon as it died down all four children began to explain at once; and though the squeaking and mewing were not at their very loudest, yet there was quite enough of both to make it very hard for the policeman to understand a single word of any of the four wholly different explanations now poured out to him.

'Stow it,' he said at last. 'I'm a-goin' into the next room in the execution of my duty. I'm a-goin' to use my eyes—my ears have gone off their chumps, what with you and them cats.'

And he pushed Robert aside, and strode through the door.

'Don't say I didn't warn you,' said Robert.

'It's tigers *really*,' said Jane. 'Father said so. I wouldn't go in, if I were you.'

But the policeman was quite stony; nothing any one said seemed to make any difference to him. Some policemen are like this, I believe. He strode down the passage, and in another moment he would have been in the room with all the cats and all the rats (musk), but at that very instant a thin, sharp voice screamed from the street outside—

'Murder—murder! Stop thief!'

The policeman stopped, with one regulation boot heavily poised in the air.

'Eh?' he said.

And again the shrieks sounded shrilly and piercingly from the dark street outside.

'Come on,' said Robert. 'Come and look after cats while somebody's being killed outside.' For Robert had an inside feeling that told him quite plainly *who* it was that was screaming.

'You young rip,' said the policeman, 'I'll settle up with you bimeby.'

And he rushed out, and the children heard his boots going weightily along the pavement, and the screams also going along, rather ahead of the policeman; and both the murder-screams and the policeman's boots faded away in the remote distance.

Then Robert smacked his knickerbocker loudly with his palm, and said—

'Good old Phoenix! I should know its golden voice anywhere.'

And then every one understood how cleverly the Phoenix had caught at what Robert had said about the real work of a policeman being to look after murderers and thieves, and not after cats, and all hearts were filled with admiring affection.

'But he'll come back,' said Anthea, mournfully, 'as soon as it finds the murderer is only a bright vision of a dream, and there isn't one at all really.'

'No he won't,' said the soft voice of the clever Phoenix, as it flew in. '*He does not know where your house is.* I heard him own as much to a fellow mercenary. Oh! what a night we are having! Lock the door, and let us rid ourselves of this intolerable smell of the perfume

peculiar to the musk-rat and to the house of the trim-
mers of beards. If you'll excuse me, I will go to bed. I
am worn out.'

It was Cyril who wrote the paper that told the carpet
to take away the rats and bring milk, because there
seemed to be no doubt in any breast that, however
Persian cats may be, they must like milk.

'Let's hope it won't be musk-milk,' said Anthea, in
gloom, as she pinned the paper face-downwards on
the carpet. 'Is there such a thing as a musk-cow?' she
added anxiously, as the carpet shrivelled and vanished. 'I do hope not. Perhaps really it *would* have been
wiser to let the carpet take the cats away. 'It's getting
quite late, and we can't keep them all night.'

'Oh, can't we?' was the bitter rejoinder of Robert,
who had been fastening the side door. 'You might
have consulted me,' he went on. 'I'm not such an idiot
as some people.'

'Why, whatever—'

'Don't you see? We've jolly well *got* to keep the cats
all night—oh, get down, you furry beasts!—because
we've had three wishes out of the old carpet now, and
we can't get any more till tomorrow.'

The liveliness of Persian mews alone prevented the
occurrence of a dismal silence.

Anthea spoke first.

'Never mind,' she said. 'Do you know, I really do
think they're quieting down a bit. Perhaps they heard
us say milk.'

'They can't understand English,' said Jane.

'You forget they're Persian cats, Panther.'

'Well,' said Anthea, rather sharply, for she was tired
and anxious, 'who told you "milk" wasn't Persian for
milk. Lots of English words are just the same in
French—at least I know "miaw" is, and "croquet",
and "fiancé". Oh, pussies, do be quiet! Let's stroke
them as hard as we can with both hands, and perhaps
they'll stop.'

So every one stroked grey fur till their hands were tired, and as soon as a cat had been stroked enough to make it stop mewing it was pushed gently away, and another mewing mouser was approached by the hands of the strokers. And the noise was really more than half purr when the carpet suddenly appeared in its proper place, and on it, instead of rows of milk-cans, or even of milk-jugs, there was a *cow*. Not a Persian cow, either, nor, most fortunately, a musk-cow, if there is such a thing, but a smooth, sleek, dun-coloured Jersey cow, who blinked large soft eyes at the gas-light and mooed in an amiable if rather inquiring manner.

Anthea had always been afraid of cows; but now she tried to be brave.

'Anyway, it can't run after me,' she said to herself. 'There isn't room for it even to begin to run.'

The cow was perfectly placid. She behaved like a strayed duchess till some one brought a saucer for the milk, and some one else tried to milk the cow into it. Milking is very difficult. You may think it is easy, but it is not. All the children were by this time strung up to a pitch of heroism that would have been impossible to them in their ordinary condition. Robert and Cyril held the cow by the horns; and Jane, when she was quite sure that their end of the cow was quite secure, consented to stand by, ready to hold the cow by the tail should occasion arise. Anthea, holding the saucer, now advanced towards the cow. She remembered to have heard that cows, when milked by strangers, are susceptible to the soothing influence of the human voice. So, clutching her saucer very tight, she sought for words to whose soothing influence the cow might be susceptible. And her memory, troubled by the events of the night, which seemed to go on and on for ever and ever, refused to help her with any form of words suitable to address a Jersey cow in.

'Poor pussy, then. Lie down, then, good dog, lie down!' was all that she could think of to say, and she said it.

And nobody laughed. The situation, full of grey mewing cats, was too serious for that.

Then Anthea, with a beating heart, tried to milk the cow. Next moment the cow had knocked the saucer out of her hand and trampled on it with one foot, while with the other three she had walked on a foot each of Robert, Cyril, and Jane.

Jane burst into tears.

'Oh, how much too horrid everything is!' she cried. 'Come away. Let's go to bed and leave the horrid cats with the hateful cow. Perhaps somebody will eat somebody else. And serve them right.'

They did not go to bed, but they had a shivering council in the drawing-room, which smelt of soot —and, indeed, a heap of this lay in the fender. There had been no fire in the room since mother went away, and all the chairs and tables were in the wrong places, and the chrysanthemums were dead, and the water in the pot nearly dried up. Anthea wrapped the embroidered woolly sofa blanket round Jane and herself, while Robert and Cyril had a struggle, silent and brief, but fierce, for the larger share of the fur hearthrug.

'It is most truly awful,' said Anthea, 'and I *am* so tired. Let's let the cats loose.'

'And the cow, perhaps?' said Cyril. 'The police would find us at once. That cow would stand at the gate and mew—I mean moo—to come in. And so would the cats. No; I see quite well what we've got to do. We must put them in baskets and leave them on people's doorsteps, like orphan foundlings.'

'We've got three baskets, counting mother's work one,' said Jane brightening.

'And there are nearly 200 cats,' said Anthea, 'besides the cow—and it would have to be a different-

sized basket for her; and then I don't know how you'd
carry it, and you'd never find a doorstep big enough to
put it on. Except the church one—and—'

'Oh, well,' said Cyril, 'If you simply *make* diffi-
culties—'

'I'm with you,' said Robert. 'Don't fuss about the
cow, Panther. It's simply *got* to stay the night, and I'm
sure I've read that the cow is a remunerating creature,
and that means it will sit still and think for hours. The
carpet can take it away in the morning. And as for the
baskets, we'll do them up in dusters, or pillow-cases,
or bath-towels. Come on, Squirrel. You girls can be
out of it if you like.'

His tone was full of contempt, but Jane and Anthea
were too tired and desperate to care; even being 'out of
it', which at other times they could not have borne,
now seemed quite a comfort. They snuggled down in
the sofa blanket, and Cyril threw the fur hearthrug
over them.

'Ah,' he said, 'that's all women are fit for—to keep
safe and warm, while the men do the work and run
dangers and risks and things.'

'I'm not,' said Anthea, 'you know I'm not.'

But Cyril was gone.

It was warm under the blanket and the hearthrug, and Jane snuggled up close to her sister; and
Anthea cuddled Jane closely and kindly, and in a sort of
dream they heard the rise of a wave of mewing as
Robert opened the door of the nursery. They heard the
booted search for baskets in the back kitchen. They
heard the side door open and close, and they knew
that each brother had gone out with at least one cat.
Anthea's last thought was that it would take at least
all night to get rid of 199 cats by twos. There would be
ninety-nine journeys of two cats each, and one cat
over.

'I almost think we might keep the one cat over,' said
Anthea. 'I don't seem to care for cats just now, but I

daresay I shall again some day.' And she fell asleep. Jane also was sleeping.

It was Jane who awoke with a start, to find Anthea still asleep. As, in the act of awakening, she kicked her sister, she wondered idly why they should have gone to bed in their boots; but the next moment she remembered where they were.

There was a sound of muffled, shuffled feet on the stairs. Like the heroine of the classic poem, Jane 'thought it was the boys', and as she felt quite wide awake, and not nearly so tired as before, she crept gently from Anthea's side and followed the footsteps. They went down into the basement; the cats, who seemed to have fallen into the sleep of exhaustion, awoke at the sound of the approaching footsteps and mewed piteously. Jane was at the foot of the stairs before she saw it was not her brothers whose coming had roused her and the cats, but a burglar. She knew he was a burglar at once, because he wore a fur cap and a red and black charity-check comforter, and he had no business where he was.

If you had been stood in Jane's shoes you would no doubt have run away in them, appealing to the police and neighbours with horrid screams. But Jane knew better. She had read a great many nice stories about burglars, as well as some affecting pieces of poetry, and she knew that no burglar will ever hurt a little girl if he meets her when burgling. Indeed, in all the cases Jane had read of, his burglarishness was almost at once forgotten in the interest he felt in the little girl's artless prattle. So if Jane hesitated for a moment before addressing the burglar, it was only because she could not at once think of any remark sufficiently prattling and artless to make a beginning with. In the stories and the affecting poetry the child could never speak plainly, though it always looked old enough to in the pictures. And Jane could not make up her mind to lisp and 'talk baby', even to a burglar. And while she hesitated he softly opened the nursery door and went in.

Jane followed—just in time to see him sit down flat on the floor, scattering cats as a stone thrown into a pool splashes water.

She closed the door softly and stood there, still wondering whether she *could* bring herself to say, 'What's 'oo doing here, Mithter Wobber?' and whether any other kind of talk would do.

Then she heard the burglar draw a long breath, and he spoke.

'It's a judgement,' he said, 'so help me bob if it ain't. Oh, 'ere's a thing to 'appen to a chap! Makes it come 'ome to you, don't it neither? Cats an' cats an' cats. There couldn't be all them cats. Let alone the cow. If she ain't the moral of the old man's Daisy. She's a dream out of when I was a lad—I don't mind 'er so much. 'Ere, Daisy, Daisy?'

The cow turned and looked at him.

'*She's* all right,' he went on. 'Sort of company, too. Though them above knows how she got into this downstairs parlour. But them cats—oh, take 'em away, take 'em away! I'll chuck the 'ole show—Oh, take 'em away.'

'Burglar,' said Jane, close behind him, and he started convulsively, and turned on her a blank face, whose pale lips trembled. 'I can't take those cats away.'

'Lor-lumme!' exclaimed the man; 'if 'ere ain't another on 'em. Are you real, miss, or something I'll wake up from presently?'

'I am quite real,' said Jane, relieved to find that a lisp was not needed to make the burglar understand her. 'And so,' she added, 'are the cats.'

'Then send for the police, send for the police, and I'll go quiet. If you ain't no realler than them cats, I'm done, spunchuck—out of time. Send for the police. I'll go quiet. One thing, there'd not be room for 'arf them cats in no cell as ever I see.'

He ran his fingers through his hair, which was short, and his eyes wandered wildly round the roomful of cats.

'Burglar,' said Jane, kindly and softly, 'if you didn't like cats, what did you come here for?'

'Send for the police,' was the unfortunate criminal's only reply. 'I'd rather you would—honest, I'd rather.'

'I daren't,' said Jane, 'and besides, I've no one to send. I hate the police. I wish he'd never been born.'

'You've a feeling 'art, miss,' said the burglar; 'but them cats is really a little bit too thick.'

'Look here,' said Jane, 'I won't call the police. And I am quite a real little girl, though I talk older than the kind you've met before when you've been doing your burglings. And they *are* real cats—and they want real milk—and—Didn't you say the cow was like somebody's Daisy that you used to know?'

'Wish I may die if she ain't the very spit of her,' replied the man.

'Well, then,' said Jane—and a thrill of joyful pride ran through her—'Perhaps you know how to milk cows?'

'Perhaps I does,' was the burglar's cautious rejoinder.

'Then,' said Jane, 'if you will *only* milk ours—you don't know how we shall always love you.'

The burglar replied that loving was all very well.

'If those cats only had a good long, wet, thirsty drink of milk,' Jane went on with eager persuasion, 'they'd lie down and go to sleep as likely as not, and then the

police won't come back. But if they go on mewing like this he will, and then I don't know what'll become of us, or you either.'

This argument seemed to decide the criminal. Jane fetched the wash-bowl from the sink, and he spat on his hands and prepared to milk the cow. At this instant boots were heard on the stairs.

'It's all up,' said the man, desperately, 'this 'ere's a plant. *'Ere*'s the police.' He made as if to open the window and leap from it.

'It's all right, I tell you,' whispered Jane, in anguish. 'I'll say you're a friend of mine, or the good clergyman called in, or my uncle, or *anything*—only do, do, do milk the cow. Oh, *don't* go—oh—, thank goodness it's only the boys!'

It was; and their entrance had awakened Anthea, who, with her brothers, now crowded through the doorway. The man looked about him like a rat looks round a trap.

'This is a friend of mine,' said Jane; 'he's just called in, and he's going to milk the cow for us. *Isn't* it good and kind of him?'

She winked at the others, and though they did not understand they played up loyally.

'How do?' said Cyril, 'Very glad to meet you. Don't let us interrupt the milking.'

'I shall 'ave a 'ead and a 'arf in the morning, and no bloomin' error,' remarked the burglar; but he began to milk the cow.

Robert was winked at to stay and see that he did not leave off milking or try to escape, and the others went to get things to put the milk in; for it was now spurting and foaming in the wash-bowl, and the cats had ceased from mewing and were crowding round the cow, with expressions of hope and anticipation on their whiskered faces.

'We can't get rid of any more cats,' said Cyril, as he and his sisters piled a tray high with saucers and soup-plates and platters and pie-dishes, 'the police nearly got us as it was. Not the same one—a much stronger sort. He thought it really was a foundling orphan we'd got. If it hadn't been for me throwing the two bags of cat slap in his eye and hauling Robert over a railing, and lying like mice under a laurel-bush—Well, it's jolly lucky I'm a good shot, that's all. He pranced off when he'd got the cat-bags off his face—thought we'd bolted. And here we are.'

The gentle samishness of the milk swishing into the hand-bowl seemed to have soothed the burglar very much. He went on milking in a sort of happy dream, while the children got a cap and ladled the warm milk out into the pie-dishes and plates, and platters and saucers, and set them down to the music of Persian purrs and lappings.

'It makes me think of old times,' said the burglar, smearing his ragged coat-cuff across his eyes—'about the apples in the orchard at home, and the rats at threshing time, and the rabbits and the ferrets, and how pretty it was seeing the pigs killed.'

Finding him in this softened mood, Jane said—

'I wish you'd tell us how you came to choose our house for your burglaring tonight. I am awfully glad you did. You *have* been so kind. I don't know what we should have done without you,' she added hastily. 'We all love you ever so. Do tell us.'

The others added their affectionate entreaties, and at last the burglar said—

'Well, it's my first job, and I didn't expect to be made
so welcome, and that's the truth, young gents and
ladies. And I don't know but what it won't be my last.
For this 'ere cow, she reminds me of my father, and I
know 'ow 'e'd 'ave 'ided me, if I'd laid 'ands on a
'a'penny as wasn't my own.'

'I'm sure he would,' Jane agreed kindly; 'but what
made you come here?'

'Well, miss,' said the burglar, 'you know best 'ow
you come by them cats, and why you don't like the
police, so I'll give myself away free, and trust to your
noble 'earts. (You'd best bale out a bit, the pan's getting fullish.) I was a-selling oranges off of my barrow—for I ain't a burglar by trade, though you 'ave
used the name so free—an' there was a lady bought
three 'a'porth off me. An' while she was a-pickin' of
them out—very careful indeed, and I'm always glad
when them sort gets a few over-ripe ones—there was
two other ladies talkin' over the fence. An' one on 'em
said to the other on 'em just like this—

' "I've told both gells to come, and they can doss in
with M'ria and Jane, 'cause their boss and his missis is
miles away and the kids too. So they can just lock up
the 'ouse and leave the gas a-burning, so's no one
won't know, and get back bright an' early by 'leven
o'clock. And we'll make a night of it, Mrs Prosser, so
we will. I'm just a-going to run out to pop the letter in
the post." And then the lady what had chosen the
three ha'porth so careful, she said: "Lor, Mrs Wigson,
I wonder at you, and your hands all over suds. This
good gentleman'll slip it into the post for yer, I'll be
bound, seeing I'm a customer of his." So they give me
the letter, and of course I read the direction what was
written on it afore I shoved it into the post. And then
when I'd sold my barrowful, I was a-goin' 'ome with
the chink in my pocket, and I'm blowed if some
bloomin' thievin' beggar didn't nick the lot whilst I
was just a-wettin' of my whistle, for callin' of oranges

is dry work. Nicked the bloomin' lot 'e did—and me with not a farden to take 'ome to my brother and his missus.'

'How awful!' said Anthea, with much sympathy.

'Horful indeed, miss, I believe yer,' the burglar rejoined, with deep feeling. 'You don't know her temper when she's roused. An' I'm sure I 'ope you never may, neither. And I'd 'ad all my oranges off of 'em. So it came back to me what was wrote on the ongverlope, and I says to myself, "Why not, seein' as I've been done myself, and if they keeps two slaveys there must be some pickings?" An' so 'ere I am. But them cats, they've brought me back to the ways of honestness. Never no more.'

'Look here,' said Cyril, 'these cats are very valuable—very indeed. And we will give them all to you, if only you will take them away.'

'I see they're a breedy lot,' replied the burglar. 'But I don't want no bother with the coppers. Did you come by them honest now? Straight?'

'They are all our very own,' said Anthea, 'we wanted them, but the confidement—'

'Consignment,' whispered Cyril.

'—was larger than we wanted, and they're an awful bother. If you got your barrow, and some sacks or baskets, you brother's missus would be awfully pleased. My father says Persian cats are worth pounds and pounds each.'

'Well,' said the burglar—and he was certainly moved by her remarks—'I see you're in a hole—and I don't mind lending a helping 'and. I don't ask 'ow you come by them. But I've got a pal—'e's a mark on cats. I'll fetch him along, and if he thinks they'd fetch anything above their skins I don't mind doin' you a kindness.'

'You won't go away and never come back,' said Jane, 'because I don't think I *could* bear that.'

The burglar, quite touched by her emotion, swore

sentimentally that, alive or dead, he would come back.

Then he went, and Cyril and Robert sent the girls to bed and sat up to wait for his return. It soon seemed absurd to await him in a state of wakefulness, but his stealthy tap on the window awoke them readily enough. For he did return, with the pal and the barrow and the sacks. The pal approved of the cats, now dormant in Persian repletion, and they were bundled into the sacks, and taken away on the barrow—mewing, indeed, but with mews too sleepy to attract public attention.

'I'm a fence—that's what I am,' said the burglar gloomily. 'I never thought I'd come down to this, and all acause er my kind 'eart.'

Cyril knew that a fence is a receiver of stolen goods, and he replied briskly—

'I give you my sacred the cats aren't stolen. What do you make the time?'

'I ain't got the time on me,' said the pal—'but it was just about chucking-out time as I come by the "Bull and Gate". I shouldn't wonder if it was nigh upon one now.'

When the cats had been removed, and the boys and the burglar had parted with warm expressions of friendship, there remained only the cow.

'She must stay all night,' said Robert. 'Cook'll have a fit when she sees her.'

'All night?' said Cyril. 'Why—it's tomorrow morning if it's one. We can have another wish!'

So the carpet was urged, in a hastily written note, to remove the cow to wherever she belonged, and to return to its proper place on the nursery floor. But the cow could not be got to move on to the carpet. So Robert got the clothes line out of the back kitchen, and tied one end very firmly to the cow's horns, and the other end to a bunched-up corner of the carpet, and said 'Fire away.'

And the carpet and cow vanished together, and the

boys went to bed, tired out and only too thankful that the evening at last`was over.

Next morning the carpet lay calmly in its place, but one corner was very badly torn. It was the corner that the cow had been tied on to.

DOCTOR DOLITTLE'S REWARD

Hugh Lofting

aving travelled to far-distant Africa to cure an outbreak of sickness among the monkeys, Doctor Dolittle now plans to return home to Puddleby. The animals, grateful for his help, decide to give the good doctor a leaving present—but what should it be . . . ?

Chee-Chee stood outside the Doctor's door, keeping everybody away till he woke up. Then John Dolittle told the monkeys that he must now go back to Puddleby.

They were very surprised at this; for they had thought that he was going to stay with them for ever. And that night all the monkeys got together in the jungle to talk it over.

And the Chief Chimpanzee rose up and said:

'Why is it the good man is going away? Is he not happy here with us?'

But none of them could answer him.

Then the Grand Gorilla got up and said: 'I think we all should go to him and ask him to stay. Perhaps if we made him a new house and a bigger bed, and promise him plenty of monkey-servants to work for him and to make life pleasant for him—perhaps then he will not wish to go.'

Then Chee-Chee got up; and all the others whispered, 'Sh! Look! Chee-Chee, the great Traveller, is about to speak!'

And Chee-Chee said to the other monkeys: 'My friends, I am afraid it is useless to ask the Doctor to stay. He owes money in Puddleby; and he says he must go back and pay it.'

And the monkeys asked him, 'What is *money*?'

Then Chee-Chee told them that in the Land of the White Men you could get nothing without money; you could *do* nothing without money—that it was almost impossible to *live* without money.

And some of them asked, 'But can you not even eat and drink without paying?'

But Chee-Chee shook his head. And then he told them that even he, when he was with the organ-grinder, had been made to ask the children for money.

And the Chief Chimpanzee turned to the Oldest Orang-outang and said, 'Cousin, surely these Men be strange creatures! Who would wish to live in such a land? My gracious, how paltry!'

Then Chee-Chee said:

'When we were coming to you we had no boat to cross the sea in and no money to buy food to eat on our journey. So a man lent us some biscuits; and we said we would pay him when we came back. And we borrowed a boat from a sailor; but it was broken on the rocks when we reached the shores of Africa. Now the Doctor says he must go back and get the sailor another boat—because the man was poor and his ship was all he had.'

And the monkeys were all silent for awhile, sitting quite still upon the ground and thinking hard.

At last the Biggest Baboon got up and said:

'I do not think we ought to let this good man leave our land till we have given him a fine present to take with him, so that he may know we are grateful for all that he has done for us.'

And a little, tiny, red monkey who was sitting up in a tree shouted down: 'I think that too!'

And then they all cried out, making a great noise, 'Yes, yes. Let us give him the finest present a White Man ever had!'

Now they began to wonder and ask one another what would be the best thing to give him. And one said, 'Fifty bags of coconuts!' And another—'a hundred bunches of bananas!—at least he shall not have to buy his fruit in the Land Where You Pay to Eat!'

But Chee-Chee told them that all these things would be too heavy to carry so far and would go bad before half was eaten.

'If you want to please him,' he said, 'give him an animal. You may be sure he will be kind to it. Give him some rare animal they have not got in the menageries.'

And the monkeys asked him, 'What are *menageries*?'

Then Chee-Chee explained to them that menageries were places in the Land of the White Men where animals were put in cages for people to come and look at. And the monkeys were very shocked and said to one another:

'These Men are like thoughtless young ones— stupid and easily amused. Sh! it is a prison he means.'

So then they asked Chee-Chee what rare animal it could be that they should give the Doctor—one the White Man had not seen before. And the Major of the Marmosettes asked:

'Have they an iguana over there?'

But Chee-Chee said, 'Yes, there is one in the London Zoo.'

And another asked, 'Have they an okapi?'

But Chee-Chee said, 'Yes. In Belgium, where my organ-grinder took me five years ago, they had an okapi in a big city they call Antwerp.'

And another asked, 'Have they a pushmi-pullyu?'

Then Chee-Chee said, 'No. No White Man has ever seen a pushmi-pullyu. Let us give him that.'

*

Pushmi-pullyus are now extinct. That means, there aren't any more. But long ago, when Doctor Dolittle was alive, there were some of them still left in the deepest jungles of Africa; and even then they were very, very scarce. They had no tail, but a head at each end, and sharp horns on each head. They were very shy and terribly hard to catch. The black men get most of their animals by sneaking up behind them while they are not looking. But you could not do this with the pushmi-pullyu—because, no matter which way you came towards him, he was always facing you. And besides, only one-half of him slept at a time. The other head was always awake—and watching. This was why they were never caught and never seen in Zoos. Though many of the greatest huntsmen and the cleverest menagerie-keepers spent years of their lives searching through the jungles in all weathers for pushmi-pullyus, not a single one had ever been caught. Even then, years ago, he was the only animal in the world with two heads.

Well, the monkeys set out hunting for this animal through the forest. And after they had gone a good many miles, one of them found peculiar footprints near the edge of a river; and they knew that a pushmi-pullyu must be very near that spot.

Then they went along the bank of the river a little way and they saw a place where the grass was high and thick; and they guessed that he was in there.

So they all joined hands and made a great circle round the high grass. The pushmi-pullyu heard them coming, and he tried hard to break through the ring of monkeys. But he couldn't do it. When he saw that it was no use trying to escape, he sat down and waited to see what they wanted.

They asked him if he would go with Doctor Dolittle and be put on show in the Land of the White Men.

But he shook both his heads hard and said, 'Certainly not!'

They explained to him that he would not be shut up in a menagerie but would just be looked at. They told him that the Doctor was a very kind man but hadn't any money; and people would pay to see a two-headed animal and the Doctor would get rich and could pay for the boat he had borrowed to come to Africa in.

But he answered, 'No. You know how shy I am —I hate being stared at.' And he almost began to cry.

Then for three days they tried to persuade him.

And at the end of the third day he said he would come with them and see what kind of a man the Doctor was, first.

So the monkeys travelled back with the pushmi-pullyu. And when they came to where the Doctor's little house of grass was, they knocked on the door.

The duck, who was packing the trunk, said, 'Come in!'

And Chee-Chee very proudly took the animal inside and showed him to the Doctor.

'What in the world is it?' asked John Dolittle, gazing at the strange creature.

'Lord save us!' cried the duck. 'How does it make up its mind?'

'It doesn't look to me as though it had any,' said Jip, the dog.

'This, Doctor,' said Chee-Chee, 'is the pushmi-pullyu—the rarest animal of the Africa jungles, the only two-headed beast in the world! Take him home with you and your fortune's made. People will pay any money to see him.'

'But I don't want any money,' said the Doctor.

'Yes, you do,' said Dab-Dab, the duck. 'Don't you remember how we had to pinch and scrape to pay the butcher's bill in Puddleby? And how are you going to get the sailor the new boat you spoke of—unless we have the money to buy it?'

'I was going to make him one,' said the Doctor.

'Oh, do be sensible!' cried Dab-Dab. 'Where would you get all the wood and the nails to make one with? —And besides, what are we going to live on? We shall be poorer than ever when we get back. Chee-Chee's perfectly right: take the funny-looking thing along, do!'

'Well, perhaps there is something in what you say,' murmured the Doctor. 'It certainly would make a nice new kind of pet. But does the er—what-do-you-call-it really want to go abroad?'

'Yes, I'll go,' said the pushmi-pullyu, who saw at once, from the Doctor's face, that he was a man to be trusted. 'You have been so kind to the animals here—and the monkeys tell me that I am the only one who will do. But you must promise me that if I do not like it in the Land of the White Men you will send me back.'

'Why, certainly—of course, of course,' said the Doc-

tor. 'Excuse me, surely you are related to the Deer
Family, are you not?'

'Yes,' said the pushmi-pullyu—'to the Abyssinian
Gazelles and the Asiatic Chamois—on my mother's
side. My father's great-grandfather was the last of the
Unicorns.'

'Most interesting!' murmured the Doctor; and he
took a book out of the trunk which Dab-Dab was
packing and began turning the pages. 'Let us see if
Buffon says anything—'

'I notice,' said the duck, 'that you only talk with one
of your mouths. Can't the other head talk as well?'

'Oh, yes,' said the pushmi-pullyu. 'But I keep the
other mouth for eating—mostly. In that way I can talk
while I am eating without being rude. Our people have
always been very polite.'

When the packing was finished and everything was
ready to start, the monkeys gave a grand party for the
Doctor, and all the animals of the jungle came. And
they had pineapples and mangoes and honey and all
sorts of good things to eat and drink.

After they had all finished eating, the Doctor got up
and said:

'My friends: I am not clever at speaking long words
after dinner, like some men; and I have just eaten
many fruits and much honey. But I wish to tell you that
I am very sad at leaving your beautiful country.
Because I have things to do in the Land of the White
Men, I must go. After I have gone, remember never to
let the flies settle on your food before you eat it; and do
not sleep on the ground when the rains are coming.
I—er—er—I hope you will all live happily ever after.'

When the Doctor stopped speaking and sat down,
all the monkeys clapped their hands a long time and
said to one another, 'Let it be remembered always
among our people that he sat and ate with us, here,
under the trees. For surely he is the Greatest of Men!'

And the Grand Gorilla, who had the strength of

seven horses in his hairy arms, rolled a great rock up to the head of the table and said:

'This stone for all time shall mark the spot.'

And even to this day, in the heart of the jungle, that stone still is there. And monkey-mothers, passing through the forest with their families, still point down at it from the branches and whisper to their children, 'Sh! There it is—look—where the Good White Man sat and ate food with us in the Year of the Great Sickness!'

Then, when the party was over, the Doctor and his pets started out to go back to the seashore. And all the monkeys went with him as far as the edge of their country, carrying his trunk and bags, to see him off.

THE WHITE-HAIRED CHILDREN

Ruth Ainsworth

The children in the village of Cockle knew each other very well. They all went to the same school, and they bought their sweets at the same shop. The same cobbler put hobnails in their thick shoes, and they had the same doctor to look after them when they were ill. They lived within a stone's throw of each other, except for a few children whose fathers were farmers, and they lived only a few fields away.

William and Mary had been born in the village, and like all their friends they knew every cottage and garden, every stream and tree. They were as surprised as everyone else when they first saw the strange, white-haired children.

It was a very hot day, and the village children were playing by the stream, some actually in the water, and others sitting on the grassy bank, dangling their feet. Suddenly William noticed a tall, fair girl standing near by. She held two small children by the hand, and three slightly bigger ones stood behind. Each of the new family was as fair as a lily, that is, so fair that their hair was almost white.

They quietly began to take off their sandals, the little ones tugging at the tall girl's shorts as a sign that they needed some help. She unfastened buckles where necessary, and soon they were all standing in the stream.

By now, all the village children were watching the strangers. Till this moment, there had been a cheerful bustle going on, children shouting, children splashing, children singing, but now all was quiet. The new children were as silent as rushes. They moved a little, the taller ones into deeper water, but there was neither splash nor shout.

The eldest girl was called Primrose, as the little ones sometimes said her name to draw her attention to this or that. She had long, thin, white arms, and long, thin, white legs, and her face was pale too. Her three brothers and two sisters were just the same, except that they were of different sizes and the boys had their hair cut shorter. They were all alike, wearing faded shirts and faded cotton shorts. But they did not look poor. They just looked different.

William showed one of the boys a frog and he smiled shyly. Mary showed Primrose a patch of orchids and invited her to smell them, and she smelled them and said, 'Lovely.' But they were not easy to talk to, and when Primrose began gathering her family to her and telling them it was time to go home, no one had found out much about them. They set off towards the hill, turning to wave white hands to the village children who waved their brown ones back.

'We ought to have asked them where they lived,' said someone.

'And what their names are,' added someone else.

'And if they're coming to our school.'

'And how old they are.'

'We know the tall girl is Primrose.'

'And one of the boys is Cedar.'

'And I think another sounded like Holly.'

The children all hoped they would meet these new friends again and get to know them better, but they didn't turn up at school and were never seen in the village shop. They were always spoken of as 'the white-haired children'.

William and Mary tried asking their parents if they had seen a family with white hair, but for some reason their parents were not helpful. They seemed to think the children were teasing them, or describing some game they had played or a story they had read. But their mother said in a comforting way,

'Of course we'll tell you if we see any strange white-haired children, or white-haired grown-up people, either. Of course we'll keep our eyes open and tell you.'

But William and Mary knew by her tone of voice that she didn't fully believe in Primrose and Cedar and the others. She still thought they might be made-up.

It was very hot when Farmer Brown cut his hay, with not a breath of air stirring. 'There'll be a storm before the hay is in,' people said. 'You mark my words.'

On Saturday the children went to help with the hay. The shady side of the hedge was hung with rucksacks and baskets containing picnic food. The grown-up people drank cider and the children lemonade or pop. During the afternoon, when the hay-makers were getting hot and tired, they suddenly noticed some strange children had joined them. The girls wore sun-bonnets and the boys floppy straw hats.

'They're the white-haired children,' whispered William and Mary. 'Look! They've brought their hay-forks and they know just how to use them. Even the tiny one has a tiny fork.'

Primrose was showing this smallest one what to do. 'Toss like this, Pimpernel, and don't try to turn too much at once. That's right. That's a clever girl!'

'Hullo, Primrose,' said Mary. 'Hot, isn't it?'

'Yes,' said Primrose with a quick smile, working away steadily and only pausing a sympathize with a scratched leg, or to wipe a damp face.

'Where do you come from, little maiden?' asked
Farmer Brown, in his loud, jolly voice.

'Over the hill,' said Primrose, pointing to the green
slope of Hunter's Hill.

'Will your father or mother be coming to fetch you
home when it's time?' he went on cunningly.

'Oh no, we look after ourselves, don't we, children?'

'Yes, Primrose,' echoed the other five voices.

The village children felt a little envious. They loved
their parents dearly, and needed them, but it might be
a nice change to look after themselves when it came to
deciding when to go to bed, or when to go out to play.

While they had a break for tea, the white-haired
children took off their hats and everyone could see
their pale hair, pressed flat on their heads by the heat.
The hotter they got the whiter their skins looked,
which was odd as the village children were mostly
scarlet after their hard work in the hot sun.

They discovered that the third girl was called Pansy
and the third boy Willow. Farmer Brown didn't give up
easily and he tried to collect some more information.

'Now Primrose is a pretty name to be sure, but what
comes after? What is your full name?'

'Primrose is my name and I don't need any other,'
said Primrose in her cool, low voice. 'You are Farmer
Brown and I am Primrose. Isn't that enough?' She
looked bewildered and Farmer Brown said heartily:

''Course it is, enough for me, anyhow. Primrose you
are and Primrose you shall stay.'

Before the tea-break was over, Primrose had gathered her flock round her and they started off towards Hunter's Hill, turning at intervals to wave their hay-forks. The other haymakers waved back.

Haymaking lost most of its pleasure for the other children when the white-haired ones were out of sight. Squabbles broke out and little ones complained that midges were biting them and that they were thirsty. Soon they were taken home and bathed and put to bed.

As her mother drew her curtains, Mary wondered who was putting the white-haired children to bed. She tried to imagine a tall pale lady like Primrose, only grown-up. Though Primrose was always quiet, and busy with the little ones, Mary felt that she liked her. She almost felt they were friends. They had exchanged smiles and glances.

During the autumn the white-haired children appeared once, when William and Mary and some friends were picking blackberries. But while William and Mary were collecting all the berries they picked in baskets, the white-haired children were simply eating. Their faces and hands were stained purple, and they had reached the stage when only a very plump and perfect berry tempted them.

'If you eat them all you won't have any to take home,' said William severely.

'We don't need to take them home if we don't want,' said Cedar.

'Then how can your mother make blackberry jelly—'

'And blackberry jam—'

'And blackberry pie—'

'And blackberry pudding—'

'Perhaps we don't want all these things,' said Primrose. 'Perhaps we just live on ice-cream.'

'And pancakes,' said Pansy.

'And lollipops,' said Pimpernel.

'And plum pudding,' said Cedar.

'And meringues,' said Holly.

'And strawberries,' said Willow.

'Perhaps!' teased William. 'You and your perhapses! Do you think we believe you? You'd have to be princes and princesses to eat party food all the year round.'

'Perhaps we are princes and princesses!'

'Perhaps! Perhaps!' mocked the village children. 'Perhaps pigs can fly.'

Primrose slipped a handful of berries into Mary's basket, and Mary whispered, 'Thank you. Don't mind what the others say. I do believe you. I always will.'

'I know,' said Primrose. 'I know you do.'

'All the same,' Mary said to William as they carried their brimming baskets home, 'it must be rather fun just to eat what you fancy, and not pick—pick—pick—a whole afternoon, as we've done, and hardly eat more than about six because we promised mother we wouldn't.'

'I'd rather live in a proper home like we do,' said William, 'with proper parents who know how to behave, and who know how we ought to behave. Why, I said to Pimpernel: 'Your mother will be cross when she sees all those squashed blackberries on your dress,' and she said: "Why? I'm not cross. Why should anyone be cross?" I think it's very odd.'

'Kind of odd but kind of nice,' said Mary. 'Nice if no one were ever cross.'

Blackberries were over, and leaves fallen, and holly

berries shining scarlet, when the snow came. As the children were going to bed they saw the first, slow flakes whirling past the window. The next day the world was white. As the Christmas holidays had begun they could play all day in the snow. Sledges were got down from attics and out of sheds, and dusted and examined.

Many of the sledges seemed smaller than they had done the winter before.

'This can't be my sledge, it's so narrow.'

'I thought my sledge was heavy—now it's light. I can lift it with one hand.'

'There's hardly room for two on this, whatever can have happened?'

'You've grown,' said the fathers and mothers. 'You're a big boy now. You're a tall, strong girl. We shan't need to pull you along for a treat this year as we did last.'

Hunter's Hill was just right for sledging. There were short, gentle slopes near the foot where the very youngest and smallest could sledge. The big ones made a barricade of snow across the bottom so the small sledges could come to a stop safely.

Then the middle-sized children had a longer, steeper run, starting higher up the hill, and the biggest children of all, and the most fearless, had a long, steep run right from the top to the bottom.

This long, steep run was so swift and exciting that even grown-up people used it at week-ends, flashing down like an aeroplane about to take off. Once in motion, there was no question of stopping till the sledge came to rest in the middle of the field.

William and Mary had a heavy, solid sledge that had belonged to their father when he was a boy. It was hard work dragging it up the hill, but once launched, it went like the wind. The runners were shod with iron which slid beautifully over the hard, packed snow.

The cold weather went on and on, and the children

could hardly believe their eyes when every morning they saw the same, crisp, even snow, and the same white roofs on the houses, and the same bright icicles on gates and railings.

William and Mary sledged all day long, only going home for meals. William sat in the front and steered, and Mary sat behind. If they changed seats, they did not get on so well. They became skilful and daring, racing all the other sledges in the middle-sized group. Sometimes they almost felt they were flying, as the polished runners skimmed so lightly over the surface of the snow, hardly seeming to touch.

The other children were full of admiration at first, stopping to watch and cheer as they flashed past, but they soon got used to the sight and took no notice except to keep out of the way.

It was a proud day when some big children, some of whom had left school, called out to William and Mary:

'Would you two like to have a go on the long run down? You could manage it, judging by your present form. We'll give you a hand in dragging the sledge up to the top.'

William and Mary were excited and breathless when they got to the top, even though a big boy had done most of the pulling. His long strides had meant that they had to run to keep up. From the top, the run down looked difficult and dangerous. Because of the uneven hillside, there was a slow, wide curve, ending in a perfectly straight, steep finish.

'You won't find the curve too bad,' said the boy. 'Watch one or two other sledges first. You just have to lean before you pass the clump of bushes and brake with your foot to make sure you clear them. The rest is plain sailing—or plain sledging, if you like.'

'And if you *do* land in the bushes,' said a girl, 'you won't be the first. I've been tipped out there lots of times. Once you get the knack, there's nothing to it.'

William and Mary watched three sledges take the

run with perfect success. Then it was their turn.

'Sure you'd like to have a go?'

''Course we're sure,' said William.

'Certain sure,' said Mary.

'Ready! Steady! Go!' They were given a friendly push and were off. The curve round the bushes was not as bad as it looked. Mary, with her arms round William's waist, leaned when he leaned, and straightened when he straightened, and it was only a few moments before the steep, downward run lay in front and they took it at top speed, the cold air catching their breath.

'It's the best thing I've done in my life,' said William, as the sledge came to rest. 'It's like flying.'

'However shall we get right up to the top?' sighed Mary. But she need not have worried. Each time they toiled up the hill someone passing gave them a hand, and many willing hands were eager to give them a push and launch them on the downward run.

Sometimes one of them would be asked to join a team on a big sledge, and though this was exciting too, they liked their own sledge best. It was so familiar that it did just what they wanted, more like something alive than an object made of wood and metal and a length of rope.

Once, plodding up the hill, Mary spoke of the white-haired children.

'I can only imagine them in the summer, can't you?' she said. 'But I suppose there must be snow the other side of the hill, where they live, and they're sure to be playing in it like us. They'll need several sledges for the six of them. But perhaps Pimpernel and Willow aren't big enough to sledge yet. I expect Primrose pulls them along for a ride. She's like a mother.'

'She isn't really,' said William, 'because she doesn't mind what they do and mothers are always minding about something or other.'

'But she keeps an eye on them, doesn't she?'

'Yes, in a way. But not a mother's eye.'

The very next day the white-haired children appeared on the village side of Hunter's Hill. There they were, all six of them, with fur hats and fur mittens, each with his or her own sledge, painted scarlet. Primrose's was the biggest, then Cedar's, then Pansy's, then Holly's, right down to little Willow and Pimpernel who had sledges almost doll size.

The little ones joined the group of youngest children, the middle-sized ones the middle group, and Primrose and Cedar climbed confidently to the top of the long run.

'Can you manage it?' asked one of the leaders among the big boys.

'It's faster than you think.'

'And there's the bend by the bushes.'

'There's no hope of braking when you're under way. You just have to sit tight and hope for the best.'

'It's kind of you to take so much trouble,' said Primrose, 'but my brother and I are quite safe. Why, on the other side of the hill, we have a much longer run with three bends—sharp ones—and a steep finish like the side of a house. This is easy as pie compared with the other.'

'Very well. Please yourselves. We only wanted to help.'

The group of older children went on chatting and paying no more attention to the newcomers, but when Primrose got her sledge in position, every eye was quietly fixed on her. She lay on her sledge, pulled her fur hat further on her head, and kicked off.

Down the run she sped, curving round the bushes, on till she reached the last steep pitch.

'Well done!' said some of the watchers when she rejoined them. 'I wouldn't be surprised if you've beaten the record for speed.'

The white-haired children were all experts, and very willing to lend their sledges and accept turns on other people's. Although Mary never said more to Primrose than, 'Have a go on mine' or, 'shall we both try a run on yours?' she felt they were getting to know each other. William and Cedar, too, were like old friends without many words being spoken. If Primrose were late, Mary felt unsettled till she came, and when Primrose had gone home, the best of the day's fun seemed over. The two boys felt the same about each other.

One day, Mary was surprised when Primrose drew her aside and said:

'We are giving a party. Will you and your brother come?'

'Yes, we'd love to. That is, if mother says we may. When is it to be?'

'Actually it's tonight, when we go home.'

'I'll ask mother at lunch time and tell you this afternoon. But perhaps you won't be coming this afternoon as you'll be getting things ready for the party.'

'Oh, we shall come. There's nothing to get ready. But please don't ask your mother. Please don't. She might say no.'

'Why should she?'

'Children think we are queer and grown-up people think we are very queer indeed. We have queer names and peculiar hair, and we look after ourselves. Please don't ask permission. Just come, both of you.'

'But we mustn't be late back. Mother would worry terribly if it got pitch dark and we weren't home.'

'Would she think you'd been eaten by wolves, or stolen by robbers?'

Mary wasn't sure if Primrose were serious or teasing.

'Not exactly,' she said. 'She'd just worry. You know how mothers worry.'

'I don't, but never mind. We'll leave earlier than usual, before the sun sets, and we'll sledge down the other side of the hill and the sledge run ends at our front door. Do, please come. We want you and William specially. As a matter of fact, we've arranged a surprise for you. Just for you.'

'What about our clothes?'

'Everyone will come in sledging clothes because they'll come on sledges. So you'll come? And please don't mention it to any of the other children because we're not asking anyone else from this village.'

'Yes, we'll come. I'll go and ask William now.'

William was not even anxious about getting home in good time. He just said yes. The idea of going in sledging clothes was an added attraction. No washings of neck or knees, or nonsense about clean nails. A party after his own heart.

That afternoon, when the red sun ball was still above the horizon, Primrose began collecting her family together, and William and Mary joined them. They followed a path leading round the side of the hill, and when they were right round to the opposite side, they struck the top of the sledge run Primrose had described.

'I'll go first,' said Primrose. 'Then you, Mary, with William. Then Cedar, and then the little ones can come as they please. Don't be frightened if you go rather fast because it's quite, quite safe, there's only one way home from here, and you can't get lost. Just be careful when you go through the gates of the drive. Of course the gates will be wide open, but you don't want to hit a gate post.'

She got ready on her sledge.

'The next person had better count ten slowly before pushing off. That ought to prevent any collisions. Ten slowly—don't forget!'

'Ten slowly—we won't forget.'

Then, in a flash, Primrose was off down the hillside.

It was several seconds before William and Mary remembered to begin counting, and they counted rather quickly for fear that Primrose would be out of sight. When they pushed off, she was still visible, a moving dot swinging round a curve.

It was a wonderful sledge run, polished and smooth, with the bends banked so the sledge slid round with no anxiety about steering or braking. The sledge was out of their control, but they never doubted they would end up at the right place. After the first steep rush, the run flattened out and they saw the gate posts as they slipped between them, then down a drive where two rows of snowy trees met in a series of arches. Then the front of a great house sprang up, brilliantly lit.

'It must be a palace,' thought Mary, gazing up at the rows of bright windows. Doors were open into the hall, and the light streamed out upon the sparkling snow.

The courtyard was packed with sledges of all sizes and colours and kinds, some expensive and new, some home-made and old. The rest of the white-

haired children arrived, one by one, and many other children. These must have come from other villages as they were strangers.

'Come in, everybody!' said Primrose, from the open door. 'Go where you like. Do what you like. The whole house is ours tonight, every nook and cranny. Come in and make yourselves at home. We only want to please you.'

At first the guests were shy, and stood about in the hall where there was a blazing log fire. Then some of the bolder ones began to explore, opening a door here, going up a few stairs with their hand on the banister, and at last swarming everywhere, upstairs, down-stairs, in attics and cellars, peeping in cupboards and on shelves.

There were games laid out in some rooms. Toys in others. Puzzles and tricks in others. Music came from a room cleared for dancing, and there was even a quiet room with books lying around. The smallest children found their way to a nursery and were soon riding rocking-horses and building with bricks the size of real ones, but light to handle. Little girls played with a dolls' house or busied themselves putting dolls to bed in cots and cradles, with a musical box to play a lullaby.

William played darts with some other boys and Mary found a box of beads, all the colours of the rainbow, with a label on the box which said: PLEASE MAKE WHAT YOU LIKE AND TAKE IT HOME WITH YOU

She began to thread herself a necklace, using the crystal beads which sparkled like the frost outside. Sometimes Primrose put her head round the door, smiling and nodding, but did not stay.

Everyone was laughing and many were shouting and racing about, but the house was so large that the party did not seem noisy. It did not seem crowded, either, with so many rooms for the guests to use, and so many different things for them to do. When a loud gong sounded there was a rush for the stairs and the dining-room, where a round table was spread with a white cloth and covered with delicious food. Whatever any child liked best was sure to be there, whether it was pancakes or peaches, sausages or strawberries, lobster or lollipops. The children moved round helping themselves to whatever took their fancy.

In the middle of the table was a wonderful frozen pudding, like a mountain made of snowy ice-cream. At the top was a sledge with two tiny figures on it, a boy and a girl. They looked as though, any minute, they would start their run down the mountain side where a winding track was clearly marked. This track went in and out of silvery fir trees, down to the valley below and over a bridge which spanned a stream.

'When do we eat the iced pudding?' asked someone.

'Last thing of all,' said Primrose, 'not till it's time to go home. When the pudding is eaten the party is over.'

Mary could not take her eyes off the iced mountain and while she ate boats made of celery with lettuce sails, she stared and stared.

She knew that some very skilful cook had made this wonderful confection, yet she felt it was more than just a pudding for a party. It was a real scene of snow and ice and frosty trees and sparkling water. The bridge had a handrail at one side and the snow on it was scuffled. It looked as if some passer-by had gripped it to steady himself. Then she saw something else that made her open her eyes even wider.

'William,' whispered Mary, 'William, look at the children on the sledge.'

William leaned forward so his eyes were level with the top of the pudding and the sledge.

'They're very well made,' he said.

'But don't you see who they are—don't you recognize them? Look properly!'

William looked again. 'Goodness, they're you and me! Your blue cap and my red, our navy wind-jackets

and your red trousers and my brown. They're us, all right. But why doesn't someone else notice? It's so obvious.'

'It's obvious to us, of course, but not many people here have even seen us before. And lots of children wear clothes very like ours when they sledge.'

'But not *exactly* like ours! You agree that it couldn't possibly be just chance? Someone meant it. Someone took a great deal of trouble to get it right. Why, even your hair is darker than mine!'

'Ought we to thank Primrose?'

'I'm not sure. She hasn't mentioned it to us. When we go we can just say we thought the pudding was marvellous, or something like that.'

'All right,' said Mary. 'Everything is so strange tonight, I feel anything could happen. It's this huge house and all these children and no one looking after us.'

'I'm going back upstairs,' said William. 'I saw a room with a model railway simply covering the whole floor, with stations and bridges and tunnels. I'm going to play with it.'

He ran off, and Mary, who was wearing her crystal necklace, followed. She went into a room where music was being played and children were dancing. At once a boy in a kilt asked her to be his partner.

'Do you live far away?' he asked.

'Just over the hill,' said Mary.

'So do I. Isn't it funny, we all come from just over the hill but I don't think it can be the same hill, do you?'

'No, it can't be, or we should all know each other. Did you come on a sledge?'

'Yes, like everyone else.'

As they danced near the platform Mary noticed that the musicians were all children too. She felt sure it must be getting late and she said goodbye to her partner and went to look for William. She met him on the landing, looking for her.

'Ought we to go?' said Mary. 'It feels late.'

'Yes, it does, and there aren't any clocks in this place. I've looked specially. I asked Primrose what the time was and she just said, "still very early—you mustn't dream of going yet."'

They sat down on a window seat, half hidden by heavy red curtains, and looked down on to the court-yard with its rows and rows of sledges. They picked out their own, near to the stone steps leading to the front door. Just then, they heard Primrose's voice speaking quietly to Cedar.

'Not long to wait now,' she said.

'But I haven't seen William and Mary lately,' said Cedar.

'Oh, they're still here. William was getting anxious about the time but I told him it was still early.'

'Have they noticed anything?'

'I don't think they have. They haven't said any-thing. Oh, won't it be lovely to have them here always, to play with whenever we want?'

'Yes, it will be fun, but we mustn't be too sure. I feel that something could go wrong even now. They might escape.'

'No! no! no!' said Primrose. 'It will be all right—you'll see. I'll sound the gong now, this minute, and then we'll serve the iced pudding. When that's gone, they won't be able to get back!'

'No, they won't. There won't be a way back!'

William and Mary heard the other two running towards the stairs.

'We must get away as quickly as we can,' said William. 'We haven't a minute to lose.'

'I don't understand—but I'm frightened,' said Mary.

Just then the gong sounded and there was a mad rush towards the dining-room, the children all calling out, as they ran:

'Now for the iced pudding! The iced pudding is to be

served now! Come along, everyone, and have your share!'

William and Mary wanted to go through the hall, but the press of children carried them along, willy-nilly, into the dining-room.

Primrose stood by the table with a large silver spoon, calling out as she scooped it into the mountain side:

'Hold out your plates! A helping for everyone!'

When they saw the spoon buried in the pudding, and the sledge with its tiny occupants poised on the top, William and Mary knew that they must be out of the house in a matter of seconds. They tore on their boots, dashed out of the door, snatched up the rope on their sledge, and ran. They did not look back once at the house with its lighted windows, but ran faster than they had ever run before. Only at the top of the hill they paused and looked back. The landscape behind was completely different. Sloping hill side, trees, track, all had disappeared. There was only a blank stretch of snow.

'Just in time,' said William. 'Now for the homeward run.'

When they arrived at their own home, their parents were not cross or alarmed. They smiled and remarked that the children must have had an extra good time playing as they were rather late.

'We sledged on the other side of the hill,' said William.

'And went home with some children we knew.'

'You look tired, anyhow,' said their mother. 'I'll read to you while you have your tea.'

'We've had tea—' began William, but by then she had fetched *Robinson Crusoe* from the shelf, taken out the marker, and begun to read, while the children tried to manage at least their cocoa and a toasted tea-cake.

As they went to bed, they planned, at the very first chance, to visit the white-haired children again, and to see what the house looked like in daylight. But it was several months before they were able to do this.

That night the thaw set in, and there was no more playing in the snow—only slogging along in the slush. Then school started again and whenever they suggested a Sunday walk right over Hunter's Hill their father said it was private land, and they had better not go without permission.

It was not till summer that their chance came. An older cousin came to stay, a tall boy almost grown-up, and he was willing to explore on the other side of the hill, striding off at such a pace that they had to run to keep up with him.

The hill was green now, with sheep on the higher slopes and buttercups at the bottom. As they went down, they searched the landscape for a big house, but they searched in vain.

'We're looking for a house we once went to,' said William.

'A house as big as a palace,' said Mary, 'with stone gate posts and a drive.'

'And the trees in the drive had branches meeting to make arches.'

'Can't see a thing!' said the cousin, 'not even a cow shed. Sounds like a fairy-tale to me. But we'll walk on for another quarter of an hour and then we'll turn back.'

Before this quarter of an hour was up they came to a pair of old, stone gate posts, green with moss. Beyond was an overgrown drive, thick with weeds. Several trees had fallen right across it, and others had lost branches in storms.

'I suppose this isn't what you were looking for?' laughed the cousin. 'Let's go up the drive, anyway.'

They climbed over the fallen trees and scrambled over the dead branches, scratching their legs while their feet sank deep in a thick, soft carpet of decaying leaves. A startled bird rose with a cry and made them jump. Then they came to the house, or what had once been the house. It was a ruin, with no glass in the windows, the doors swinging on broken hinges, and great, gaping holes in the roof. Nettles and docks grew in the hall, and the window sills were hung with ivy.

'If we had more time we'd go in and explore,' said the cousin, but neither William nor Mary wanted to set foot over that doorstep again. They knew that whatever was inside, they would not find the white-haired children.

They were silent on the way home, but the cousin did not notice as he was not used to children, and did not know what to say to them anyway. He left them to their own disturbing, puzzling thoughts.

As they changed their shoes for tea, William whispered to Mary:

'Was it all a dream?' and Mary whispered back:

'How can you say that? You know it wasn't. It really happened. Anyhow, I still have the crystal necklace I threaded. That's proof, isn't it?'

'We've lots to ask Primrose if we ever see her again.'

'Yes, we have. She must have wondered what went wrong with her plan, and why we ran away when we did.'

But the white-haired children never visited the village of Cockle again, though William and Mary looked for them by the river and in the hayfield, and among the blackberry bushes, and most of all on Hunter's Hill, when the snow came and sledging began again.

HARRIET'S HAIRLOOM

Joan Aiken

h, Mother,' Harriet said as she did every year. 'Can't I open my birthday presents at breakfast?'

And as she did every year, Mrs Armitage replied,

'Certainly not! You know perfectly well that you weren't born till half past four. You get your birthday presents at tea-time, not before.'

'We could change the custom now we're in our teens,' Harriet suggested cunningly. 'You know you hate having to get up at half past two in the morning for Mark's presents.'

But Mark objected strongly to any change, and Mrs Armitage added,

'In any case, don't forget that as it's your thirteenth birthday you have to be shown into the Closed Room; there'd never be time to do that before school. Go and collect your schoolbooks now, and, Mark, wash the soot from behind your ears; if you must hunt for Lady Anne's pearls in the chimney, I wish you'd clean up before coming to breakfast.'

'You'd be as pleased as anyone else if I found them,' Mark grumbled, going off to put sooty marks all over the towels.

'What do you suppose is in the Closed Room?' Mark said later, as he and Harriet walked to the school bus. 'I think it's a rotten swindle that only girls in the family are allowed to go inside when they get to be thirteen.

Suppose it's a monster like at Glamis, what'll you do?'

'Tame it,' said Harriet promptly. 'I shall feed it on bread-and-milk and lettuce.'

'That's hedgehogs, dope! Suppose it has huge teeth and tentacles and a poisonous sting three yards long?'

'Shut up! Anyway I don't suppose it is a monster. After all we never see Mother going into the Closed Room with bowls of food. It's probably just some mouldering old great-aunt in her coffin or something boring like that.'

Still, it was nice to have a Closed Room in the family, Harriet reflected, and she sat in the bus happily speculating about what it might contain—jewels, perhaps, rubies as big as tomatoes, or King Arthur's sword Excalibur, left with the Armitage family for safe keeping when he went off to Avalon, or the Welsh bard Taliesin, fallen asleep in the middle of a poem—or a Cockatrice—or the vanished crew of the *Marie Celeste*, playing cards and singing shanties—

Harriet was still in a dreamy state when school began. The first lesson was geography with old Mr Gubbins so there was no need to pay attention; she sat trying to think of suitable pet names for Cockatrices until she heard a stifled sobbing on her left.

'. . . is of course the Cathay of the ancients,' Mr Gubbins was rambling on. 'Marco Polo in his travels . . .'

Harriet looked cautiously round and saw that her best friend, and left-hand neighbour Desiree, or Dizzry as everyone called her, was crying bitterly, hunched over the inkwell on her desk so that the tears ran into it.

Dizzry was the daughter of Ernie Perrow, the village chimney-sweep; the peculiarity of the Perrow family was that none of them ever grew to be more than six inches high. Dizzry travelled to school every day in Harriet's pocket and instead of sitting at her desk in the usual way had a small table and chair, which Mark had obligingly made her out of matchboxes, on the top of it.

'What's the matter?' whispered Harriet. 'Here, don't cry into the ink—you'll make it weaker than it is already. Haven't you a handkerchief?'

She pulled sewing things out of her own desk, snipped a shred off the corner of a tablecloth she was embroidering, and passed it to Dizzry, who gulped, nodded, took a deep breath, and wiped her eyes on it.

'What's the matter?' Harriet asked again.

'It was what Mr Gubbins said that started me off,' Dizzry muttered. 'Talking about Cathay. Our Min always used to say she'd a fancy to go to Cathay. She'd got it muddled up with café. She thought she'd get cake and raspberryade and ice-cream there.'

'Well, so what?' said Harriet, who saw nothing to cry about in that.

'Haven't you heard? We've lost her—we've lost our Min!'

'Oh, my goodness! You mean she's dead?'

'No, not died. Just lost. Nobody's seen her since yesterday breakfast time!'

Harriet privately thought this ought to have been rather a relief for the family but was too polite to say so. Min, the youngest of the Perrow children, was a perfect little fiend, always in trouble of one kind or another. When not engaged in entering sweet jars in the village shop and stealing Butter Kernels or Quince Drops, she was probably worming her way through keyholes and listening to people's secrets, or hitching a free lift round the houses in her enemy the postman's pocket and jabbing him with a darning needle as a reward for the ride, or sculling about the pond on Farmer Beezeley's ducks and driving them frantic by tickling them under their wings, or galloping down the street on somebody's furious collie, or climbing into the vicar's TV and frightening him half to death by shouting 'Time is short!' through the screen. She fre-

quently ran fearful risks but seemed to have a charmed
life. Everybody in the village heartily detested Min
Perrow, but her elder brothers and sisters were
devoted to her and rather proud of her exploits.

Poor Dizzry continued to cry, on and off, for the rest
of the day. Harriet tried to console her but it seemed
horribly probable that Min had at last gone too far and
had been swallowed by a cow or drowned in a sump or
rolled into a Swiss roll at the bakery while stealing
jam—so many ill fates might easily have befallen her
that it was hard to guess the likeliest.

'I'll help you hunt for her this evening,' Harriet
promised, however, 'and so will Mark. As soon as my
birthday tea's finished.'

Dizzry came home with Harriet for the birthday tea
and was a little cheered by the cake made in the shape
of a penguin with blackcurrant icing and an orange
beak, and Harriet's presents, which included a do-it-
yourself water-divining kit from Mark (a hazel twig and
a bucket of water), an electronic guitar which could
sing as well as play, a little pocket computer for working out sums and, from Harriet's fairy godmother,
a tube of everlasting toothpaste. Harriet was not particularly grateful for this last; the thought of toothpaste
supplied for the rest of her life left her unmoved.

'I'd rather have had an endless stick of liquorice,'
she said crossly. 'Probably I shan't have any teeth left
by the time I'm ninety; what use will toothpaste be
then?'

Her presents from Dizzry were by far the nicest: a pink-and-orange necklace of spindleberries, beautifully carved, and a starling named Alastair whom Dizzry had trained to take messages, answer the telephone or the front door, and carry home small quantities of shopping.

'Now,' said Mrs Armitage rather nervously when the presents had been admired, 'I'd better show Harriet the Closed Room.'

Mr Armitage hurriedly retired to his study while Mark, controlling some natural feelings of envy, kindly said he would help Dizzry hunt for Min, and carried her off to inspect all the reapers and binders in Mr Beezeley's farmyard.

Harriet and Mrs Armitage went up to the attic floor and Mrs Armitage paused before a cobweb-shrouded door and pulled a rusty old key out of her pocket.

'Now you must say "I, Harriet Armitage, solemnly swear not to reveal the secret of this room to any other soul in the world."'

'But when I grow up and have a daughter,' objected Harriet, 'won't I have to tell her, just as Granny told you and you're telling me?'

'Well, yes, I suppose so,' Mrs Armitage said uncertainly. 'I've rather forgotten how the oath went, to tell you the truth.'

'Why do we have to promise not to tell?'

'To be honest, I haven't the faintest idea.'

'Let's skip that bit—there doesn't seem much point

to it—and just go in,' Harriet suggested. So they opened the door (it was very stiff, for it had been shut at least twenty years) and went in.

The attic was dim, lit only by a patch of green glass tiles in the roof; it was quite empty except for a small, dusty loom, made of black wood, with a stool to match.

'A loom?' said Harriet, very disappointed. 'Is that all?'

'It isn't an ordinary loom,' her mother corrected her. 'It's a hairloom. For weaving human hair.'

'Who wants to weave human hair? What can you make?'

'I suppose you make a human hair mat. You must only use hair that's never been cut since birth.'

'Haven't you ever tried?'

'Oh, my dear, I never seemed to get a chance. When I was your age and Granny first showed me the loom everyone wore their hair short; you couldn't get a bit long enough to weave for love or money. And then you children came along—somehow I never found time.'

'Well I jolly well shall,' Harriet said. 'I'll try and get hold of some hair. I wonder if Miss Pring would let me have hers? I bet it's never been cut—she must have yards. Maybe you can make a cloak of invisibility, or the sort that turns swans into humans.'

She was so pleased with this notion that only as they went downstairs did she think to ask, 'How did the loom get into the family?'

'I'm a bit vague about that,' Mrs Armitage admitted. 'I believe it belonged to a Greek ancestress that one of the crusading Armitages married and brought back to England. She's the one I'm called Penelope after.'

Without paying much attention, Harriet went off to find Mark and Dizzry. Her father said they were along at the church, so she followed, pausing at the post office to ask elderly Miss Pring the postmistress if she would sell her long grey hair to be woven into a rug.

'It would look very pretty,' she coaxed. 'I could dye some of pink or blue.'

Miss Pring was not keen.

'Sell my hair? Cut it off? The idea! Dye it? What impertinence! Get along with you, sauce-box!'

So Harriet had to abandon that scheme, but she stuck up a postcard on the notice-board: HUMAN HAIR REQUIRED, UNCUT: BEST PRICES PAID, and posted off another to the local paper. Then she joined Mark and Dizzry, who were searching the church organ pipes, but without success.

Harriet had met several other members of the Perrow family on her way: Ernie, Min's father, driving an old dolls' push-chair which he had fitted with an engine and turned into a convertible like a Model T Ford; old Gran Perrow, stomping along and gloomily shouting 'Min!' down all the drain-holes; and Sid, one of the boys, riding a bike made from cocoa tins and poking out nests from the hedge with a bamboo in case Min had been abducted.

When it was too dark to go on searching Harriet and Mark left Dizzry at Rose Cottage, where the Perrows lived.

'We'll go on looking tomorrow!' they called. And Harriet said, 'Don't worry too much.'

'I expect she'll be all right wherever she is,' Mark said. 'I'd back Min against a mad bull any day.'

As they walked home he asked Harriet,

'What about the Closed Room, then? Any monster?'

'No, very dull—just a hairloom.'

'I say, you shouldn't tell me, should you?'

'It's all right—we agreed to skip the promise to keep it secret.'

'What a let-down,' Mark said. 'Who wants an old loom?'

They arrived home to trouble. Their father was complaining, as he did every day, about soot on the carpets and black tide-marks on the bathroom basin and towels.

'Well, if you don't want me to find Lady Anne's necklace—' Mark said aggrievedly. 'If it was worth a thousand pounds when she lost it in 1660, think what it would fetch now.'

'Why in heaven's name would it be up the chimney? Stop arguing and go to bed. And brush your teeth!'

'I'll lend you some of my toothpaste,' Harriet said.

'Just the same,' Mark grumbled, brushing his teeth with yards of toothpaste so that the foam stood out on either side of his face like Dundreary whiskers and flew all over the bathroom, 'Ernie Perrow definitely told me that his great-great-great-grandfather Oliver Perrow had a row with Lady Anne Armitage because she ticked him off for catching field-mice in her orchard; Oliver was the village sweep, and her pearls vanished just after; Ernie thinks old Oliver stuck them in the chimney to teach her a lesson, and then he died, eaten by a fox before he had a chance to tell anyone. But Ernie's sure that's where the pearls are.'

'Perhaps Min's up there looking for them too.'

'Not her! She'd never do anything as useful as that.'

Harriet had asked Alastair the starling to call her at seven; in fact she was roused at half past six by loud bangs on the front door.

'For heaven's sake, somebody, tell that maniac to go away!' shouted Mr Armitage from under his pillow.

Harriet flung on a dressing-gown and ran downstairs. What was her surprise to find at the door a little old man in a white duffel-coat with the hood up. He carried a very large parcel, wrapped in sacking. Harriet found the sharp look he gave her curiously disconcerting.

'Would it be Miss Armitage now, the young lady who put the advertisement in the paper then?'

'About hair?' Harriet said eagerly. 'Yes, I did. Have you got some, Mr—?'

'Mr Thomas Jones, the Druid, I am. Beautiful hair I have then, look you—finer than any lady's in the land.'

Only see now till I get this old parcel undone!' And he dumped the bundle down at her feet and started un-knotting the cords. Harriet helped. When the last half-hitch twanged apart a great springy mass of hair came boiling out. It was soft and fine, dazzlingly white with just a few strands of black, and smelt slightly of tobacco.

'There, now indeed to goodness! Did you ever see finer?'

'But,' said Harriet, 'has it ever been cut short?' She very much hoped that it had not; it seemed impossible that they would ever be able to parcel it up again.

'Never has a scissor-blade been laid to it, till I cut it all off last night,' the old man declared.

Harriet wondered whose it was; something slightly malicious and self-satisfied about the old man's grin as he said, 'I cut it all off' prevented her from asking.

'Er—how much would you want for it?' she inquired cautiously.

'Well, indeed,' he said. 'It would be hard to put a price on such beautiful hair, whatever.'

At this moment there came an interruption. A large van drew up in front of the Armitage house. On its sides iridescent bubbles were painted, and, in rainbow colours, the words SUGDEN'S SOAP.

A uniformed driver jumped out, consulting a piece of paper.

'Mr Mark Armitage live here?' he asked Harriet. She nodded.

'Will he take delivery of one bathroom, complete with shower, tub, footbath, de-luxe basin, plastic curtains, turkish towelling, chrome sponge-holder, steel-and-enamel hair drier, and a six years' supply of Sugden's Soap?'

'I suppose so,' Harriet said doubtfully. 'You're sure there's no mistake?'

The delivery note certainly had Mark's name and address.

'Mark!' Harriet yelled up the stairs, forgetting it was

still only seven a.m. 'Did you order a bathroom? Because it's come.'

'Merciful goodness!' groaned the voice of Mr Armitage. 'Has no one any consideration for my hours of rest?'

Mark came running down, looking slightly embarrassed.

'Darn it,' he said as he signed the delivery note, 'I never expected I'd get a bathroom; I was hoping for the free cruise to Saposoa.'

'Where shall we put it, guv?' said the driver, who was plainly longing to be away and get some breakfast at the nearest carmen's pull-in.

Mark looked about him vaguely. At this moment Mr Armitage came downstairs in pyjamas and a very troublesome frame of mind.

'Bathroom? Bathroom?' he said. 'You've bought a bathroom? What the blazes did you want to go and get a bathroom for? Isn't the one we have good enough for you, pray? You leave it dirty enough. Who's going to pay for this? And why has nobody put the kettle on?'

'I won it,' Mark explained, blushing. 'It was the second prize in the Sugden's Soap competition. In the *Radio Times*, you know.'

'What did you have to do?' Harriet asked.

'Ten uses for soap in correct order of importance.'

'I bet washing came right at the bottom,' growled his father. 'Greased stairs and fake soft-centres are more your mark.'

'Anyway he won!' Harriet pointed out. 'Was that all you had to do?'

'You had to write a couplet too.'

'What was yours?'

Mark blushed even pinker. 'Rose or White or Heliotrope, Where there's life there's Sugden's Soap.'

'Come on now,' said the van driver patiently, 'we don't want to be here all day, do we? Where shall we put it, guv? In the garden?'

'Certainly not,' snapped Mr Armitage. He was proud of his garden.

'How about in the field?' suggested Harriet diplomatically. 'Then Mark and I can wash in it, and you needn't be upset by soot on the towels.'

'That's true,' her father said, brightening a little. 'All right, stick it in the field. And now will somebody please put on a kettle and make a cup of tea, is that too much to ask?' And he stomped back to bed, leaving Mark and the driver to organize the erection of the bathroom in the field beside the house. Harriet put a kettle on the stove and went back to Mr Jones the Druid who was sunning himself in the front porch.

'Have you decided what you want for your hair?' she asked.

'Oh,' he said. 'There is a grand new bathroom you have with you! Lucky that is, indeed. Now I am thinking I do not want any money at all for my fine bundle of hair, but only to strike a bargain with you.'

'Very well,' Harriet said cautiously.

'No bathroom I have at my place, see? Hard it is to wash the old beard, and chilly of a winter morning in the stream. But if you and your brother, that I can see is a kind-hearted obliging young gentleman, would let me come and give it a bit of a lather now and again in your bathroom—'

'Why yes, of course,' Harriet said. 'I'm sure Mark won't mind at all.'

'So it shall be, then. Handy that will be, indeed. Terrible deal of the old beard there is, look you, and grubby she do get.'

With that he undid his duffel-coat and pulled back the hood. All round his head and wound about his body like an Indian Sari was a prodigiously long white beard which he proceeded to untwine until it trailed on the ground. It was similar to the white hair in the bundle, but not so clean.

'Is that somebody's beard, then?' Harriet asked, pointing to the bundle.

'My twin brother, Dai Jones the Bard. Bathroom he has by him, the lucky old cythryblwr! But soon I will be getting a bigger one. Made a will, my Dad did, see, leaving all his money to the one of us who has the longest and whitest beard on our ninetieth birthday, that falls tomorrow on Midsummer Day. So I crept into his house last night and cut his beard off while he slept; hard he'll find it now to grow another in time! All Dad's money I will be getting, he, he, he!'

Mr Jones the Druid chuckled maliciously.

Harriet could not help thinking he was rather a wicked old man, but a bargain was a bargain, so she picked up the bundle of beard, with difficulty, and was about to say goodbye when he stopped her.

'Weaving the hair into a mat, you would be, isn't it?' he said wheedlingly. 'There is a fine bath-mat it would make! Towels and curtains there are in that grand new bathroom of yours but no bath-mat—pity that is, indeed.' He gave her a cunning look out of the corners of his eyes, but Harriet would not commit herself.

'Come along this evening, then, I will, for a good old wash-up before my birthday,' Mr Jones said. He wound himself in his beard again and went off with many nods and bows. Harriet ran to the field to see how the bathroom was getting on. Mark had it nearly finished. True enough, there was no bath-mat. It struck Harriet that Mr Jones's suggestion was not a bad one.

'I'll start weaving a mat as soon as we've had another thorough hunt for Min Perrow,' she said. 'Saturday, thank goodness, no school.'

However during breakfast (which was late, owing to these various events) Ernie Perrow drove along in the push-chair with Lily and Dizzry to show the Armitages an air letter which had arrived from the British Consul in Cathay.

Dear Sir or Madam,

Kindly make earliest arrangements to send passage money back to England for your daughter Hermione who has had herself posted here, stowed away in a box of Health Biscuits. Please forward without delay fare and expenses totalling £1,093 7s. 1d.

A postscript, scrawled by Min, read: 'Dun it at last! Sux to silly old postmun!'

'Oh, what shall we do?' wept Mrs Perrow. 'A thousand pounds! How can we ever find it?'

While the grown-ups discussed ways and means, Mark went back to his daily search for Lady Anne's pearls, and Harriet took the woebegone Dizzry up to the attic, hoping to distract her by a look at the hairloom.

Dizzry was delighted with it. 'Do let's do some weaving!' she said. 'I like weaving better than anything.'

So Harriet lugged in the great bundle of beard and they set up the loom. Dizzry was an expert weaver. She had been making beautiful scarves for years on a child's toy loom—she could nip to and fro with the shuttle almost faster than Harriet's eyes could follow. By teatime they had woven a handsome thick white mat with the words BATH MA across the middle (there had not been quite enough black for the final T).

'Anyway you can see what it's meant to be,' Harriet said. They took the new mat and spread it in their elegant bathroom.

'Tell you what,' Mark said, 'we'd better hide the bath and basin plugs when Min gets back or she'll climb in and drown herself.'

'Oh, I do wonder what Dad and Mum are doing about getting her back,' sighed Dizzry, who was sitting on a sponge. She wiped her eyes on a corner of Harriet's face-cloth.

'Let's go along to your house,' Harriet said, 'and find out.'

There was an atmosphere of deep gloom in the Perrow household. Ernie had arranged to sell his Model T push-chair, the apple of his eye, to the Motor Museum at Beaulieu.

'A thousand pounds they say they'll give for it,' he said miserably. 'With that and what I've saved from the chimney sweeping, we can just about pay the fare. Won't I half clobber young Min when I get her back, the little varmint!'

'Mrs Perrow,' Harriet said, 'may Dizzry come and spend the evening at our house, as Mother and Daddy are going to a dance? And have a bath in our new bathroom? Mother says it's all right and I'll take great care of her.'

'Oh, very well, if your Ma doesn't mind,' sighed Mrs Perrow. 'I'm so distracted I hardly know if I'm coming or going. Don't forget your wash things, Diz, and the bath-salts.'

Harriet was enchanted with the bath-salts, no bigger than hundreds-and-thousands.

On Midsummer Eve the Armitage children were allowed to stay up as late as they liked. Mark, a single-minded boy, said he intended to go on hunting for Lady Anne's necklace in the chimney. The girls had their baths and then went up to Harriet's room with a bagful of apples and the gramophone, intending to have a good gossip.

At half past eleven Harriet, happening to glance out of the window, saw a light in the field.

'That must be Mr Jones,' she said. 'I'd forgotten he was coming to shampoo his beard. It's not Mark, I can still hear him bumping around in the chimney.'

There was indeed an excited banging to be heard from the chimney-breast, but it was as nothing compared with the terrible racket that suddenly broke out in the field. They heard shouts and cries of rage, thuds, crashes, and the tinkle of smashed glass.

'Heavens, what can be going on?' cried Harriet. She flung up the sash and prepared to climb out of the window.

'Wait for me!' said Dizzry.

'Here, jump into my pocket. Hold tight!'

Harriet slid down the wisteria and dashed across the garden. A moment later they arrived at the bathroom door and witnessed a wild scene.

Evidently Mr Jones the Druid had finished washing his beard and been about to leave when he saw his doom waiting for him outside the door in the form of another, very angry, old man who was trying to batter his way in.

'It must be his brother!' Harriet whispered. 'Mr Jones the Bard!'

The second old man had no beard, only a ragged white frill cut short round his chin. He was shouting.

'Wait till I catch you, you hocsdwr, you herwhaliwr, you ffrawddunio, you wicked old llechwr! A snake would think shame to spit on you! Cutting off your brother's beard, indeed! Just let me get at you and I'll trim you to spillikins. I'll shave your beard round your eyebrows!' And he beat on the door with a huge pair of shears. A pane of glass fell in and broke on the bathroom tiles; then the whole door gave way.

Dizzry left Harriet's pocket and swarmed up on to her head to see what was happening. They heard a fearful bellow from inside the bathroom, a stamping and crashing, fierce grunts, the hiss of the shower and more breaking glass.

'Hey!' Harriet shouted. 'Stop wrecking our bathroom!'

No answer. The noise of battle went on.

Then the bathroom window flew open and Jones the Druid shot out, all tangled in his beard which was snowy white now, but still damp. He had the bath-mat rolled up under his arm. As soon as he was out he flung it down, leapt on it, and shouted, 'Take me out of here!'

The mat took off vertically and hovered, about seven feet up, while Mr Jones began hauling in his damp beard, hand over hand. 'Come back!' Harriet cried. 'You've no right to go off with our bath-mat.'

Jones the Bard came roaring out of the window, waving his shears.

'Come back, ystraffaldiach! Will you come down off there and let me mince you into macaroni! Oh, you wicked old weasel, I'll trim your beard shorter than an earwig's toe-nails!'

He made a grab for the bath-mat but it was just out of reach.

'He, he, he!' cackled Jones the Druid up above. 'You didn't know your fine beard would make up so nice into a flying carpet, did you, brother? Has to be woven on a hair-loom on Midsummer Eve and then it'll carry you faster than the Aberdovey Flyer.'

'Just let me get at you, rheibiwr!' snarled Jones the Bard, making another vain grab.

But Dizzry, who was now jumping up and down on the top of Harriet's head, made a tremendous spring, grabbed hold of a trailing strand of Mr Jones's beard, and hauled herself up on to a corner of the flying bath-mat.

'Oh dammo!' gasped the Druid at the sight of her. He was so taken aback that he lost his balance, staggered, and fell headlong on top of his brother. There was a windmill confusion of arms and legs, all swamped by the foaming mass of beard. Then Jones the Bard grabbed his shears with a shout of triumph and began chopping away great sways of white hair.

Harriet, however, paid no heed to these goings-on.

'Dizzry!' she shouted, cupping her hands round her mouth. 'It's a wishing-mat. Make it take you—'

Dizzry nodded. She needed no telling. 'Take me to Cathay!' she cried, and the mat soared away through the milky air of midsummer night.

At this moment Mark came running across the field.

'Oh, Mark!' Harriet burst out. 'Look what those old fiends have done to our bathroom! It's ruined. They ought to be made to pay for it.'

Mark glanced through the broken window. The place was certainly a shambles: bath and basin were both smashed, the sponge-rack was wrapped round the hair-drier, the towels were trodden into a soggy pulp and the curtains were in ribbons.

The Jones brothers were in equally bad shape. Jones the Bard was kneeling on Jones the Druid's stomach; he had managed to trim every shred of hair off his brother's head, but he himself was as bald as a coot. Both had black eyes and swollen lips.

'Oh, well,' Mark said. 'They seem to have trouble of their own. I bet neither of them comes into that legacy now. And I never did care much for washing anyway. Look, here comes Dizzry back.'

The bath-mat swooped to a three-point landing, Dizzry and Min rolled off it, laughing and crying.

'You wicked, wicked, bad little girl,' Dizzry cried, shaking and hugging her small sister at the same time. 'Don't you ever dare do such a thing again.'

'Now I will take my own property which is my lawful beard,' said Mr Jones the Bard, and he jumped off his brother's stomach on to the mat and addressed it in a flood of Welsh, which it evidently understood, for it rose into the air and flew off in a westerly direction. Mr Jones the Druid slunk away across the field looking, Dizzry said, as hangdog as a cat that has fallen into the milk.

'Now we've lost our bath-mat,' Harriet sighed.

'I'll help you make another,' Dizzry said. 'There's plenty of hair lying about. And at least we've got Min back.'

'Was it nice in Cathay, Min?' Mark said.

'Smashing. I had rice-cake and cherry ice and Coca-Cola.'

At this point Mr and Mrs Armitage returned from their dance and kindly drove Dizzry and Min to break the joyful news to their parents.

Harriet and Mark had a try at putting the bathroom to rights, but it was really past hope.

'I must say, trouble certainly haunts this household,' remarked Mr Armitage, when he came back and found them at it. 'Hurry up and get to bed, you two. Do you realize it's four o'clock on midsummer morning? Oh, Lord, I suppose now we have to go back to the old regime of sooty footmarks all over the bathroom.'

'Certainly not,' said Mark. 'I'd forgotten to tell you. I found Lady Anne's pearls.'

He pulled them out and dangled them: a soot-black, six-foot double strand of pearls as big as cobnuts, probably worth a king's ransom.

'Won't Ernie Perrow be pleased to know they really were in the chimney?' he said.

'Oh, get to bed!' snapped his father. 'I'm fed up with hearing about the Perrows.'

THE WAY OUT

Mary Norton

he borrowers—Pod, Homily and their daughter Arrietty—are tiny people living in the secret places of an old cottage, borrowing match-boxes, needles and other small objects to make their clothes and furniture. But when the humans decide to leave the cottage, the borrowers must leave too. Their friend Spiller suggests a way out—through the drain...

'What drain?' asked Homily, staring.

'The one in the floor,' said Spiller as though she ought to have known. 'The sink's no good—got an S-bend. And they keep the lid on the copper.'

'I didn't see any drain in the floor ...' said Pod.

'It's under the mangle,' explained Spiller.

'But,' went on Homily, 'I mean, do you always come by the drain?'

'And go,' said Spiller.

'Under cover, like,' Pod pointed out to Homily, 'doesn't have to bother with the weather.'

'Or the woods,' said Homily.

'That's right,' agreed Spiller; 'you don't want to bother with the woods. Not the woods,' he repeated thoughtfully.

'Where does the drain come out?' asked Pod.

'Down by the kettle,' said Spiller.

'What kettle?'

'His kettle,' put in Arrietty excitedly. 'That kettle he's got by the stream...'

'That's right,' said Spiller.

Pod looked thoughtful. 'Do the Hendrearys know this?'

Spiller shook his head. 'Never thought to tell them,' he said.

Pod was silent a moment and then he said: 'Could anyone use this drain?'

'No reason why not,' said Spiller. 'Where you making for?'

'We don't know yet,' said Pod.

Spiller frowned and scratched his knee where the black mud, drying in the warmth of the ash, had turned to a powdery grey. 'Ever thought of the town?' he asked.

'Leighton Buzzard?'

'No,' exclaimed Spiller scornfully, 'Little Fordham.'

Had Spiller suggested a trip to the moon they could not have looked more astonished. Homily's face was a study in disbelief as though she thought Spiller was romancing. Arrietty became very still—she seemed to be holding her breath. Pod looked ponderously startled.

'So there is such a place?' he said slowly.

'Of course there is such a place,' snapped Homily; 'everyone knows that: what they don't know exactly is—*where*? And I doubt if Spiller does either.'

'Two days down the river,' said Spiller, 'if the stream's running good.'

'Oh,' said Pod.

'You mean we have to swim for it?' snapped Homily.

'I got a boat,' said Spiller.

'Oh, my goodness ...' murmured Homily, suddenly deflated.

'Big?' asked Pod.

'Fair,' said Spiller.

'Could she take passengers?' asked Pod.

'Could do,' said Spiller.

'Oh, my goodness . . .' murmured Homily again.

'What's the matter, Homily?' asked Pod.

'Can't see myself in a boat,' said Homily, 'not on the water, I can't.'

'Well, a boat's not much good on dry land,' said Pod. 'To get something you got to risk something—that's how it goes. We got to find somewhere to live.'

'There might be something, say, in walking distance,' faltered Homily.

'Such as?'

'Well,' said Homily unhappily, throwing a quick glance at Spiller, 'say, for instance . . . Spiller's kettle.'

'Not much accommodation in a kettle,' said Pod.

'More than there was in a boot,' retorted Homily.

'Now, Homily,' said Pod, suddenly firm, 'you wouldn't be happy, not for twenty-four hours, in a kettle; and inside a week you'd be on at me night and day to find some kind of craft to get you down-stream to Little Fordham. Here you are with the chance of a good home, fresh start, and a free passage, and all you do is go on like a maniac about a drop of clean running water. Now, if it was the drain you objected to—'

Homily turned to Spiller. 'What sort of boat?' she asked nervously. 'I mean, if I could picture it like . . .'

Spiller thought a moment. 'Well,' he said, 'it's wooden.'

'Yes?' said Homily.

Spiller tried again. 'Well, it's like . . . you might say it was something like a knife-box.'

'How much like?' asked Pod.

'Very like,' said Spiller.

'In fact,' declared Homily triumphantly, 'it *is* a knife-box?'

Spiller nodded. 'That's right,' he admitted.

'Flat-bottomed?' asked Pod.

'With divisions, like, for spoons, forks, and so on?' put in Homily.

'That's right,' agreed Spiller, replying to both.

'Tarred and waxed at the seams?'

'Waxed,' said Spiller.

'Sounds all right to me,' said Pod. 'What do you say, Homily?' It sounded better to her too, Pod realized, but he saw she was not quite ready to commit herself. He turned again to Spiller. 'What do you do for power?'

'Power?'

'Got some kind of sail?'

Spiller shook his head. 'Take her down-stream, loaded—with a paddle; pole her back up-stream in ballast...'

'I see,' said Pod. He sounded rather impressed. 'You go often to Little Fordham?'

'Pretty regular,' said Spiller.

'I see,' said Pod again. 'Sure you could give us a lift?'

'Call back for you,' said Spiller, 'at the kettle, say. Got to go up-stream to load.'

'Load what?' asked Homily bluntly.

'The boat,' said Spiller.

'I know that,' said Homily, 'but with what?'

'Now, Homily,' put in Pod, 'that's Spiller's business. No concern of ours. Does a bit of trading up and down the river, I shouldn't wonder. Mixed cargo, eh, Spiller? Nuts, birds' eggs, meat, minnows ... that sort of tackle—more or less what he brings Lupy.'

'Depends what they're short of,' said Spiller.

'They?' exclaimed Homily.

'Now, Homily,' Pod admonished her, 'Spiller's got his customers. Stands to reason. We're not the only borrowers in the world, remember. Not by a long chalk...'

'But these ones at Little Fordham,' Homily pointed out. 'They say they're made of plaster?'

'That's right,' said Spiller, 'painted over. All of a
piece . . . Except one,' he added.

'One live one?' said Pod.

'That's right,' said Spiller.

'Oh, I wouldn't like that,' exclaimed Homily, 'I
wouldn't like that at all: not to be the one live borrower
among a lot of dummy waxworks or whatever they call
themselves. Get on my nerves that would . . .'

'They don't bother him,' said Spiller, 'leastways not
as much, he says, as a whole lot of live ones might.'

'Well, that's a nice friendly attitude, I must say,'
snapped Homily. 'Nice kind of welcome we'll get, I
can see, when we turn up there unexpected.'

'Plenty of houses,' said Spiller; 'no sort of need to
live close . . .'

'And he doesn't own the place,' Pod reminded her.

'That's true,' said Homily.

'What about it, Homily?' said Pod.

'I don't mind,' said Homily, 'providing we live near
the shops.'

'There's nothing in the shops,' explained Pod in a
patient voice, 'or so I've heard tell, but bananas and
suchlike made of plaster and all stuck down in a lump.'

'No, but it sounds nice,' said Homily, 'say you were
talking to Lupy—'

'But you won't be talking to Lupy,' said Pod. 'Lupy
won't even know we're gone until she wakes up
tomorrow morning thinking that she's got to get us
breakfast. No, Homily,' he went on earnestly, 'you
don't want to make for shopping centres and all that
sort of caper: better some quiet little place down by the
water's edge. You won't want to be everlastingly carting water. And, say Spiller comes down pretty regular
with a nice bit of cargo, you want somewhere he can tie
up and unload . . . Plenty of time, once we get there, to
have a look round and take our pick.'

'Take our pick . . .' Suddenly Homily felt the magic
of these words: they began to work inside her—cham-

pagne bubbles of excitement welling up and up—
until, at last, she flung her hands together in a sudden
joyful clap. 'Oh, Pod,' she breathed, her eyes brimming as, startled by the noise, he turned sharply
towards her, 'think of it—all those houses ... we
could try them *all* out if we wanted, one after another.
What's to prevent us?'

'Common sense,' said Pod; he smiled at Arrietty:
'What do you say, lass? Shops or water?'

Arrietty cleared her throat. 'Down by water,' she
whispered huskily, her eyes shining and her face
tremulous in the dancing light of the dip. 'At least to
start with ...'

There was a short pause. Pod glanced down at his
tackle strapped to the hat-pin and up at the clock on
the wall. 'Getting on for half past one,' he said; 'time
we had a look at this drain. What do you say, Spiller?
Could you spare us a minute? And show us the ropes
like?'

'Oh,' exclaimed Homily, dismayed, 'I thought
Spiller was coming with us.'

'Now, Homily,' explained Pod, 'it's a long trek and
he's only just arrived—he won't want to go back right
away.'

'I don't see why not if his clothes aren't ready—
that's what you came for, isn't it, Spiller?'

'That and other things,' said Pod; 'dare say he's
brought a few oddments for Lupy.'

'That's all right,' said Spiller, 'I can tip 'em out on the
floor.'

'And you will come?' cried Homily.

Spiller nodded. 'Might as well.'

Even Pod seemed slightly relieved. 'That's very civil
of you, Spiller,' he said, 'very civil indeed.' He turned
to Arrietty: 'Now, Arrietty, take a dip and go and fetch
the egg.'

'Oh, don't let's bother with the egg,' said Homily.

Pod gave her a look. 'You go and get that egg,

Arrietty. Just roll it along in front of you into the wash-house, but be careful with the light near those shavings. Homily, you bring the other two dips and I'll get the tackle . . .'

*

As they filed through the crack of the door on to the stone flags of the wash-house they heard the ferret again. But Homily now felt brave. 'Scratch away,' she dared it happily, secure in their prospect of escape. But when they stood at last, grouped beneath the mangle and staring down at the drain, her new-found courage ebbed a little and she murmured: 'Oh, my goodness . . .'

Very deep and dark and well-like, it seemed, sunk below the level of the floor. The square grating which usually covered it lay beside it at an angle and in the yawning blackness she could see the reflections of their dips. A dank draught quivered round the candle flames and there was a sour smell of yellow soap, stale disinfectant, and tea leaves.

'What's that at the bottom?' she asked, peering down. 'Water?'

'Slime,' said Spiller.

'Jellied soap,' put in Pod quickly.

'And we've got to wade through that?'

'It isn't deep,' said Spiller.

'Not as though this drain was a sewer,' said Pod, trying to sound comforting and hearty. 'Beats me though,' he went on to Spiller, 'how you manage to move this grating.'

Spiller showed him. Lowering the dip, he pointed out a short length of what looked like brass curtain rod, strong but hollow, perched on a stone at the bottom of the well and leaning against the side. The top of this rod protruded slightly above the mouth of the drain. The grating, when in place, lay loosely on its worn rim of cement. Spiller explained how, by exerting all his strength on the rod from below, he could raise one corner of the grating—as a washerwoman with a prop can raise up a clothes-line. He would then slide the base of the prop on to the raised stone in the base of the shaft, thus holding the contraption in place. Spiller would then swing himself up to the mouth of the drain on a piece of twine tied to a rung of the grating: 'only about twice my height,' he explained. The twine, Pod gathered, was a fixture. The double twist round the light iron rung was hardly noticeable from above and the length of the twine, when not in use, hung downwards into the drain. Should Spiller want to remove the grating entirely, as was the case today, after scrambling through the aperture raised by the rod he would pull the twine after him, fling it around one of the stays of the mangle above his head, and would drag and pull on the end. Sometimes, Spiller explained, the grating slid easily, at other times it stuck on an angle. In which event Spiller would produce a small but heavy bolt, kept specially for the purpose, which he would wind into the free end of his halyard and, climbing into the girder-like structure at the base of the mangle, would swing himself out on the bolt which, sinking under his weight, exerted a pull on the grating.

'Very ingenious,' said Pod. Dip in hand he went deeper under the mangle, examined the wet twine, pulled on the knots and finally, as though to test its weight, gave the grating a shove—it slid smoothly on the worn flagstones. 'Easier to shove than to lift,' he

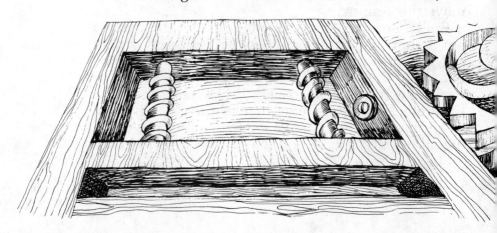

remarked. Arrietty, glancing upwards, saw vast shadows on the wash-house ceiling—moving and melting, advancing and receding—in the flickering light from their dips: wheels, handles, rollers, shifting spokes . . . as though, she thought, the great mangle under which they stood was silently and magically turning . . .

On the ground, beside the drain, she saw an object she recognized: the lid of an aluminium soap-box, the one in which the summer before last Spiller had spun her down the river, and from which he used to fish. It was packed now with some kind of cargo and covered with a piece of worn hide—possibly a rat skin—strapped over lid and all with lengths of knotted twine. From a hole bored in one end of the rim a second piece of twine protruded. 'I pull her up by that,' explained Spiller, following the direction of her eyes.

'I see how you get up,' said Homily unhappily, peering into the slime, 'but it's how you get down that worries me.'

'Oh, you just drop,' said Spiller. He took hold of the twine as he spoke and began to drag the tin lid away towards the door.

'It's all right, Homily,' Pod promised hurriedly, 'we'll let you down on the bolt,' and he turned quickly to Spiller. 'Where you going with that?' he asked.

Spiller, it seemed, not wishing to draw attention to the drain, was going to unpack next door. The house being free of humans and the log-box pulled out there

was no need to go upstairs—he could dump what he'd brought beside the hole in the skirting.

While he was gone Pod outlined a method of procedure: '... if Spiller agrees,' he kept saying, courteously conceding the leadership.

Spiller did agree, or rather he raised no objections. The empty soap-box lid, lightly dangling, was lowered on to the mud: into this they dropped the egg—rolling it to the edge of the drain as though it were a giant rugby football, with a final kick from Pod to send it spinning and keep it clear of the sides. It plopped into the soap-box lid with an ominous crack. This did not matter, however, the egg being hard-boiled.

Homily, with not a few nervous exclamations, was lowered next seated astride the bolt; with one hand she clung to the twine, in the other she carried a lighted dip. When she climbed off the bolt into the lid of the soap-box the latter slid swiftly away on the slime, and Homily, for an anxious moment, disappeared down the drain. Spiller drew her back, however, hand over hand. And there she sat behind the egg, grumbling a little, but with her candle still alight. 'Two can go in the lid,' Spiller had announced, and Arrietty (who secretly had longed to try the drop) was lowered considerately, dip in hand, in the same respectful way. She settled herself opposite her mother with the egg wobbling between them.

'You two are the light-bearers,' said Pod. 'All you've got to do is to sit quite still and—steady the egg—move the lights as we say ...'

There was a little shuffling about in the lid and some slightly perilous balancing as Homily, who had never liked travelling—as human beings would say—back to the engine, stood up to change seats with Arrietty. 'Keep a good hold on that string,' she kept imploring Spiller as she completed this manoeuvre, but soon she and Arrietty were seated again face to face, each with their candle and the egg between their knees. Arrietty was laughing.

'Now I'm going to let you go a little ways,' warned Spiller and paid out a few inches of twine. Arrietty and Homily slid smoothly under the roof of their arched tunnel, which gleamed wetly in the candlelight. Arrietty put out a finger and touched the gleaming surface: it seemed to be made of baked clay.

'Don't touch *anything*,' hissed Homily shudderingly, 'and don't breathe either—not unless you have to.'

Arrietty, lowering her dip, peered over the side at the mud. 'There's a fishbone,' she remarked, 'and a tin bottle top. And a hairpin . . .' she added on a pleased note.

'Don't even *look*,' shuddered Homily.

'A hairpin would be useful,' Arrietty pointed out.

Homily closed her eyes. 'All right,' she said, her face drawn with the effort not to mind. 'Pick it out quickly and drop it, sharp, in the bottom of the boat. And wipe your hands on my apron.'

'We can wash it in the river,' Arrietty pointed out.

Homily nodded: she was trying not to breathe.

Over Homily's shoulder Arrietty could see into the well of the drain; a bulky object was coming down the shaft: it was Pod's tackle, waterproof wrapped and strapped securely to his hat-pin. It wobbled on the mud with a slight squelch. Pod, after a while, came after it. Then came Spiller. For a moment the surface seemed to bear their weight then, knee deep, they sank in slime.

Spiller removed the length of curtain rod from the stone and set it up inconspicuously in the corner of the shaft. Before their descent he and Pod must have placed the grating above more conveniently in position: a deft pull by Spiller on the twine and they heard it clamp down into place—a dull metallic sound which echoed hollowly along the length of their tunnel. Homily gazed into the blackness ahead as though following its flight. 'Oh, my goodness,' she breathed as the sound died: she felt suddenly shut in.

'Well,' announced Pod in a cheerful voice, coming up behind them, and he placed a hand on the rim of their lid, 'we're off!'

*

Spiller, they saw, to control them on a shorter length, was rolling up the towline. Not that towline was quite the right expression under the circumstances. The drain ran ahead on a slight downwards incline and Spiller functioned more as a sea anchor and used the twine as a brake.

'Here we go,' said Pod, and gave the lid a slight push. They slid ahead on the slippery scum, to be lightly checked by Spiller. The candlelight danced and shivered on the arched roof and about the dripping walls. So thick and soapy was the scum on which they rode that Pod, behind them, seemed more to be leading his bundle than dragging it behind him. Sometimes, even, it seemed to be leading him.

'Whoa, there!' he would cry on such occasions. He was in very good spirits, and had been, Arrietty noticed, from the moment he set foot in the drain. She too felt strangely happy: here she was, with the two she held most dear, with Spiller added, making their way towards the dawn. The drain held no fears for Arrietty: leading as it did towards a life to be lived away from dust and candlelight and confining shadows—a life on which the sun would shine by day and the moon by night.

She twisted round in her seat in order to see ahead, and as she did so a great aperture opened to her left and a dank draught flattened the flame of the candle. She shielded it quickly with her hand and Homily did the same.

'That's where the pipe from the sink comes in,' said Spiller, 'and the overflow from the copper . . .'

There were other openings as they went along, drains which branched into darkness and ran away uphill. Where these joined the main drain a curious

collection of flotsam and jetsam piled up over which
they had to drag the soap-box lid. Arrietty and Homily
got out for this to make less weight for the men. Spiller
knew all these branch drains by name and the exact
position of each cottage or house concerned. Arrietty
began, at last, to understand the vast resources of
Spiller's trading. 'Not that you get up into all of 'em,'
he explained. 'I don't mind an S-bend, but where you
get an S-bend you're apt to get a brass grille or suchlike
in the plug hole.'

Once he said, jerking his head towards the mouth of
a circular cavern: 'Holmcroft, that is . . . nothing but
bath water from now on . . .' And, indeed, this cavern
as they slid past it had looked cleaner than most—a
shining cream-coloured porcelain, and the air from
that point onwards, Arrietty noticed, smelled far less
strongly of tea leaves.

Every now and again they came across small
branches—of ash or holly—rammed so securely into
place that they would have difficulty manoeuvring
round them. They were set, Arrietty noticed, at almost
regular intervals. 'I can't think how these tree things
get down drains, anyway,' Homily exclaimed irritably
when, for about the fifth time, the soap-box lid was
turned up sideways and eased past and she and
Arrietty stood ankle deep in jetsam, shielding their
dips with their hands.

'I put them there,' said Spiller, holding the boat for
them to get in again. The drain at this point dropped
more steeply. As Homily stepped in opposite Arrietty
the soap-box lid suddenly slid away, dragging Spiller
after: he slipped and skidded on the surface of the mud
but miraculously he kept his balance. They fetched up
in a tangle against the trunk of one of Spiller's tree-like
erections and Arrietty' dip went overboard. 'So that's
what they're for,' exclaimed Homily as she coaxed her
own flattened wick back to brightness to give Arrietty
a light.

But Spiller did not answer straight away. He pushed past the obstruction and, as they waited for Pod to catch up, he said suddenly: 'Could be . . .'

Pod looked weary when he came up to them. He was panting a little and had stripped off his jacket and slung it round his shoulders. 'That last lap's always the longest,' he pointed out.

'Would you care for a ride in the lid?' asked Homily. 'Do, Pod!'

'No, I'm better walking,' said Pod.

'Then give me your jacket,' said Homily. She folded it gently across her knees and patted it soberly as though (thought Arrietty watching) it too were tired, like Pod.

And then they were off again—an endless, monotonous vista of circular walls. Arrietty after a while began to doze: she slid forward against the egg, her head caught up on one knee. Just before she fell asleep she felt Homily slide the dip from her drooping fingers and wrap her round with Pod's coat.

When she awoke the scene was much the same: shadows sliding and flickering on the wet ceiling, Spiller's narrow face palely lit as he trudged along and the bulky shape beyond which was Pod; her mother, across the egg, smiling at her bewilderment. 'Forgotten where you were?' asked Homily.

Arrietty nodded. Her mother held a dip in either hand and the wax, Arrietty noticed, had burned very low. 'Must be nearly morning,' Arrietty remarked. She still felt very sleepy.

'Shouldn't wonder . . .' said Homily.

The walls slid by, unbroken except for arch-like thickening at regular intervals where one length of pipe joined another. And when they spoke their voices echoed hollowly, back and forth along the tunnel.

'Aren't there any more branch drains?' Arrietty asked after a moment.

Spiller shook his head. 'No more now. Holmcroft was the last . . .'

'But that was ages ago . . . we must be nearly there.'

'Getting on,' said Spiller.

Arrietty shivered and drew Pod's coat more tightly around her shoulders: the air seemed fresher suddenly and curiously free from smell. 'Or perhaps,' she thought, 'we've grown more used to it . . .' There was no sound except for the whispering slide of the soap-box lid and the regular plop and suction of Pod's and Spiller's footsteps. But the silt seemed rather thinner: there was an occasional grating sound below the base of the tin-lid as though it rode on grit. Spiller stood still. 'Listen,' he said.

They were all quiet but could hear nothing except Pod's breathing and a faint musical drip somewhere just ahead of them. 'Better push on,' said Homily suddenly, breaking the tension; 'these dips aren't going to last for ever.'

'Quiet!' cried Spiller again. Then they heard a faint drumming sound, hardly more than a vibration.

'Whatever is it?' asked Homily.

'Can only be Holmcroft,' said Spiller. He stood rigid, with one hand raised, listening intently. 'But,' he said, turning to Pod, 'whoever'd be having a bath at this time o' night?'

Pod shook his head. 'It's morning by now,' he said; 'must be getting on for six.'

The drumming sound grew louder, less regular, more like a leaping and a banging . . .

'We've got to run for it!' cried Spiller. Towline in hand he swung the tin-lid round and, taking the lead, flew ahead into the tunnel. Arrietty and Homily banged and rattled behind him. Dragged on the short line they swung shatteringly, thrown from wall to wall. But, panic-stricken at the thought of total dark-ness, each shielded the flame of her candle. Homily stretched out a free hand to Pod who caught hold of it

just as his bundle bore down on him, knocking him over. He fell across it, still gripping Homily's hand, and was carried swiftly along.

'Out and up!' cried Spiller from the shadows ahead, and they saw the glistening twigs wedged tautly against the roof. 'Let the traps go!' he was shouting. 'Come on—climb!'

They each seized a branch and swung themselves up and wedged themselves tight against the ceiling. The over-turned dips lay guttering in the tin-lid and the air was filled with the sound of galloping water. In the jerking light from the dips they saw the first pearly bubbles and the racing, dancing, silvery bulk behind. And then all was choking, swirling, scented darkness.

After the first few panic-stricken seconds Arrietty found she could breathe and that the sticks still held. A mill-race of hot, scented water swilled through her clothes, piling against her at one moment, falling away the next. Sometimes it bounced above her shoulders, drenching her face and hair, at others it swirled steadily about her waist and tugged at her legs and feet. 'Hold on!' shouted Pod above the turmoil.

'Die down soon!' shouted Spiller.

'You there, Arrietty?' gasped Homily. They were all there and all breathing and, even as they realized this, the water began to drop in level and run less swiftly. Without the brightness of the dips the darkness about them seemed less opaque, as though a silvery haze rose from the water itself, which seemed now to be running well below them and, from the sound of it, as innocent and steady as a brook.

After a while they climbed down into it and felt a smoothly running warmth about their ankles. At this level they could see a faint translucence where the surface of the water met the blackness of the walls. 'Seems lighter,' said Pod wonderingly. He seemed to perceive some shifting in the darkness where Spiller splashed and probed. 'Anything there?' he asked.

'Not a thing,' said Spiller.

Their baggage had disappeared—egg, soap-box lid, and all—swept away on the flood.

'And now what?' asked Pod dismally.

But Spiller seemed quite unworried. 'Pick it up later,' he said; 'nothing to hurt. And saves carting.'

Homily was sniffing the air. 'Sandalwood!' she exclaimed suddenly to Arrietty. 'Your father's favourite soap.'

But Arrietty, her hand on a twig to steady herself against the warm flow eddying past her ankles, did not reply; she was staring straight ahead down the incline of the drain. A bead of light hung in the darkness. For a moment she thought that, by some miraculous chance, it might be one of the dips— then she saw it was completely round and curiously steady. And mingled with the scent of sandalwood she smelled another smell—minty, grassy, mildly earthy...

'It's dawn,' she announced in a wondering voice; 'and what's more,' she went on, staring spellbound at the distant pearl of light, 'that's the end of the drain.'

RIDDLES IN THE DARK

J. R. R. Tolkien

Having left Bag End, his comfortable home, the hobbit Bilbo Baggins sets off with the wizard Gandalf and a company of dwarfs to recover a hoard of gold stolen by the dragon Smaug. Now, separated from his friends by a sudden goblin attack, Bilbo finds himself lost and alone in the eery depths of the Lonely Mountain . . .

When Bilbo opened his eyes, he wondered if he had; for it was just as dark as with them shut. No one was anywhere near him. Just imagine his fright! He could hear nothing, see nothing, and he could feel nothing except the stone of the floor.

Very slowly he got up and groped about on all fours, till he touched the wall of the tunnel; but neither up nor down it could he find anything: nothing at all, no sign of goblins, no sign of dwarves. His head was swimming, and he was far from certain even of the direction they had been going in when he had his fall. He guessed as well as he could, and crawled along for a good way, till suddenly his hand met what felt like a tiny ring of cold metal lying on the floor of the tunnel. It was a turning point in his career, but he did not know it. He put the ring in his pocket almost without thinking; certainly it did not seem of any particular use at the moment. He did not go much further, but sat down on the cold floor and gave himself up to complete miserableness, for a long while. He thought of himself frying bacon and eggs in his own kitchen at home—for he could feel inside that it was high time for some meal or other; but that only made him miserabler.

He could not think what to do; nor could he think what had happened; or why he had been left behind; or why, if he had been left behind, the goblins had not caught him; or even why his head was so sore. The truth was he had been lying quiet, out of sight and out of mind, in a very dark corner for a long while.

After some time he felt for his pipe. It was not broken, and that was something. Then he felt for his pouch, and there was some tobacco in it, and that was something more. Then he felt for matches and he could not find any at all, and that shattered his hopes completely. Just as well for him, as he agreed when he came to his senses. Goodness knows what the striking of matches and the smell of tobacco would have brought on him out of dark holes in that horrible place. Still at the moment he felt very crushed. But in slapping all his pockets and feeling all round himself for matches his hand came on the hilt of his little sword—the little dagger that he got from the trolls, and that he had quite forgotten; nor fortunately had the goblins noticed it, as he wore it inside his breeches.

Now he drew it out. It shone pale and dim before his eyes. 'So it is an elvish blade, too,' he thought; 'and goblins are not very near, and yet not far enough.'

But somehow he was comforted. It was rather splendid to be wearing a blade made in Gondolin for the goblin-wars of which so many songs had sung; and also he had noticed that such weapons made a great impression on goblins that came upon them suddenly.

'Go back?' he thought. 'No good at all! Go sideways!

Impossible! Go forward? Only thing to do! On we go!'
So up he got, and trotted along with his little sword
held in front of him and one hand feeling the wall, and
his heart all of a patter and a pitter.

*

Now certainly Bilbo was in what is called a tight place.
But you must remember it was not quite so tight for
him as it would have been for me or for you. Hobbits
are not quite like ordinary people; and after all if their
holes are nice cheery places and properly aired, quite
different from the tunnels of the goblins, still they are
more used to tunnelling than we are, and they do not
easily lose their sense of direction underground—not
when their heads have recovered from being bumped.
Also they can move very quietly, and hide easily, and
recover wonderfully from falls and bruises, and they
have a fund of wisdom and wise sayings that men
have mostly never heard or have forgotten long ago.

I should not have liked to have been in Mr Baggins'
place, all the same. The tunnel seemed to have no end.
All he knew was that it was still going down pretty
steadily and keeping in the same direction in spite of a
twist and a turn or two. There were passages leading
off to the side every now and then, as he knew by the
glimmer of his sword, or could feel with his hand on
the wall. Of these he took no notice, except to hurry
past for fear of goblins or half-imagined dark things
coming out of them. On and on he went, and down
and down; and still he heard no sound of anything
except the occasional whirr of a bat by his ears, which
startled him at first, till it became too frequent to bother
about. I do not know how long he kept on like this,
hating to go on, not daring to stop, on, on, until he was
tireder than tired. It seemed like all the way to
tomorrow and over it to the days beyond.

Suddenly without any warning he trotted splash
into water! Ugh! it was icy cold. That pulled him up
sharp and short. He did not know whether it was just a

pool in the path, or the edge of an underground stream that crossed the passage, or the brink of a deep dark subterranean lake. The sword was hardly shining at all. He stopped, and he could hear, when he listened hard, drops drip-drip-dripping from an unseen roof into the water below; but there seemed no other sort of sound.

'So it is a pool or a lake, and not an underground river,' he thought. Still he did not dare to wade out into the darkness. He could not swim; and he thought, too, of nasty slimy things, with big bulging blind eyes, wriggling in the water. There are strange things living in the pools and lakes in the hearts of mountains: fish whose fathers swam in, goodness only knows how many years ago, and never swam out again, while their eyes grew bigger and bigger and bigger from trying to see in the blackness; also there are other things more slimy than fish. Even in the tunnels and caves the goblins have made for themselves there are other things living unbeknown to them that have sneaked in from outside to lie up in the dark. Some of these caves, too, go back in their beginnings to ages before the goblins, who only widened them and joined them up with passages, and the original owners are still there in odd corners slinking and nosing about.

Deep down here by the dark water lived old Gollum, a small slimy creature. I don't know where he came from, nor who or what he was. He was a Gollum—as dark as darkness, except for two big round pale eyes in his thin face. He had a little boat, and he rowed about quite quietly on the lake; for lake it was, wide and deep and deadly cold. He paddled it with large feet dangling over the side, but never a ripple did he make. Not he. He was looking out of his pale lamp-like eyes for blind fish, which he grabbed with his long fingers as quick as thinking. He liked meat too. Goblin he thought good, when he could get it; but he took care they never found him out. He just

throttled them from behind, if they ever came down
alone anywhere near the edge of the water, while he
was prowling about. They very seldom did, for they
had a feeling that something unpleasant was lurking
down there, down at the very roots of the mountain.
They had come on the lake, when they were tunnelling down long ago, and they found they could go no
further; so there their road ended in that direction, and
there was no reason to go that way—unless the Great
Goblin sent them. Sometimes he took a fancy for fish
from the lake, and sometimes neither goblin nor fish
came back.

Actually Gollum lived on a slimy island of rock in
the middle of the lake. He was watching Bilbo now
from the distance with his pale eyes like telescopes.
Bilbo could not see him, but he was wondering a lot
about Bilbo, for he could see that he was no goblin at all.

Gollum got into his boat and shot off from the
island, while Bilbo was sitting on the brink altogether
flummoxed and at the end of his way and his wits.
Suddenly up came Gollum and whispered and hissed:

'Bless us and splash us, my preciousss! I guess it's a
choice feast; at least a tasty morsel it'd make us, gollum!' And when he said *gollum* he made a horrible
swallowing noise in his throat. That is how he got his
name, though he always called himself 'my precious'.

The hobbit jumped nearly out of his skin when the
hiss came in his ears, and he suddenly saw the pale
eyes sticking out at him.

'Who are you?' he said, thrusting his dagger in front
of him.

'What iss he, my preciouss?' whispered Gollum
(who always spoke to himself through never having
anyone else to speak to). This is what he had come to
find out, for he was not really very hungry at the
moment, only curious; otherwise he would have
grabbed first and whispered afterwards.

'I am Mr Bilbo Baggins. I have lost the dwarves and I

have lost the wizard, and I don't know where I am; and
I don't want to know, if only I can get away.'

'What's he got in his handses?' said Gollum, looking
at the sword, which he did not quite like.

'A sword, a blade which came out of Gondolin!'

'Sssss,' said Gollum, and became quite polite.
'Praps ye sits here and chats with it a bitsy, my
preciouss. It like riddles, praps it does, does it?' He
was anxious to appear friendly, at any rate for the
moment, and until he found out more about the sword
and the hobbit, whether he was quite alone really,
whether he was good to eat, and whether Gollum was
really hungry. Riddles were all he could think of. Asking them, and sometimes guessing them, had been the
only game he had ever played with other funny
creatures sitting in their holes in the long, long ago,
before he lost all his friends and was driven away,
alone, and crept down, down, into the dark under the
mountains.

'Very well,' said Bilbo, who was anxious to agree,
until he found out more about the creature, whether
he was quite alone, whether he was fierce or hungry,
and whether he was a friend of the goblins.

'You ask first,' he said, because he had not had time
to think of a riddle.

So Gollum hissed:

> *What has roots as nobody sees,*
> *Is taller than trees*
> > *Up, up it goes,*
> > *And yet never grows?*

'Easy!' said Bilbo. 'Mountain, I suppose.'

'Does it guess easy? It must have a competition with
us, my preciouss! If precious asks, and it doesn't
answer, we eats it, my preciouss. If it asks us, and we
doesn't answer, then we does what it wants, eh? We
shows it the way out, yes!'

'All right!' said Bilbo, not daring to disagree, and nearly bursting his brain to think of riddles that could save him from being eaten.

> Thirty white horses on a red hill,
>   First they champ,
>   Then they stamp,
> Then they stand still.

That was all he could think of to ask—the idea of eating was rather on his mind. It was rather an old one, too, and Gollum knew the answer as well as you do.

'Chestnuts, chestnuts,' he hissed. 'Teeth! teeth! my preciousss; but we has only six!' Then he asked his second:

> Voiceless it cries,
> Wingless flutters,
> Toothless bites,
> Mouthless mutters.

'Half a moment!' cried Bilbo, who was still thinking uncomfortably about eating. Fortunately he had once heard something rather like this before, and getting his wits back he thought of the answer. 'Wind, wind of course,' he said, and he was so pleased that he made up one on the spot. 'This'll puzzle the nasty little underground creature,' he thought:

> An eye in a blue face
> Saw an eye in a green face.
> 'That eye is like to this eye'
> Said the first eye,
> 'But in low place,
> Not in high place.'

'Ss, ss, ss,' said Gollum. He had been underground a long long time, and was forgetting this sort of thing.

But just as Bilbo was beginning to hope that the wretch would not be able to answer, Gollum brought up memories of ages and ages and ages before, when he lived with his grandmother in a hole in a bank by a river, 'Sss, sss, my preciouss,' he said. 'Sun on the daisies it means, it does.'

But these ordinary above ground everyday sort of riddles were tiring for him. Also they reminded him of days when he had been less lonely and sneaky and nasty, and that put him out of temper. What is more they made him hungry; so this time he tried something a bit more difficult and more unpleasant:

> *It cannot be seen, cannot be felt,*
> *Cannot be heard, cannot be smelt,*
> *It lies behind stars and under hills,*
> > *And empty holes it fills.*
> *It comes first and follows after,*
> > *Ends life, kills laughter.*

Unfortunately for Gollum Bilbo had heard that sort of thing before; and the answer was all round him anyway. 'Dark!' he said without even scratching his head or putting on his thinking cap.

> *A box without hinges, key, or lid.*
> *Yet golden treasure inside is hid,*

he asked to gain time, until he could think of a really hard

one. This he thought a dreadfully easy chestnut, though he had not asked it in the usual words. But it proved a nasty poser for Gollum. He hissed to himself, and still he did not answer; he whispered and spluttered.

After some while Bilbo became impatient. 'Well, what is it?' he said. 'The answer's not a kettle boiling over, as you seem to think from the noise you are making.'

'Give us a chance; let it give us a chance, my preciouss—ss—ss.'

'Well,' said Bilbo after giving him a long chance, 'what about your guess?'

But suddenly Gollum remembered thieving from nests long ago, and sitting under the river bank teaching his grandmother, teaching his grandmother to suck—'Eggses!' he hissed. 'Eggses it is!' Then he asked:

> *Alive without breath,*
> *As cold as death;*
> *Never thirsty, ever drinking,*
> *All in mail never clinking.*

He also in his turn thought this was a dreadfully easy one, because he was always thinking of the answer. But he could not remember anything better at the moment, he was so flustered by the egg-question. All the same it was a poser for poor Bilbo, who never had anything to do with the water if he could help it. I

imagine you know the answer, of course, or can guess
it as easy as winking, since you are sitting comfortably
at home and have not the danger of being eaten to
disturb your thinking. Bilbo sat and cleared his throat
once or twice, but no answer came.

After a while Gollum began to hiss with pleasure to
himself: 'Is it nice, my preciousss? Is it juicy? Is it
scrumptiously crunchable?' He began to peer at Bilbo
out of the darkness.

'Half a moment,' said the hobbit shivering. 'I gave
you a good long chance just now.'

'It must make haste, haste!' said Gollum, beginning
to climb out of his boat on to the shore to get at Bilbo.
But when he put his long webby foot in the water, a
fish jumped out in fright and fell on Bilbo's toes.

'Ugh!' he said, 'it is cold and clammy!'—and so he
guessed. 'Fish! fish!' he cried. 'It is fish!'

Gollum was dreadfully disappointed: but Bilbo
asked another riddle as quick as ever he could, so that
Gollum had to get back into his boat and think.

No-legs lay on one-leg, two-legs sat near on three-legs,
four-legs got some.

It was not really the right time for this riddle, but
Bilbo was in a hurry. Gollum might have had some
trouble guessing it, if he had asked it at another time.
As it was, talking of fish, 'no-legs' was not so very
difficult, and after that the rest was easy. 'Fish on a
little table, man at table sitting on a stool, and cat has
the bones' that of course is the answer, and Gollum
soon gave it. Then he thought the time had come to ask
something hard and horrible. This is what he said:

This thing all things devours:
Birds, beasts, trees, flowers;
Gnaws iron, bites steel;
Grinds hard stones to meal;
Slays king, ruins town,
And beats high mountain down.

Poor Bilbo sat in the dark thinking of all the horrible names of all the giants and ogres he had ever heard told of in tales, but not one of them had done all these things. He had a feeling that the answer was quite different and that he ought to know it, but he could not think of it. He began to get frightened, and that is bad for thinking. Gollum began to get out of his boat. He flapped into the water and paddled to the bank; Bilbo could not see his eyes coming towards him. His tongue seemed to stick in his mouth; he wanted to shout out: 'Give me more time! Give me time!' But all that came out with a sudden squeal was:

'Time! Time!'

Bilbo was saved by pure luck. For that of course was the answer.

Gollum was disappointed once more; and now he was getting angry, and also tired of the game. It had made him very hungry indeed. This time he did not go back to the boat. He sat down in the dark by Bilbo. That made the hobbit most dreadfully uncomfortable and scattered his wits.

'It's got to ask uss a quesstion, my preciouss, yes, yess, yesss. Jusst one more question to guess, yes, yess,' said Gollum.

But Bilbo simply could not think of any question with that nasty wet cold thing sitting next to him, and pawing and poking him. He scratched himself, he pinched himself; still he could not think of anything.

'Ask us! ask us!' said Gollum.

Bilbo pinched himself and slapped himself; he gripped on his little sword; he even felt in his pocket with his other hand. There he found the ring he had picked up in the passage and forgotten about.

'What have I got in my pocket?' he said aloud. He was talking to himself, but Gollum thought it was a riddle, and he was frightfully upset.

'Not fair! not fair!' he hissed. 'It isn't fair, my precious, is it, to ask us what it's got in its nassty little pocketses?'

Bilbo seeing what had happened and having nothing better to ask stuck to his question, 'What have I got in my pocket?' he said louder.

'S-s-s-s-s,' hissed Gollum. 'It must give us three guesseses, my preciouss, three guesseses.'

'Very well! Guess away!' said Bilbo.

'Handses!' said Gollum.

'Wrong,' said Bilbo, who had luckily just taken his hand out again. 'Guess again!'

'S-s-s-s-s,' said Gollum more upset than ever. He thought of all the things he kept in his own pockets: fish-bones, goblins' teeth, wet shells, a bit of bat-wing, a sharp stone to sharpen his fangs on, and other nasty things. He tried to think what other people kept in their pockets.

'Knife!' he said at last.

'Wrong!' said Bilbo, who had lost his some time ago. 'Last guess!'

Now Gollum was in a much worse state than when Bilbo had asked him the egg-question. He hissed and spluttered and rocked himself backwards and for-wards, and slapped his feet on the floor, and wriggled and squirmed; but still he did not dare to waste his last guess.

'Come on!' said Bilbo. 'I am waiting!' He tried to sound bold and cheerful, but he did not feel at all sure how the game was going to end, whether Gollum guessed right or not.

'Time's up!' he said.

'String, or nothing!' shrieked Gollum, which was not quite fair—working in two guesses at once.

'Both wrong,' cried Bilbo very much relieved; and he jumped at once to his feet, put his back to the nearest wall, and held out his little sword. He knew, of course, that the riddle-game was sacred and of immense antiquity, and even wicked creatures were afraid to cheat when they played at it. But he felt he could not trust this slimy thing to keep any promise at a pinch. Any excuse would do for him to slide out of it. And after all that last question had not been a genuine riddle according to the ancient laws.

But at any rate Gollum did not at once attack him. He could see the sword in Bilbo's hand. He sat still, shivering and whispering. At last Bilbo could wait no longer.

'Well?' he said. 'What about your promise? I want to go. You must show me the way.'

'Did we say so, precious? Show the nassty little Baggins the way out, yes, yes. But what has it got in its pocketses, eh? Not string, precious, but not nothing. Oh no! gollum!'

'Never you mind,' said Bilbo. 'A promise is a promise.'

'Cross it is, impatient, precious,' hissed Gollum. 'But it must wait, yes it must. We can't go up the tunnels so hasty. We must go and get some things first, yes, things to help us.'

'Well, hurry up!' said Bilbo, relieved to think of Gollum going away. He thought he was just making an excuse and did not mean to come back. What was Gollum talking about? What useful thing could he keep out on the dark lake? But he was wrong. Gollum did mean to come back. He was angry now and hungry. And he was a miserable wicked creature, and already he had a plan.

Not far away was his island, of which Bilbo knew nothing, and there in his hiding-place he kept a few wretched oddments, and one very beautiful thing, very beautiful, very wonderful. He had a ring, a golden ring, a precious ring.

'My birthday-present!' he whispered to himself, as he had often done in the endless dark days. 'That's what we wants now, yes; we wants it!'

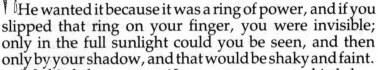

He wanted it because it was a ring of power, and if you slipped that ring on your finger, you were invisible; only in the full sunlight could you be seen, and then only by your shadow, and that would be shaky and faint.

'My birthday-present! It came to me on my birthday, my precious.' So he had always said to himself. But who knows how Gollum came by that present, ages ago in the old days when such rings were still at large in the world? Perhaps even the Master who ruled them could not have said. Gollum used to wear it at first, till it tired him; and then he kept it in a pouch next his skin, till it galled him; and now usually he hid it in a hole in the rock on his island, and was always going back to look at it. And still sometimes he put it on, when he could not bear to be parted from it any longer, or when he was very, very, hungry, and tired of fish. Then he would creep along dark passages looking for stray goblins. He might even venture into places where the torches were lit and made his eyes blink and smart; for he would be safe. Oh yes, quite safe. No one would see him, no one would notice him, till he had his fingers on their throat. Only a few hours ago he had worn it, and caught a small goblin-imp. How it squeaked! He still had a bone or two left to gnaw, but he wanted something softer.

'Quite safe, yes,' he whispered to himself. 'It won't see us, will it, my precious? No. It won't see us, and its nasty little sword will be useless, yes quite.'

That is what was in his wicked little mind, as he slipped suddenly from Bilbo's side, and flapped back to his boat, and went off into the dark. Bilbo thought he had heard the last of him. Still he waited a while; for he had no idea how to find his way out alone.

Suddenly he heard a screech. It sent a shiver down his back. Gollum was cursing and wailing away in the gloom, not very far off by the sound of it. He was on his island, scrabbling here and there, searching and seeking in vain.

'Where is it? Where iss it?' Bilbo heard him crying. 'Losst it is, my precious, lost, lost! Curse us and crush us, my precious is lost!'

'What's the matter?' Bilbo called. 'What have you lost?'

'It mustn't ask us,' shrieked Gollum. 'Not its business, no, gollum! It's losst, gollum, gollum, gollum.'

'Well, so am I,' cried Bilbo, 'and I want to get unlost. And I won the game, and you promised. So come along! Come and let me out, and then go on with your looking!' Utterly miserable as Gollum sounded, Bilbo could not find much pity in his heart, and he had a feeling that anything Gollum wanted so much could hardly be something good. 'Come along!' he shouted.

'No, not yet, precious!' Gollum answered. 'We must search for it, it's lost, gollum.'

'But you never guessed my last question, and you promised,' said Bilbo.

'Never guessed!' said Gollum. Then suddenly out of the gloom came a sharp hiss. 'What has it got in its pocketses? Tell us that. It must tell first.'

As far as Bilbo knew, there was no particular reason why he should not tell. Gollum's mind had jumped to a guess quicker than his; naturally, for Gollum had brooded for ages on this one thing, and he was always afraid of its being stolen. But Bilbo was annoyed at the delay. After all, he had won the game, pretty fairly, at a horrible risk. 'Answers were to be guessed not given,' he said.

'But it wasn't a fair question,' said Gollum. 'Not a riddle, precious, no.'

'Oh well, if it's a matter of ordinary questions,' Bilbo replied, 'then I asked one first. What have you lost? Tell me that!'

'What has it got in its pocketses?' The sound came hissing louder and sharper, and as he looked towards it, to his alarm Bilbo now saw two small points of light peering at him. As suspicion grew in Gollum's mind, the light of his eyes burned with a pale flame.

'What have you lost?' Bilbo persisted.

But now the light in Gollum's eyes had become a green fire, and it was coming swiftly nearer. Gollum was in his boat again, paddling wildly back to the dark shore; and such a rage of loss and suspicion was in his heart that no sword had any more terror for him.

Bilbo could not guess what had maddened the wretched creature, but he saw that all was up, and that Gollum meant to murder him at any rate. Just in time he turned and ran blindly back up the dark passage down which he had come, keeping close to the wall and feeling it with his left hand.

'What has it got in its pocketses?' he heard the hiss loud behind him, and the splash as Gollum leapt from his boat. 'What have I, I wonder?' he said to himself, as he panted and stumbled along. He put his left hand in his pocket. The ring felt very cold as it quietly slipped on to his groping forefinger.

The hiss was close behind him. He turned now and saw Gollum's eyes like small green lamps coming up the slope. Terrified he tried to run faster, but suddenly he struck his toes on a snag in the floor, and fell flat with his little sword under him.

In a moment Gollum was on him. But before Bilbo could do anything, recover his breath, pick himself up, or wave his sword, Gollum passed by, taking no notice of him, cursing and whispering as he ran.

What could it mean? Gollum could see in the dark. Bilbo could see the light of his eyes palely shining even from behind. Painfully he got up, and sheathed his sword, which was now glowing faintly again, then very cautiously he followed. There seemed nothing else to do. It was no good crawling back down to Gollum's water. Perhaps if he followed him, Gollum might lead him to some way of escape without meaning to.

'Curse it! curse it! curse it!' hissed Gollum. 'Curse the Baggins! It's gone! What has it got in its pocketses?

Oh we guess, we guess, my precious. He's found it, yes he must have. My birthday-present.'

Bilbo pricked up his ears. He was at last beginning to guess himself. He hurried a little, getting as close as he dared behind Gollum, who was still going quickly, not looking back, but turning his head from side to side, as Bilbo could see from the faint glimmer on the walls.

'My birthday-present! Curse it! How did we lose it, my precious? Yes, that's it. When we came this way last, when we twisted that nassty young squeaker. That's it. Curse it! It slipped from us, after all these ages and ages! It's gone, gollum.'

Suddenly Gollum sat down and began to weep, a whistling and gurgling sound horrible to listen to. Bilbo halted and flattened himself against the tunnel-wall. After a while Gollum stopped weeping and began to talk. He seemed to be having an argument with himself.

'It's no good going back there to search, no. We doesn't remember all the places we've visited. And it's no use. The Baggins has got it in its pocketses; the nassty noser has found it, we says.

'We guesses, precious, only guesses. We can't know till we find the nassty creature and squeezes it. But it doesn't know what the present can do, does it? It'll just keep it in its pocketses. It doesn't know, and it can't go far. It's lost itself, the nassty nosey thing. It doesn't know the way out. It said so.

'It said so, yes; but it's tricksy. It doesn't say what it means. It won't say what it's got in its pocketses. It knows. It knows a way in, it must know a way out, yes. It's off to the back-door. To the back-door, that's it.

'The goblinses will catch it then. It can't get out that way, precious.

'Ssss, sss, gollum! Goblinses! Yes, but if it's got the present, our precious present, then goblinses will get it, gollum! They'll find it, they'll find out what it does.

We shan't ever be safe again, never, gollum! One of the goblinses will put it on, and then no one will see him. He'll be there but not seen. Not even our clever eyeses will notice him; and he'll come creepsy and tricksy and catch us, gollum, gollum!

'Then let's stop talking, precious, and make haste. If the Baggins has gone that way, we must go quick and see. Go! Not far now. Make haste!'

With a spring Gollum got up and started shambling off at a great pace. Bilbo hurried after him, still cautiously, though his chief fear now was of tripping on another snag and falling with a noise. His head was in a whirl of hope and wonder. It seemed that the ring he had was a magic ring: it made you invisible! He had heard of such things, of course in old old tales; but it was hard to believe that he really had found one, by accident. Still there it was: Gollum with his bright eyes had passed him by, only a yard to one side.

On they went, Gollum flip-flapping ahead, hissing and cursing; Bilbo behind going as softly as a hobbit can. Soon they came to places where, as Bilbo had noticed on the way down, side-passages opened, this way and that. Gollum began at once to count them.

'One left, yes. One right, yes. Two right, yes, yes. Two left, yes, yes.' And so on and on.

As the count grew he slowed down, and he began to get shaky and weepy; for he was leaving the water further and further behind, and he was getting afraid. Goblins might be about, and he had lost his ring. At last he stopped by a low opening, on their left as they went up.

'Seven right, yes. Six left, yes!' he whispered. 'This is it. This is the way to the back-door, yes. Here's the passage!'

He peered in, and shrank back. 'But we durstn't go in, precious, no we durstn't. Goblinses down there. Lots of goblinses. We smells them. Ssss!

'What shall we do? Curse them and crush them! We

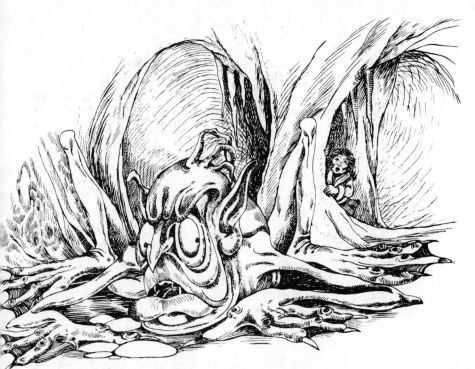

must wait here, precious, wait a bit and see.'

So they came to a dead stop. Gollum had brought
Bilbo to the way out after all, but Bilbo could not get in!
There was Gollum sitting humped up right in the
opening, and his eyes gleamed cold in his head, as he
swayed it from side to side between his knees.

Bilbo crept away from the wall more quietly than a
mouse; but Gollum stiffened at once, and sniffed, and
his eyes went green. He hissed softly but menacingly.
He could not see the hobbit, but now he was on the
alert, and he had other senses that the darkness had
sharpened: hearing and smell. He seemed to be
crouched right down with his flat hands splayed on
the floor, and his head thrust out, nose almost to the
stone. Though he was only a black shadow in the
gleam of his own eyes, Bilbo could see or feel that he
was tense as a bowstring, gathered for a spring.

Bilbo almost stopped breathing, and went stiff himself. He was desperate. He must get away, out of this

horrible darkness, while he had any strength left. He must fight. He must stab the foul thing, put its eyes out, kill it. It meant to kill him. No, not a fair fight. He was invisible now, Gollum had no sword. Gollum had not actually threatened to kill him, or tried to yet. And he was miserable, alone, lost. A sudden understanding, a pity mixed with horror, welled up in Bilbo's heart: a glimpse of endless unmarked days without light or hope of betterment, hard stone, cold fish, sneaking and whispering. All these thoughts passed in a flash of a second. He trembled. And then quite suddenly in another flash, as if lifted by a new strength and resolve, he leaped.

No great leap for a man, but a leap in the dark. Straight over Gollum's head he jumped, seven feet forward and three in the air; indeed, had he known it, he only just missed cracking his skull on the low arch of the passage.

Gollum threw himself backwards, and grabbed as the hobbit flew over him, but too late: his hands snapped on thin air, and Bilbo, falling fair on his sturdy feet, sped off down the new tunnel. He did not turn to see what Gollum was doing. There was a hissing and cursing almost at his heels at first, then it stopped. All at once there came a blood-curdling shriek, filled with hatred and despair. Gollum was defeated. He dared go no further. He had lost: lost his prey, and lost, too, the only thing he had ever cared for, his precious. The cry brought Bilbo's heart to his mouth, but still he held on. Now faint as an echo, but menacing, the voice came behind:

'Thief, thief, thief! Baggins! We hates it, we hates it, we hates it for ever!'

Then there was a silence. But that too seemed menacing to Bilbo. 'If goblins are so near that he smelt them,' he thought, 'then they'll have heard his shrieking and cursing. Careful now, or this way will lead you to worse things.'

The passage was low and roughly made. It was not too difficult for the hobbit, except when, in spite of all care, he stubbed his poor toes again, several times, on nasty jagged stones in the floor. 'A bit low for goblins, at least for the big ones,' thought Bilbo, not knowing that even the big ones, the orcs of the mountains, go along at a great speed stooping low with their hands almost on the ground.

Soon the passage that had been sloping down began to go up again, and after a while it climbed steeply. That slowed Bilbo down. But at last the slope stopped, the passage turned a corner, and dipped down again, and there, at the bottom of a short incline, he saw, filtering round another corner—a glimpse of light. Not red light, as of fire or lantern, but a pale out-of-doors sort of light. Then Bilbo began to run.

Scuttling as fast as his legs would carry him he turned the last corner and came suddenly right into an open space, where the light, after all that time in the dark, seemed dazzlingly bright. Really it was only a leak of sunshine in through a doorway, where a great door, a stone door, was left standing open.

Bilbo blinked, and then suddenly he saw the goblins: goblins in full armour with drawn swords sitting just inside the door, and watching it with wide eyes, and watching the passage that led to it. They were aroused, alert, ready for anything.

They saw him sooner than he saw them. Yes, they saw him. Whether it was an accident, or a last trick of the ring before it took a new master, it was not on his finger. With yells of delight the goblins rushed upon him.

A pang of fear and loss, like an echo of Gollum's misery, smote Bilbo, and forgetting even to draw his sword he stuck his hands into his pockets. And there was the ring still, in his left pocket, and it slipped on his finger. The goblins stopped short. They could not see a sign of him. He had vanished. They yelled twice as loud as before, but not so delightedly.

'Where is it?' they cried.

'Go back up the passage!' some shouted.

'This way!' some yelled. 'That way!' others yelled.

'Look out for the door,' bellowed the captain.

Whistles blew, armour clashed, swords rattled, goblins cursed and swore and ran hither and thither, falling over one another and getting very angry. There was a terrible outcry, to-do, and disturbance.

Bilbo was dreadfully frightened, but he had the sense to understand what had happened and to sneak behind a big barrel which held drink for the goblin-guards, and so get out of the way and avoid being bumped into, trampled to death, or caught by feel.

'I must get to the door, I must get to the door!' he kept on saying to himself, but it was a long time before he ventured to try. Then it was like a horrible game of blind-man's-buff. The place was full of goblins running about, and the poor little hobbit dodged this way and that, was knocked over by a goblin who could not make out what he had bumped into, scrambled away on all fours, slipped between the legs of the captain just in time, got up, and ran for the door.

It was still ajar, but a goblin had pushed it nearly to. Bilbo struggled but he could not move it. He tried to squeeze through the crack. He squeezed and squeezed, and he stuck! It was awful. His buttons had got wedged on the edge of the door and the door-post. He could see outside into the open air: there were a few steps running down into a narrow valley between tall mountains; the sun came out from behind a cloud and shone bright on the outside of the door—but he could not get through.

Suddenly one of the goblins inside shouted: 'There is a shadow by the door. Something is outside!'

Bilbo's heart jumped into his mouth. He gave a terrific squirm. Buttons burst off in all directions. He was through, with a torn coat and waistcoat, leaping down the steps like a goat, while bewildered goblins were still picking up his nice brass buttons on the door-step.

Of course they soon came down after him, hooting and hallooing, and hunting among the trees. But they don't like the sun: it makes their legs wobble and their heads giddy. They could not find Bilbo with the ring on, slipping in and out of the shadow of the trees, running quick and quiet, and keeping out of the sun; so soon they went back grumbling and cursing to guard the door. Bilbo had escaped.

THE PHANTOM
TOLLBOOTH

Norton Juster

here was once a boy named Milo who didn't know what to do with himself—not just sometimes, but always.

When he was in school he longed to be out, and when he was out he longed to be in. On the way he thought about coming home, and coming home he thought about going. Wherever he was he wished he was somewhere else, and when he got there he wondered why he'd bothered. Nothing really interested him—least of all the things that should have.

'It seems to me that almost everything is a waste of time,' he remarked one day as he walked dejectedly home from school. 'I can't see the point in learning to solve useless problems, or subtracting turnips from turnips, or knowing where Ethiopia is, or how to spell February.' And, since no one bothered to explain otherwise, he regarded the process of seeking knowledge as the greatest waste of time of all.

As he and his unhappy thoughts hurried along (for while he was never anxious to be where he was going, he liked to get there as quickly as possible) it seemed a great wonder that the world, which was so large, could sometimes feel so small and empty.

'And worst of all,' he continued sadly, 'there's nothing for me to do, nowhere I'd care to go, and hardly anything worth seeing.' He punctuated this last thought with such a deep sigh that a house sparrow singing near by stopped and rushed home to be with his family.

Without stopping or looking up, he rushed past the buildings and busy shops that lined the street and in a few minutes reached home—dashed through the hall—hopped into the lift—two, three, four, five, six, seven, eight, and off again—opened the door of the flat—rushed into his room—flopped dejectedly into a chair, and grumbled softly, 'Another long afternoon.'

He looked glumly at all the things he owned. The books that were too much trouble to read, the tools he'd never learned to use, the small electric car he hadn't driven for months—or was it years?—and the hundreds of other games and toys, and bats and balls, and bits and pieces scattered around him. And then, on the far side of the room he noticed something he had certainly never seen before.

Who could possibly have left such an enormous package and such a strange one? For, while it was not quite square, it was definitely not round, and for its size it was larger than almost any other big package of smaller dimension that he'd ever seen.

Attached to one side was a bright-blue envelope which said simply: FOR MILO, WHO HAS PLENTY OF TIME.

Of course, if you've ever received a surprise package, you can imagine how puzzled and excited Milo was; and if you've never received one, pay close attention, because some day you might.

'I don't think it's my birthday,' he puzzled, 'and Christmas must be months away, and I haven't been outstandingly good, or even good at all.' (He had to admit this, even to himself.) 'Probably I won't like it anyway, but since I don't know where it came from, I can't possibly send it back.' He thought about it for quite a while and then opened the envelope, but just to be polite.

ONE GENUINE TURNPIKE TOLLBOOTH, it stated—and then it went on:

EASILY ASSEMBLED AT HOME, AND FOR USE BY THOSE WHO HAVE NEVER TRAVELLED IN LANDS BEYOND.

'Beyond what?' thought Milo as he continued to read.

THIS PACKAGE CONTAINS THE FOLLOWING ITEMS:

One (1) genuine turnpike tollbooth to be erected according to directions.

Three (3) precautionary signs to be used in a precautionary fashion.

Assorted coins for use in paying tolls.

One (1) map, up-to-date and carefully drawn by master cartographers, depicting natural and man-made features.

One (1) book of rules and traffic regulations, which may not be bent or broken.

And in smaller letters at the bottom it concluded:

Results are not guaranteed, but if not perfectly satisfied, your wasted time will be refunded.

Following the instructions, which told him to cut here, lift there, and fold back all around, he soon had the tollbooth unpacked and set up on its stand. He fitted the windows in place and attached the roof, which extended out on both sides and fastened on the coin box. It was very much like the tollbooths he'd seen on family trips, except of course it was much smaller and purple.

'What a strange present,' he thought to himself. 'The least they could have done was to send a motorway with it, for it's terribly impractical without one.'

But since, at the time, there was nothing else he wanted to play with, he set up the three signs,

SLOW DOWN APPROACHING TOLLBOOTH
PLEASE HAVE YOUR FARE READY
HAVE YOUR DESTINATION IN MIND

and slowly unfolded the map.

As the announcement stated, it was a beautiful map, in many colours, showing principal roads, rivers, and seas, towns and cities, mountain and valleys, intersections and detours, and sites of outstanding interest both beautiful and historic.

The only trouble was that Milo had never heard of any of the places it indicated, and even the names sounded most peculiar.

'I don't think there really is such a country,' he concluded after studying it carefully. 'Well, it doesn't matter anyway.' And he closed his eyes and poked a finger at the map.

'Dictionopolis,' read Milo slowly when he saw what his finger had chosen. 'Oh, well, I might as well go there as anywhere.'

He walked across the room and dusted the car carefully. Then, taking the map and rule book with him, he hopped in and, for lack of anything better to do, drove slowly up to the tollbooth. As he deposited his coin and rolled past he remarked wistfully, 'I do hope this is an interesting game, otherwise the afternoon will be so terribly dull.'

*

Suddenly he found himself speeding along an unfamiliar country road, and as he looked back over his shoulder neither the tollbooth nor his room nor even the house was anywhere in sight. What had started as make-believe was now very real.

'What a strange thing to happen,' he thought (just as you must be thinking). 'This game is much more

serious than I thought, for here I am riding on a road
I've never seen, going to a place I've never heard of,
and all because of a tollbooth which came from
nowhere. I'm certainly glad that it's a nice day for a
trip,' he concluded hopefully, for, at the moment, this
was the one thing he definitely knew.

The sun sparkled, the sky was clear, and all the
colours he saw seemed to be richer and brighter than
he could ever remember. The flowers shone as if
they'd been cleaned and polished, and the tall trees
that lined the road shimmered in silvery green.

WELCOME TO EXPECTATIONS, said a carefully lettered
sign on a small house at the side of the road.
INFORMATION, PREDICTIONS, AND ADVICE CHEER-
FULLY OFFERED. PARK HERE AND BLOW HORN.

With the first sound from the horn a little man in a
long coat came rushing from the house, speaking as
fast as he could, and repeating everything several
times:

'My, my, my, my, my, welcome, welcome, welcome, welcome to the land of Expectations, to the land
of Expectations, to the land of Expectations. We don't
get many travellers these days; we certainly don't get
many travellers these days. Now what can I do for
you? I'm the Whether Man.'

'Is this the right road for Dictionopolis?' asked Milo,
a little bowled over by the effusive greeting.

'Well now, well now, well now,' he began again, 'I
don't know of any wrong road to Dictionopolis, so if
this road goes to Dictionopolis at all it must be the right
road, and if it doesn't it must be the right road to
somewhere else, because there are no wrong roads to
anywhere. Do you think it will rain?'

'I thought you were the Weather Man,' said Milo,
very confused.

'Oh no,' said the little man, 'I'm the Whether Man,

not the Weather Man, for after all it's more important to know whether there will be weather than what the weather will be.' And with that he released a dozen balloons that sailed off into the sky. 'Must see which way the wind is blowing,' he said, chuckling over his little joke and watching them disappear in all directions.

'What kind of a place is Expectations?' inquired Milo, unable to see the joke and feeling very doubtful of the little man's sanity.

'Good question, good question,' he exclaimed. 'Expectations is the place you must always go to before you get to where you're going. Of course, some people never go beyond Expectations, but my job is to hurry them along whether they like it or not. Now what else can I do for you?' And before Milo could reply he rushed into the house and reappeared a moment later with a new coat and an umbrella.

'I think I can find my own way,' said Milo, not at all sure that he could. But, since he didn't understand the little man at all, he decided that he might as well move on—at least until he met someone whose sentences didn't always sound as if they would make as much sense backwards as forwards.

'Splendid, splendid, splendid,' exclaimed the Whether Man. 'Whether or not you find your own way, you're bound to find some way. If you happen to find my way, please return it, as it was lost years ago. I imagine by now it's quite rusty. You did say it was going to rain, didn't you?' And with that he opened the umbrella and walked with Milo to the car.

'I'm glad you made your own decision. I do so hate to make up my mind about anything, whether it's good or bad, up or down, in or out, rain or shine. Expect everything, I always say, and the unexpected never happens. Now please drive carefully; goodbye, goodbye, goodbye, good ...' His last goodbye was drowned out by an enormous clap of thunder, and as

Milo drove down the road in the bright sunshine he could see the Whether Man standing in the middle of a fierce cloudburst that seemed to be raining only on him.

The road dipped now into a broad green valley and stretched towards the horizon. The little car bounced along with very little effort, and Milo had hardly to touch the accelerator to go as fast as he wanted. He was glad to be on his way again.

'It's all very well to spend time in Expectations,' he thought, 'but talking to that strange man all day would certainly get me nowhere. He's the most peculiar person I've ever met,' continued Milo—unaware of how many peculiar people he would shortly encounter.

As he drove along the peaceful road he soon fell to day-dreaming and paid less and less attention to where he was going. In a short time he wasn't paying any attention at all, and that is why, at a fork in the road, when a sign pointed to the left, Milo went to the right, along a route which looked suspiciously like the wrong way.

Things began to change as soon as he left the main highway. The sky became quite grey and, along with it, the whole countryside seemed to lose its colour and assume the same monotonous tone. Everything was quiet, and even the air hung heavily. The birds sang only grey songs and the road wound back and forth in an endless series of climbing curves.

Mile after

mile after

mile after

mile he drove, and now, gradually the car went slower and slower, until it was hardly moving at all.

'It looks as though I'm getting nowhere,' yawned Milo, becoming very drowsy and dull. 'I hope I haven't taken a wrong turn.'

Mile after

mile after
mile after
mile, and everything became greyer and more monotonous. Finally, the car just stopped altogether, and, hard as he tried, it wouldn't budge another inch.

'I wonder where I am,' said Milo in a very worried tone.

'You're ... in ... the ... Dol ... drums,' wailed a voice that sounded far away.

He looked around quickly to see who had spoken. No one was there, and it was as quiet and still as one could imagine.

'Yes ... the ... Dol ... drums,' yawned another voice, but still he saw no one.

'WHAT ARE THE DOLDRUMS?' he cried loudly, and tried very hard to see who would answer this time.

'The Doldrums, my young friend, are where nothing ever happens and nothing ever changes.'

This time the voice came from so close that Milo jumped with surprise, for, sitting on his right shoulder, so lightly that he hardly noticed, was a small creature exactly the colour of his shirt.

'Allow me to introduce all of us,' the creature went on. 'We are the Lethargarians, at your service.'

Milo looked around and, for the first time, noticed dozens of them—sitting on the car, standing in the road, and lying all over the trees and bushes. They were very difficult to see, because whatever they happened to be sitting on or near was exactly the colour they happened to be. Each one looked very much like the other (except for the colour, of course) and some looked even more like each other than they did like themselves.

'I'm very pleased to meet you,' said Milo, not sure whether or not he was pleased at all. 'I think I'm lost. Can you help me please?'

'Don't say "think",' said one sitting on his shoe, for the one on his shoulder had fallen asleep. 'It's against

the law.' And he yawned and fell off to sleep, too.

'No one's allowed to think in the Doldrums,' continued a third, beginning to doze off. And as each one spoke, he fell off to sleep and another picked up the conversation with hardly any interruption.

'Don't you have a rule book? It's local ordinance 175389–J.'

Milo quickly pulled the rule book from his pocket, opened to the page, and read, 'Ordinance 175389–J: It shall be unlawful, illegal, and unethical to think, think of thinking, surmise, presume, reason, meditate, or speculate while in the Doldrums. Anyone breaking this law shall be severely punished!'

'That's a ridiculous law,' said Milo, quite indignantly. 'Everybody thinks.'

'We don't,' shouted the Lethargarians all at once.

'And most of the time *you* don't,' said a yellow one sitting in a daffodil. 'That's why you're here. You weren't thinking, and you weren't paying attention either. People who don't pay attention often get stuck in the Doldrums.' And with that he toppled out of the flower and fell snoring into the grass.

Milo couldn't help laughing at the little creature's strange behaviour, even though he knew it might be rude.

'Stop that at once,' ordered the tartan one clinging to his stocking. 'Laughing is against the law. Don't you have a rule book? It's a local ordinance 574381–W.'

Opening the book again, Milo found Ordinance

574381–W: 'In the Doldrums, laughter is frowned upon and smiling is permitted only on alternate Thursdays. Violators shall be dealt with most harshly.'

'Well, if you can't laugh or think, what can you do?' asked Milo.

'Anything as long as it's nothing, and everything as long as it isn't anything,' explained another. 'There's lots to do; we have a very busy schedule—

'At 8 o'clock we get up, and then we spend
'From 8 to 9 daydreaming.
'From 9 to 9.30 we take our early midmorning nap.
'From 9.30 to 10.30 we dawdle and delay.
'From 10.30 to 11.30 we take our late early morning nap.
'From 11.30 to 12.00 we bide our time and then eat lunch.
'From 1.00 to 2.00 we linger and loiter.
'From 2.00 to 2.30 we take our early afternoon nap.
'From 2.30 to 3.30 we put off for tomorrow what we could have done today.
'From 3.30 to 4.00 we take our early late afternoon nap.
'From 4.00 to 5.00 we loaf and lounge until dinner.
'From 6.00 to 7.00 we dilly-dally.
'From 7.00 to 8.00 we take our early evening nap, and then for an hour before we go to bed at 9.00 we waste time.

'As you can see, that leaves almost no time for brooding, lagging, plodding, or procrastinating, and if we stopped to think or laugh, we'd never get nothing done.'

'You mean you'd never get anything done,' corrected Milo.

'We don't want to get anything done,' snapped another angrily; 'we want to get nothing done, and we can do that without your help.'

'You see,' continued another in a more conciliatory tone, 'it's really quite strenuous doing nothing all day, so once a week we take a holiday and go nowhere, which was just where we were going when you came along. Would you care to join us?'

'I might as well,' thought Milo; 'that's where I seem to be going anyway.'

'Tell me,' he yawned, for he felt ready for a nap now himself, 'does everyone here do nothing?'

'Everyone but the terrible watchdog,' said two of them, shuddering in chorus. 'He's always sniffing around to see that nobody wastes time. A most unpleasant character.'

'The watchdog?' said Milo quizzically.

'THE WATCHDOG,' shouted another, fainting from fright, for racing down the road barking furiously and kicking up a great cloud of dust was the very dog of whom they had been speaking.

'RUN!'

'WAKE UP!'

'RUN!'

'HERE HE COMES!'

'THE WATCHDOG!'

Great shouts filled the air as the Lethargarians scattered in all directions and soon disappeared entirely.

'R-R-R-G-H-R-O-R-R-H-F-F,' exclaimed the watchdog as he dashed up to the car, loudly puffing and panting.

Milo's eyes opened wide, for there in front of him was a large dog with a perfectly normal head, four feet, and a tail—and the body of a loudly ticking alarm-clock.

'What are you doing here?' growled the watchdog.

'Just killing time,' replied Milo apologetically. 'You see—'

'KILLING TIME!' roared the dog—so furiously that his alarm went off. 'It's bad enough wasting time without killing it.' And he shuddered at the thought. 'Why are you in the Doldrums anyway—don't you have anywhere to go?'

'I was on my way to Dictionopolis when I got stuck here,' explained Milo. 'Can you help me?'

'Help you! You must help yourself,' the dog replied, carefully winding himself with his left hind leg. 'I suppose you know why you got stuck.'

'I suppose I just wasn't thinking,' said Milo.

'PRECISELY,' shouted the dog as his alarm went off again. 'Now you know what you must do.'

'I'm afraid I don't,' admitted Milo, feeling quite stupid.

'Well,' continued the watchdog impatiently, 'since you got here by not thinking, it seems reasonable to expect that, in order to get out, you must start thinking.' And with that he hopped into the car.

'Do you mind if I get in? I love car rides.'

Milo began to think as hard as he could (which was very difficult, since he wasn't used to it). He thought of birds that swim and fish that fly. He thought of yesterday's lunch and tomorrow's dinner. He thought of words that began with J the numbers that end in 3. And, as he thought, the wheels began to turn.

'We're moving, we're moving,' he shouted happily.

'Keep thinking,' scolded the watchdog.

The little car started to go faster and faster as Milo's brain whirled with activity, and down the road they went. In a few moments they were out of the Doldrums and back on the main road. All the colours had returned to their original brightness, and as they raced along the road Milo continued to think of all sorts of things; of the many detours and wrong turns that were so easy to take, of how fine it was to be moving along, and, most of all, how much could be accomplished with just a little thought. And the dog, his nose in the wind, just sat back, watchfully ticking.

*

'You must excuse my gruff conduct,' the watchdog said, after they'd been driving for some time, 'but you see it's traditional for watchdogs to be ferocious . . .'

Milo was so relieved at having escaped the Doldrums that he assured the dog that he bore him no ill-will and, in fact, was very grateful for the assistance.

'Splendid,' shouted the watchdog. 'I'm very pleased—I'm sure we'll be great friends for the rest of the trip. You may call me Tock.'

'That is a strange name for a dog who goes ticktick-tickticktick all day,' said Milo. 'Why didn't they call you—'

'Don't say it,' gasped the dog, and Milo could see a tear well up in his eye.

'I didn't mean to hurt your feelings,' said Milo, not meaning to hurt his feelings.

'That's all right,' said the dog, getting hold of himself. 'It's an old story and a sad one, but I can tell it to you now.

'When my brother was born, the first pup in the family, my parents were overjoyed and immediately named him Tick in expectation of the sound they were sure he'd make. On first winding him, they discovered to their horror that, instead of going tickticktickticktick, he went tocktocktocktocktocktock. They rushed to the Hall of Records to change the name, but too late. It had already been officially inscribed, and nothing could be done. When I arrived, they were determined not to make the same mistake twice and, since it seemed logical that all their children would make the same sound, they named me Tock. Of course, you know the rest—my brother is called Tick because he goes tocktocktocktocktocktocktock and I am called Tock because I go tickticktickticktickticktick, and both of us are for ever burdened with the wrong names. My parents were so overwrought that they gave up having any more children and devoted their lives to doing good work among the poor and hungry.'

'But how did you become a watchdog?' interjected Milo, hoping to change the subject, as Tock was sobbing quite loudly now.

'That,' he said, rubbing a paw in his eye, 'is also traditional. My family have always been watchdogs—from father to son, almost since time began.

'You see,' he continued, beginning to feel better, 'once there was no time at all, and people found it very inconvenient. They never knew whether they were eating lunch or dinner, and they were always missing trains. So time was invented to help them keep track of the day and get to places when they should. When they began to count all the time that was available, what with 60 seconds in a minute and 60 minutes in an hour and 24 hours in a day and 365 days in a year, it seemed as if there was much more than could ever be used. "If there's so much of it, it couldn't be very valuable," was the general opinion, and it soon fell into disrepute. People wasted it and even gave it away. Then we were given the job of seeing that no one wasted time again,' he said, sitting up proudly. 'It's hard work but a noble calling. For you see'—and now he was standing on the seat, one foot on the windscreen, shouting with his arms outstretched—'it is our most valuable possession, more precious than diamonds. It marches on, it and tide wait for no man, and—'

At that point in the speech the car hit a bump in the road and the watchdog collapsed in a heap on the front seat with his alarm again ringing furiously.

'Are you all right?' shouted Milo.

'Umphh,' grunted Tock. 'Sorry to get carried away, but I think you get the point.'

As they drove along, Tock continued to explain the

importance of time, quoting the old philosophers and poets and illustrating each point with gestures that brought him perilously close to tumbling headlong from the speeding car.

Before long they saw in the distance the towers and flags of Dictionopolis sparkling in the sunshine, and in a few moments they reached the great wall and stood at the gateway to the city.

'A-H-H-H-R-R-E-M-M-,' roared the sentry, clearing his throat and snapping smartly to attention. 'This is Dictionopolis, a happy kingdom, advantageously located in the Foothills of Confusion and caressed by gentle breezes from the Sea of Knowledge. Today, by royal proclamation, is market-day. Have you come to buy or sell?'

'I beg your pardon?' said Milo.

'Buy or sell, buy or sell,' repeated the sentry impatiently. 'Which is it? You must have come for some reason.'

'Well, I—' Milo began.

'Come now, if you don't have a reason, you must at least have an explanation or certainly an excuse,' interrupted the sentry.

Milo shook his head.

'Very serious, very serious,' the sentry said, shaking his head also. 'You can't get in without a reason.' He thought for a moment, and then continued: 'Wait a minute; maybe I have an old one you can use.'

He took a battered suitcase from the sentry-box and began to rummage busily through it, mumbling to himself, 'No . . . no . . . no . . . this won't do . . . no . . . h-m-m-m . . . ah, this is fine,' he cried triumphantly, holding up a small medallion on a chain. He dusted it off, and engraved on one side were the words 'WHY NOT?'

'That's a good reason for almost anything—a bit used perhaps, but still quite serviceable.' And with that he placed it around Milo's neck, pushed back the heavy iron gate, bowed low, and motioned them into the city.

'I wonder what the market will be like,' thought Milo as they drove through the gate; but before there was time for an answer they had driven into an immense square crowded with long lines of stalls heaped with merchandise and decorated in gaily coloured bunting. Overhead a large banner proclaimed:

WELCOME TO THE WORLD MARKET

And, from across the square, five very tall, thin gentlemen regally dressed in silks and satins, plumed hats, and buckled shoes rushed up to the car, stopped short, mopped five brows, caught five breaths, unrolled five parchments, and began talking in turn.

'Greetings!'

'Salutations!'

'Welcome!'

'Good afternoon!'

'Hello!'

Milo nodded his head, and they went on, reading from their scrolls.

'By order of Azaz the Unabridged—'

'King of Dictionopolis—'

'Monarch of letters—'

'Emperor of phrases, sentences, and miscellaneous figures of speech—'

'We offer you the hospitality of our kingdom.'

'Country,'

'Nation,'

'State,'

'Commonwealth,'

'Realm,'

'Empire,'

'Palatinate,'

'Principality.'

'Do all those words mean the same thing?' gasped Milo.

'Of course.'

'Certainly.'

'Precisely.'

'Exactly.'

'Yes,' they replied in order.

'Well, then,' said Milo, not understanding why each one said the same thing in a slightly different way, 'wouldn't it be simpler to use just one? It would certainly make more sense.'

'Nonsense.'

'Ridiculous.'

'Fantastic.'

'Absurd.'

'Bosh,' they chorused again, and continued.

'We're not interested in making sense; it's not our job,' scolded the first.

'Besides,' explained the second, 'one word is as good as another—so why not use them all?'

'Then you don't have to choose which one is right,' advised the third.

'Besides,' sighed the fourth, 'if one is right, then ten are ten times as right.'

'Obviously you don't know who we are,' sneered the fifth. And they presented themselves one by one as:

'The Duke of Definition.'

'The Minister of Meaning.'

'The Earl of Essence.'

'The Count of Connotation.'

'The Under-secretary of Understanding.'

Milo acknowledged the introduction and, as Tock growled softly, the minister explained.

'We are the king's advisers, or, in more formal terms, his cabinet.'

'Cabinet,' recited the duke: (1) a small private room or closet, case with drawers, etc., for keeping valuables

or displaying curiosities; (2) council room for chief ministers of state; (3) a body of official advisers to the chief executive of a nation.'

'You see,' continued the minister, bowing thankfully to the duke, 'Dictionopolis is the place where all the words in the world come from. They're grown right here in our orchards.'

'I didn't know that words grew on trees,' said Milo timidly.

'Where did you think they grew?' shouted the earl irritably. A small crowd began to gather to see the little boy who didn't know that letters grew on trees.

'I didn't know they grew at all,' admitted Milo even more timidly. Several people shook their heads sadly.

'Well, money doesn't grow on trees, does it?' demanded the count.

'I've heard not,' said Milo.

'Then something must. Why not words?' exclaimed the under-secretary triumphantly. The crowd cheered his display of logic and continued about its business.

'To continue,' continued the minister impatiently. 'Once a week by Royal Proclamation the world market is held here in the great square, and people come from everywhere to buy the words they need or trade in the words they haven't used.'

'Our job,' said the count, 'is to see that all the words sold are proper ones, for it wouldn't do to sell someone a word that had no meaning or didn't exist at all. For instance, if you bought a word like *ghlbtsk*, where would you use it?'

'It would be difficult,' thought Milo—but there were so many words that were difficult, and he knew hardly any of them.

'But we never choose which ones to use,' explained the earl as they walked towards the market stalls, 'for as long as they mean what they mean to mean we don't care if they make sense or nonsense.'

'Innocence or magnificence,' added the count.

'Reticence or common sense,' said the under-secretary.

'That seems simple enough,' said Milo, trying to be polite.

'Easy as falling off a log,' cried the earl, falling off a log with a loud thump.

'Must you be so clumsy?' shouted the duke.

'All I said was—' began the earl, rubbing his head.

'We heard you,' said the minister angrily, 'and you'll have to find an expression that's less dangerous.'

The earl dusted himself, as the others snickered audibly.

'You see,' cautioned the count, 'you must pick your words very carefully and be sure to say just what you intend to say. And now we must leave to make preparations for the Royal Banquet.'

'You'll be there, of course,' said the minister.

But before Milo had a chance to say anything, they

were rushing off across the square as fast as they had come.

'Enjoy yourself in the market,' shouted back the under-secretary.

'Market,' recited the duke: 'an open space or covered building in which—'

And that was the last Milo heard as they disappeared into the crowd.

RIP VAN WINKLE

Washington Irving

hoever has made a voyage up the Hudson must remember the Kaatskill mountains. They are a dismembered branch of the great Appalachian family, and are seen away to the west of the river, swelling up to a noble height, and lording it over the surrounding country. Every change of season, every change of weather, indeed, every hour of the day, produces some change in the magical hues and shapes of these mountains, and they are regarded by all the good wives, far and near, as perfect barometers. When the weather is fair and settled, they are clothed in blue and purple, and print their bold outlines on the clear evening sky; but sometimes, when the rest of the landscape is cloudless, they will gather a hood of gray vapors about their summits, which, in the last rays of the setting sun, will glow and light up like a crown of glory.

At the foot of these fairy mountains, the voyager may have descried the light smoke curling up from a village, whose shingle roofs gleam among the trees, just where the blue tints of the upland melt away into the fresh green of the nearer landscape. It is a little village, of great antiquity, having been founded by some of the Dutch colonists in the early times of the province, just about the beginning of the government of the good Peter Stuyvesant (may he rest in peace!), and there were some of the houses of the original settlers standing within a few years, built of small yellow bricks brought from Holland, having latticed windows and gable fronts, surmounted with weather-cocks.

In that same village, and in one of these very houses (which, to tell the precise truth, was sadly time-worn and weather-beaten), there lived, many years since, while the country was yet a province of Great Britain, a simple, good-natured fellow, of the name of Rip Van Winkle. He was a descendant of the Van Winkles who figured so gallantly in the chivalrous days of Peter Stuyvesant, and accompanied him to the siege of Fort Christina. He inherited, however, but little of the martial character of his ancestors. I have observed that he was a simple, good-natured man; he was, moreover, a kind neighbor, and an obedient, hen-pecked husband. Indeed, to the latter circumstance might be owing that meekness of spirit which gained him such universal popularity; for those men are most apt to be obsequious and conciliating abroad, who are under the discipline of shrews at home. Their tempers, doubtless, are rendered pliant and malleable in the fiery furnace of domestic tribulation; and a curtain-lecture is worth all the sermons in the world for teaching the virtues of patience and long-suffering. A termagant wife may, therefore, in some respects, be considered a tolerable blessing; and if so, Rip Van Winkle was thrice blessed.

Certain it is, that he was a great favorite among all the good wives of the village, who, as usual with the amiable sex, took his part in all family squabbles; and never failed, whenever they talked those matters over in their evening gossipings, to lay all the blame on Dame Van Winkle. The children of the village, too, would shout with joy whenever he approached. He assisted at their sports, made their playthings, taught them to fly kites and shoot marbles, and told them long stories of ghosts, witches, and Indians. Whenever he went dodging about the village, he was surrounded by a troop of them, hanging on his skirts, clambering on his back, and playing a thousand tricks on him with impunity; and not a dog would bark at him throughout the neighbourhood.

The great error in Rip's composition was an insuperable aversion to all kinds of profitable labor. It could not be from the want of assiduity or perseverance; for he would sit on a wet rock, with a rod as long and heavy as a Tartar's lance, and fish all day without a murmur, even though he should not be encouraged by a single nibble. He would carry a fowling-piece on his shoulder for hours together, trudging through woods and swamps, and up hill and down dale, to shoot a few squirrels or wild pigeons. He would never refuse to assist a neighbor even in the roughest toil, and was a foremost man at all country frolics for husking Indian corn, or building stone fences; the women of the village, too, used to employ him to run their errands, and to do such little odd jobs as their less obliging husbands would not do for them. In a word, Rip was ready to attend to anybody's business but his own; but as to doing family duty, and keeping his farm in order, he found it impossible.

In fact, he declared it was of no use to work on his farm; it was the most pestilent little piece of ground in the whole country; everything about it went wrong, and would go wrong, in spite of him. His fences were continually falling to pieces; his cow would either go astray, or get among the cabbages; weeds were sure to grow quicker in his fields than anywhere else; the rain always made a point of setting in just as he had some

out-door work to do; so that though his patrimonial
estate had dwindled away under his management,
acre by acre, until there was little more left than a mere
patch of Indian corn and potatoes, yet it was the worst
conditioned farm in the neighbourhood.

His children, too, were as ragged and wild as if they
belonged to nobody. His son Rip, an urchin begotten
in his own likeness, promised to inherit the habits,
with the old clothes, of his father. He was generally
seen trooping like a colt at his mother's heels, equip-
ped in a pair of his father's cast-off galligaskins, which
he had much ado to hold up with one hand, as a fine
lady does her train in bad weather.

Rip Van Winkle, however, was one of those happy
mortals, of foolish, well-oiled dispositions, who take
the world easy, eat white bread or brown, whichever
can be got with least thought or trouble, and would
rather starve on a penny than work for a pound. If left
to himself, he would have whistled life away in perfect
contentment; but his wife kept continually dinning in
his ears about his idleness, his carelessness, and the
ruin he was bringing on his family. Morning, noon,
and night, her tongue was incessantly going, and
everything he said or did was sure to produce a torrent
of household eloquence. Rip had but one way of replying to all lectures of the kind, and that, by frequent
use, had grown into a habit. He shrugged his
shoulders, shook his head, cast up his eyes, but said
nothing. This, however, always provoked a fresh volley from his wife; so that he was fain to draw off his
forces, and take to the outside of the house—the only
side which, in truth, belongs to a hen-pecked husband.

Rip's sole domestic adherent was his dog Wolf, who
was as much hen-pecked as his master; for Dame Van
Winkle regarded them as companions in idleness, and
even looked upon Wolf with an evil eye, as the cause of
his master's going so often astray. True it is, in all

points of spirit befitting an honorable dog, he was as courageous an animal as ever scoured the woods; but what courage can withstand the ever-enduring and all-besetting terrors of a woman's tongue? The moment Wolf entered the house his crest fell, his tail drooped to the ground, or curled between his legs, he sneaked about with a gallows air, casting many a sidelong glance at Dame Van Winkle, and at the least flourish of a broomstick or ladle he would fly to the door with yelping precipitation.

Times grew worse and worse with Rip Van Winkle as years of matrimony rolled on; a tart temper never mellows with age, and a sharp tongue is the only edged tool that grows keener with constant use. For a long while he used to console himself, when driven from home, by frequenting a kind of perpetual club of the sages, philosophers, and other idle personages of the village, which held its sessions on a bench before a small inn, designated by a rubicund portrait of His Majesty George the Third. Here they used to sit in the shade through a long, lazy summer's day, talking listlessly over village gossip, or telling endless sleepy stories about nothing. But it would have been worth any statesman's money to have heard the profound discussions that sometimes took place, when by chance an old newspaper fell into their hands from some passing traveller. How solemnly they would listen to the contents, as drawled out by Derrick Van Bummel, the schoolmaster, a dapper learned little man, who was not to be daunted by the most gigantic word in the dictionary; and how sagely they would deliberate upon public events some months after they had taken place.

The opinions of this junto were completely controlled by Nicholas Vedder, patriarch of the village, and landlord of the inn, at the door of which he took his seat from morning till night, just moving sufficiently to avoid the sun and keep in the shade of a large tree; so that the neighbors could tell the hour by his movements as accurately as by a sundial. It is true he was rarely heard to speak, but smoked his pipe incessantly. His adherents, however (for every great man has his adherents), perfectly understood him, and knew how to gather his opinions. When anything that was read or related displeased him, he was observed to smoke his pipe vehemently, and to send forth short, frequent, and angry puffs; but when pleased, he would inhale the smoke slowly and tranquilly, and emit it in light placid clouds; and sometimes, taking the pipe from his mouth, and letting the fragrant vapor curl about his nose, would gravely nod his head in token of perfect approbation.

From even this stronghold the unlucky Rip was at length routed by his termagant wife, who would suddenly break in upon the tranquillity of the assemblage and call the members all to naught; nor was that august personage, Nicholas Vedder himself; sacred from the daring tongue of this terrible virago, who charged him outright with encouraging her husband in habits of idleness.

Poor Rip was at last reduced almost to despair; and his only alternative, to escape from the labor of the farm and clamor of his wife, was to take gun in hand and stroll away into the woods. Here he would sometimes seat himself at the foot of a tree, and share the contents of his wallet with Wolf, with whom he sympathized as a fellow-sufferer in persecution. 'Poor Wolf,' he would say, 'thy mistress leads thee a dog's life of it, but never mind, my lad, whilst I live thou shalt never want a friend to stand by thee!' Wolf would wag his tail, look wistfully in his master's face, and if dogs can feel pity, I verily believe he reciprocated the sentiment with all his heart.

In a long ramble of the kind on a fine autumnal day, Rip had unconsciously scrambled to one of the highest parts of the Kaatskill mountains. He was after his

favorite sport of squirrel-shooting, and the still soli-
tudes had echoed and re-echoed with the reports of
his gun. Panting and fatigued, he threw himself, late
in the afternoon, on a green knoll, covered with mountain herbage, that crowned the brow of a precipice.
From an opening between the trees he could overlook
all the lower country for many a mile of rich woodland.
He saw at a distance the lordly Hudson, far, far below
him, moving on its silent but majestic course, with the
reflection of a purple cloud, or the sail of a lagging
bark, here and there sleeping on its glassy bosom, and
at last losing itself in the blue highlands.

On the other side he looked down into a deep mountain glen, wild, lonely, and shagged, the bottom filled
with fragments from the impending cliffs, and scarcely
lighted by the reflected rays of the setting sun. For
some time Rip lay musing on this scene; evening was
gradually advancing; the mountains began to throw
their long blue shadows over the valleys; he saw that it
would be dark long before he could reach the village,
and he heaved a heavy sigh when he thought of
encountering the terrors of Dame Van Winkle.

As he was about to descend, he heard a voice from a
distance, hallooing, 'Rip Van Winkle, Rip Van
Winkle!' He looked round, but could see nothing but a
crow winging its solitary flight across the mountain.
He thought his fancy must have deceived him, and
turned again to descend, when he heard the same cry
ring through the still evening air: 'Rip Van Winkle! Rip
Van Winkle!'—at the same time Wolf bristled up his
back, and giving a low growl, skulked to his master's
side, looking fearfully down into the glen. Rip now felt
a vague apprehension stealing over him; he looked
anxiously in the same direction, and perceived a
strange figure slowly toiling up the rocks, and bending
under the weight of something he carried on his back.
He was surprised to see any human being in this
lonely and unfrequented place; but supposing it to be

some one of the neighbourhood in need of his assistance, he hastened down to yield it.

On nearer approach he was still more surprised at
the singularity of the stranger's appearance. He was a
short, square-built old fellow, with thick bushy hair,
and a grizzled beard. His dress was of the antique
Dutch fashion—a cloth jerkin strapped around the
waist—several pair of breeches, the outer one of
ample volume, decorated with rows of buttons down
the sides, and bunches at the knees. He bore on his
shoulders a stout keg, that seemed full of liquor, and
made signs for Rip to approach and assist him with the
load. Though rather shy and distrustful of this new
acquaintance, Rip complied with his usual alacrity;
and mutually relieving one another, they clambered
up a narrow gully, apparently the dry bed of a mountain torrent. As they ascended, Rip every now and
then heard long, rolling peals, like distant thunder,
that seemed to issue out of a deep ravine, or rather
cleft, between lofty rocks, towards which their rugged
path conducted. He paused for an instant, but supposing it to be the muttering of one of those transient
thunder-showers which often take place in mountain
heights, he proceeded. Passing through the ravine,
they came to a hollow, like a small amphitheatre, surrounded by perpendicular precipices, over the brinks
of which impending trees shot their branches, so that
you only caught glimpses of azure sky and the bright
evening cloud. During the whole time Rip and his
companion had labored on in silence; for though the
former marvelled greatly what could be the object of
carrying a keg of liquor up this wild mountain, yet
there was something strange and incomprehensible
about the unknown, that inspired awe and checked
familiarity.

On entering the amphitheatre, new objects of wonder presented themselves. On a level spot in the centre
was a company of odd-looking personages playing at

ninepins. They were dressed in a quaint, outlandish fashion; some wore short doublets, others jerkins, with long knives in their belts, and most of them had enormous breeches, of similar style with that of the guide's. Their visages, too, were peculiar: one had a large beard, broad face, and small piggish eyes; the face of another seemed to consist entirely of nose, and was surmounted by a white sugar-loaf hat, set off with a little red cock's tail. They all had beards, of various shapes and colors. There was one who seemed to be the commander. He was a stout old gentleman, with a weather-beaten countenance; he wore a laced doublet, broad belt and hanger, high crowned hat and feather, red stockings, and high-heeled shoes, with roses in them. The whole group reminded Rip of the figures in an old Flemish painting, in the parlor of Dominie Van Shaick, the village parson, and which had been brought over from Holland at the time of the settlement.

What seemed particularly odd to Rip was, that, though these folks were evidently amusing themselves, yet they maintained the gravest faces, the most mysterious silence, and were, withal, the most melancholy party of pleasure he had ever witnessed. Nothing interrupted the stillness of the scene but the noise of the balls, which, whenever they rolled, echoed along the mountains like rumbling peals of thunder.

As Rip and his companion approached them, they suddenly desisted from their play, and stared at him

with such fixed, statue-like gaze, and such strange, uncouth, lack-lustre countenances, that his heart turned within him, and his knees smote together. His companion now emptied the contents of the keg into large flagons, and made signs to him to wait upon the company. He obeyed with fear and trembling; they quaffed the liquor in profound silence, and then' returned to their game.

By degrees Rip's awe and apprehension subsided. He even ventured, when no eye was fixed upon him, to taste the beverage, which he found had much of the flavor of excellent Hollands. He was naturally a thirsty soul, and was soon tempted to repeat the draught. One taste provoked another; and he reiterated his visits to the flagon so often that at length his senses were overpowered, his eyes swam in his head, his head gradually declined, and he fell into a deep sleep.

On waking, he found himself on the green knoll whence he had first seen the old man of the glen. He rubbed his eyes—it was a bright sunny morning. The birds were hopping and twittering among the bushes, and the eagle was wheeling aloft, and breasting the pure mountain breeze. 'Surely,' thought Rip, 'I have not slept here all night.' He recalled the occurrences before he fell asleep. The strange man with a keg of liquor—the mountain ravine—the wild retreat among the rocks—the woe-begone party at ninepins—the flagon—'Oh! that flagon! that wicked flagon!' thought Rip, 'what excuse shall I make to Dame Van Winkle?'

He looked round for his gun, but in place of the clean, well-oiled fowling-piece, he found an old firelock lying by him, the barrel encrusted with rust, the lock falling off, and the stock worm-eaten. He now suspected that the grave roisters of the mountain had put a trick upon him, and, having dosed him with liquor, had robbed him of his gun. Wolf, too, had disappeared, but he might have strayed away after a squirrel or partridge. He whistled after him, and shouted his name, but all in vain; the echoes repeated his whistle and shout, but no dog was to be seen.

He determined to revisit the scene of the last evening's gambol, and if he met with any of the party, to demand his dog and gun. As he rose to walk, he found himself stiff in the joints, and wanting in his usual activity. 'These mountain beds do not agree with me,' thought Rip, 'and if this frolic should lay me up with a fit of rheumatism, I shall have a blessed time with Dame Van Winkle.' With some difficulty he got down into the glen: he found the gully up which he and his companion had ascended the preceding evening; but to his astonishment a mountain stream was now foaming down it, leaping from rock to rock, and filling the glen with babbling murmurs. He, however, made shift to scramble up its sides, working his toilsome way through thickets of birch, sassafras, and witch-hazel, and sometimes tripped up or entangled by the wild grape-vines that twisted their coils or tendrils from tree to tree, and spread a kind of network in his path.

At length he reached to where the ravine had opened through the cliffs to the amphitheatre; but no traces of such opening remained. The rocks presented a high, impenetrable wall, over which the torrent came tumbling in a sheet of feathery foam, and fell into a broad deep basin, black from the shadows of the surrounding forest. Here, then, poor Rip was brought to a stand. He again called and whistled after his dog; he was only answered by the cawing of a flock of idle

crows, sporting high in air about a dry tree that over-
hung a sunny precipice; and who, secure in their
elevation, seemed to look down and scoff at the poor
man's perplexities. What was to be done? the morning
was passing away, and Rip felt famished for want of
his breakfast. He grieved to give up his dog and gun;
he dreaded to meet his wife; but it would not do to
starve among the mountains. He shook his head,
shouldered the rusty fire-lock, and, with a heart full of
trouble and anxiety, turned his footsteps homeward.

As he approached the village he met a number of
people, but none of whom he knew, which somewhat
surprised him, for he had thought himself acquainted
with every one in the country round. Their dress, too,
was of a different fashion from that to which he was
accustomed. They all stared at him with equal marks of
surprise, and whenever they cast their eyes upon him,
invariably stroked their chins. The constant recurrence
of this gesture induced Rip, involuntarily, to do the
same, when, to his astonishment, he found his beard
had grown a foot long!

He had now entered the skirts of the village. A troop
of children ran at his heels, hooting after him, and
pointing at his gray beard. The dogs, too, not one of
which he recognized for an old acquaintance, barked
at him as he passed. The very village was altered; it
was larger and more populous. There were rows of
houses which he had never seen before, and those
which had been his familiar haunts had disappeared.
Strange names were over the doors—strange faces at
the windows—everything was strange. His mind now
misgave him; he began to doubt whether both he and
the world around him were not bewitched. Surely
this was his native village, which he had left but
the day before. There stood the Kaatskill mountains
—there ran the silver Hudson at a distance—there
was every hill and dale precisely as it had always
been. Rip was sorely perplexed. 'That flagon last

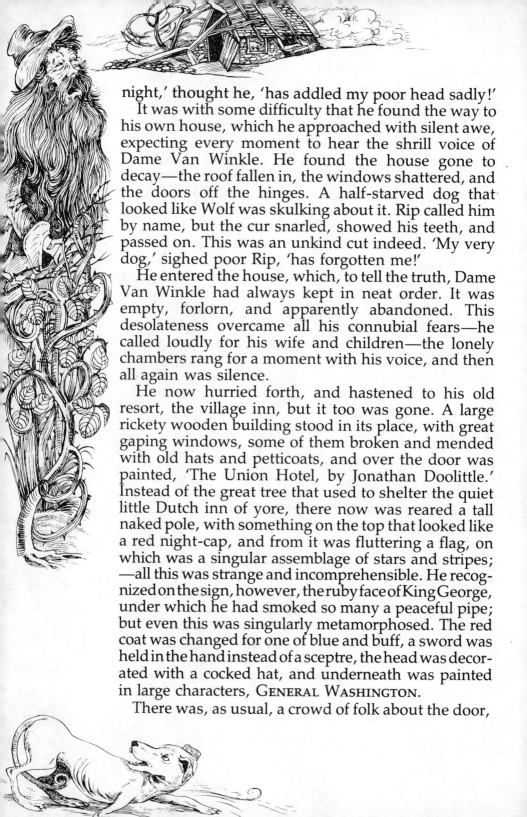

night,' thought he, 'has addled my poor head sadly!'

It was with some difficulty that he found the way to his own house, which he approached with silent awe, expecting every moment to hear the shrill voice of Dame Van Winkle. He found the house gone to decay—the roof fallen in, the windows shattered, and the doors off the hinges. A half-starved dog that looked like Wolf was skulking about it. Rip called him by name, but the cur snarled, showed his teeth, and passed on. This was an unkind cut indeed. 'My very dog,' sighed poor Rip, 'has forgotten me!'

He entered the house, which, to tell the truth, Dame Van Winkle had always kept in neat order. It was empty, forlorn, and apparently abandoned. This desolateness overcame all his connubial fears—he called loudly for his wife and children—the lonely chambers rang for a moment with his voice, and then all again was silence.

He now hurried forth, and hastened to his old resort, the village inn, but it too was gone. A large rickety wooden building stood in its place, with great gaping windows, some of them broken and mended with old hats and petticoats, and over the door was painted, 'The Union Hotel, by Jonathan Doolittle.' Instead of the great tree that used to shelter the quiet little Dutch inn of yore, there now was reared a tall naked pole, with something on the top that looked like a red night-cap, and from it was fluttering a flag, on which was a singular assemblage of stars and stripes; —all this was strange and incomprehensible. He recognized on the sign, however, the ruby face of King George, under which he had smoked so many a peaceful pipe; but even this was singularly metamorphosed. The red coat was changed for one of blue and buff, a sword was held in the hand instead of a sceptre, the head was decorated with a cocked hat, and underneath was painted in large characters, GENERAL WASHINGTON.

There was, as usual, a crowd of folk about the door,

but none that Rip recollected. The very character of the people seemed changed. There was a busy, bustling, disputatious tone about it, instead of the accustomed phlegm and drowsy tranquillity. He looked in vain for the sage Nicholas Vedder, with his broad face, double chin, and fair long pipe, uttering clouds of tobacco-smoke instead of idle speeches; or Van Bummel, the schoolmaster, doling forth the contents of an ancient newspaper. In place of these, a lean, bilious-looking fellow, with his pockets full of handbills, was haranguing vehemently about rights of citizens—elections—members of congress—liberty—Bunker's Hill—heroes of seventy-six—and other words, which were a perfect Babylonish jargon to the bewildered Van Winkle.

The appearance of Rip, with his long, grizzled beard, his rusty fowling-piece, his uncouth dress, and an army of women and children at his heels, soon attracted the attention of the tavern-politicians. They crowded round him, eyeing him from head to foot with great curiosity. The orator bustled up to him, and drawing him partly aside, inquired 'On which side he voted?' Rip stared in vacant stupidity. Another short but busy little fellow pulled him by the arm, and, rising on tiptoe, inquired in his ear, 'Whether he was Federal or Democrat?' Rip was equally at a loss to comprehend the question; when a knowing, self-important old gentleman, in a sharp cocked hat, made his way through the crowd, putting them to the right and left with his elbows as he passed, and planting himself before Van Winkle, with one arm akimbo, the other resting on his cane, his keen eyes and sharp hat penetrating, as it were, into his very soul, demanded in an austere tone, 'What brought him to the election with a gun on his shoulder, and a mob at his heels; and whether he meant to breed a riot in the village?' —'Alas! gentlemen,' cried Rip, somewhat dismayed, 'I am a poor quiet man, a native of the place, and a loyal subject of the King, God bless him!'

Here a general shout burst from the by-standers —'A tory! a tory! a spy! a refugee! hustle him! away with him!' It was with great difficulty that the self-important man in the cocked hat restored order; and, having assumed a tenfold austerity of brow, demanded again of the unknown culprit, what he came there for, and whom he was seeking? The poor man humbly assured him that he meant no harm, but merely came there in search of some of his neighbors, who used to keep about the tavern.

'Well—who are they?—name them.'

Rip bethought himself a moment, and inquired, 'Where's Nicholas Vedder?'

There was a silence for a little while, when an old man replied, in a thin piping voice, 'Nicholas Vedder! why, he is dead and gone these eighteen years! There was a wooden tombstone in the churchyard that used to tell all about him, but that's rotten and gone too.'

'Where's Brom Dutcher?'

'Oh, he went off to the army in the beginning of the war; some say he was killed at the storming of Stony Point—others say he was drowned in a squall at the foot of Antony's Nose. I don't know—he never came back again.'

'Where's Van Bummel, the schoolmaster?'

'He went off to the wars too, was a great militia general, and is now in Congress.'

Rip's heart died away at hearing of these sad changes in his home and friends, and finding himself thus alone in the world. Every answer puzzled him too, by treating of such enormous lapses of time, and of matters which he could not understand: war —Congress—Stony Point—he had no courage to ask after any more friends, but cried out in despair, 'Does nobody here know Rip Van Winkle?'

'Oh, Rip Van Winkle!' exclaimed two or three, 'oh, to be sure! that's Rip Van Winkle yonder, leaning against the tree.'

Rip looked, and he beheld a precise counterpart of himself, as he went up the mountain; apparently as lazy, and certainly as ragged. The poor fellow was now completely confounded. He doubted his own identity, and whether he was himself or another man. In the midst of his bewilderment, the man in the cocked hat demanded who he was, and what was his name.

'God knows,' exclaimed he, at his wit's end; 'I'm not myself—I'm somebody else—that's me yonder —no—that's somebody else got into my shoes—I was myself last night, but I fell asleep on the mountain, and they've changed my gun, and everything's changed, and I'm changed, and I can't tell what's my name, or who I am!'

The by-standers began now to look at each other, nod, wink significantly, and tap their fingers against their foreheads. There was a whisper, also, about securing the gun, and keeping the old fellow from doing mischief, at the very suggestion of which the self-important man in the cocked hat retired with some precipitation. At this critical moment a fresh, comely woman pressed through the throng to get a peep at the gray-bearded man. She had a chubby child in her arms, which, frightened at his looks, began to cry. 'Hush, Rip,' cried she, 'hush, you little fool; the old man won't hurt you.' The name of the child, the air of the mother, and tone of her voice, all awakened a train of recollections in his mind. 'What is your name, my good woman?' asked he.

'Judith Gardenier.'

'And your father's name?'

'Ah, poor man, Rip Van Winkle was his name, but it's twenty years since he went away from home with his gun, and never has been heard of since,—his dog came home without him; but whether he shot himself, or was carried away by the Indians, nobody can tell. I was then but a little girl.'

Rip had but one question more to ask; but he put it with a faltering voice:

'Where's your mother?'

'Oh, she too had died but a short time since; she broke a bloodvessel in a fit of passion at a New England peddler.'

There was a drop of comfort, at least, in this intelligence. The honest man could contain himself no longer. He caught his daughter and her child in his arms. 'I am your father!' cried he—'Young Rip Van Winkle once—old Rip Van Winkle now!—Does nobody know poor Rip Van Winkle?'

All stood amazed, until an old woman, tottering out from among the crowd, put her hand to her brow, and peering under it in his face for a moment, exclaimed, 'Sure enough! it is Rip Van Winkle—it is himself! Welcome home again, old neighbor. Why, where have you been these twenty long years?'

Rip's story was soon told, for the whole twenty

years had been to him but as one night. The neighbors
stared when they heard it; some were seen to wink at
each other, and put their tongues in their cheeks: and
the self-important man in the cocked hat, who, when
the alarm was over, had returned to the field, screwed
down the corners of his mouth, and shook his head
—upon which there was a general shaking of the head
throughout the assemblage.

It was determined, however, to take the opinion of
old Peter Vanderdonk, who was seen slowly advancing up the road. He was a descendant of the historian
of that name, who wrote one of the earliest accounts of
the province. Peter was the most ancient inhabitant of
the village, and well versed in all the wonderful events
and traditions of the neighbourhood. He recollected
Rip at once, and corroborated his story in the most
satisfactory manner. He assured the company that it
was a fact, handed down from his ancestor the historian, that the Kaatskill mountains had always been
haunted by strange beings. That it was affirmed that
the great Hendrick Hudson, the first discoverer of the
river and country, kept a kind of vigil there every
twenty years, with his crew of the *Half-Moon*; being
permitted in this way to revisit the scenes of his enter-
prise, and keep a guardian eye upon the river and the
great city called by his name. That his father had once
seen them in their old Dutch dresses playing at ninepins in a hollow of the mountains; and that he himself
had heard, one summer afternoon, the sound of their
balls, like distant peals of thunder.

To make a long story short, the company broke up
and returned to the more important concerns of the
election. Rip's daughter took him home to live with
her; she had a snug, well-furnished house, and a
stout, cheery farmer for a husband, whom Rip recollected for one of the urchins that used to climb upon
his back. As to Rip's son and heir, who was the ditto
of himself, seen leaning against the tree, he was

employed to work on the farm; but evinced an heredi-
tary disposition to attend to anything else but his
business.

Rip now resumed his old walks and habits; he soon
found many of his former cronies, though all rather
the worse for the wear and tear of time; and preferred
making friends among the rising generation, with
whom he soon grew into great favor.

Having nothing to do at home, and being arrived at
that happy age when a man can be idle with impunity,
he took his place once more on the bench at the inn-
door, and was reverenced as one of the patriarchs of
the village, and a chronicle of the old times 'before the
war.' It was some time before he could get into the
regular track of gossip, or could be made to comprehend the strange events that had taken place
during his torpor. How that there had been a
revolutionary war—that the country had thrown off
the yoke of old England—and that, instead of being a
subject of his Majesty George the Third, he was now a
free citizen of the United States. Rip, in fact, was no
politician; the changes of states and empires made but
little impression on him; but there was one species of
despotism under which he had long groaned, and that
was—petticoat government. Happily that was at an
end; he had got his neck out of the yoke of matrimony,
and could go in and out whenever he pleased, without
dreading the tyranny of Dame Van Winkle. Whenever
her name was mentioned, however, he shook his
head, shrugged his shoulders, and cast up his eyes;
which might pass either for an expression of resigna-
tion to his fate, or joy at his deliverance.

He used to tell his story to every stranger that
arrived at Mr Doolittle's hotel. He was observed, at
first, to vary on some points every time he told it,
which was, doubtless, owing to his having so recently
awaked. It at last settled down precisely to the tale I
have related, and not a man, woman, or child in the

neighborhood but knew it by heart. Some always pre-
tended to doubt the reality of it, and insisted that Rip
had been out of his head, and that this was one point
on which he always remained flighty. The old Dutch
inhabitants, however, almost universally gave it full
credit. Even to this day they never hear a thunderstorm of a summer afternoon about the Kaatskill, but
they say Hendrick Hudson and his crew are at their
game of ninepins; and it is a common wish of all
hen-pecked husbands in the neighborhood, when life
hangs heavy on their hands, that they might have a
quieting draught out of Rip Van Winkle's flagon.

THE LION AND THE UNICORN

Lewis Carroll

When Alice passed through the looking glass, she found herself in a world of living chessmen and characters from nursery rhymes. Sitting in a forest, recovering from an exhausting encounter with Humpty Dumpty, Alice is brought to her feet by a loud crash . . .

The next moment soldiers came running through the wood, at first in twos and threes, then tens or twenty together, and at last in such crowds that they seemed to fill the whole forest. Alice got behind a tree, for fear of being run over, and watched them go by.

She thought that in all her life she had never seen soldiers so uncertain on their feet: they were always tripping over something or other, and whenever one went down, several more always fell over him, so that the ground was soon covered with little heaps of men.

Then came the horses. Having four feet, these managed rather better than the foot-soldiers; but even *they* stumbled now and then; and it seemed to be a regular rule that, whenever a horse stumbled, the rider fell off instantly. The confusion got worse every moment, and Alice was very glad to get out of the wood into an open place, where she found the White King seated on the ground, busily writing in his memorandum-book.

'I've sent them all!' the King cried in a tone of delight, on seeing Alice. 'Did you happen to meet any soldiers, my dear, as you came through the wood?'

'Yes, I did,' said Alice: 'several thousand, I should think.'

'Four thousand two hundred and seven, that's the exact number,' the King said, referring to his book. 'I couldn't send all the horses, you know, because two of them are wanted in the game. And I haven't sent the two Messengers, either. They're both gone to the town. Just look along the road, and tell me if you can see either of them.'

'I see nobody on the road,' said Alice.

'I only wish I had such eyes,' the King remarked in a fretful tone. 'To be able to see Nobody! And at that distance too! Why, it's as much as I can do to see real people, by this light!'

All this was lost on Alice, who was still looking intently along the road, shading her eyes with one hand. 'I see somebody now!' she exclaimed at last. 'But he's coming very slowly—and what curious attitudes he goes into!' (For the Messenger kept skipping up and down, and wriggling like an eel, as he came along, with his great hands spread out like fans on each side.)

'Not at all,' said the King. 'He's an Anglo-Saxon Messenger—and those are Anglo-Saxon attitudes. He only does them when he's happy. His name is Haigha.' (He pronounced it so as to rhyme with 'mayor.')

'I love my love with an H,' Alice couldn't help beginning, 'because he is Happy. I hate him with an H, because he is Hideous. I fed him with—with—with Ham-sandwiches and Hay. His name is Haigha, and he lives—'

'He lives on the Hill,' the King remarked simply, without the least idea that he was joining in the game, while Alice was still hesitating for the name of a town beginning with H. 'The other Messenger's called

Hatta. I must have *two*, you know—to come and go. One to come, and one to go.'

'I beg your pardon?' said Alice.

'It isn't respectable to beg,' said the King.

'I only meant that I didn't understand,' said Alice. 'Why one to come and one to go?'

'Don't I tell you?' the King repeated impatiently. 'I must have *two*—to fetch and carry. One to fetch, and one to carry.'

At this moment the Messenger arrived: he was far too much out of breath to say a word, and could only wave his hands about, and make the most fearful faces at the poor King.

'This young lady loves you with an H,' the King said, introducing Alice in the hope of turning off the Messenger's attention from himself—but it was of no use—the Anglo-Saxon attitudes only got more extraordinary every moment, while the great eyes rolled wildly from side to side.

'You alarm me!' said the King. 'I feel faint—Give me a ham sandwich!'

On which the Messenger, to Alice's great amusement, opened a bag that hung round his neck, and handed a sandwich to the King, who devoured it greedily.

'Another sandwich!' said the King.

'There's nothing but hay left now,' the Messenger said, peeping into the bag.

'Hay, then,' the King murmured in a faint whisper.

Alice was glad to see that it revived him a good deal.

'There's nothing like eating hay when you're faint,' he remarked to her as he munched away.

'I should think throwing cold water over you would be better,' Alice suggested: '—or some sal-volatile.'

'I didn't say there was nothing *better*,' the King replied. 'I said there was nothing *like* it.' Which Alice did not venture to deny.

'Who did you pass on the road?' the King went on,

holding out his hand to the Messenger for some more hay.

'Nobody,' said the Messenger.

'Quite right,' said the King: 'this young lady saw him too. So of course Nobody walks slower than you.'

'I do my best,' the Messenger said in a sullen tone. 'I'm sure nobody walks much faster than I do!'

'He can't do that,' said the King, 'or else he'd have been here first. However, now you've got your breath, you may tell us what's happened in the town.'

'I'll whisper it,' said the Messenger, putting his hands to his mouth in the shape of a trumpet and stooping so as to get close to the King's ear. Alice was sorry for this, as she wanted to hear the news too. However, instead of whispering, he simply shouted, at the top of his voice, 'They're at it again!'

'Do you call *that* a whisper?' cried the poor King, jumping up and shaking himself. 'If you do such a thing again, I'll have you buttered! It went through and through my head like an earthquake!'

'It would have to be a very tiny earthquake!' thought Alice. 'Who are at it again?' she ventured to ask.

'Why, the Lion and the Unicorn, of course,' said the King.

'Fighting for the crown!'

'Yes, to be sure,' said the King: 'and the best of the joke is, that it's *my* crown all the while! Let's run and see them.' And they trotted off, Alice repeating to herself, as she ran, the words of the old song:—

The Lion and the Unicorn were fighting for the crown:
The Lion beat the Unicorn all round the town.
Some gave them white bread, some gave them brown:
Some gave them plum-cake and drummed them out of town.

'Does—the one—that wins—get the crown?' she asked, as well as she could, for the run was putting her quite out of breath.

'Dear me, no!' said the King. 'What an idea!'

'Would you—be good enough—' Alice panted out, after running a little further, 'to stop a minute—just to get—one's breath again?'

'I'm *good* enough,' the King said, 'only I'm not *strong* enough. You see, a minute goes by so fearfully quick. You might as well try to stop a Bandersnatch!'

Alice had no more breath for talking; so they trotted on in silence, till they came into sight of a great crowd, in the middle of which the Lion and Unicorn were fighting. They were in such a cloud of dust, that at first Alice could not make out which was which; but she soon managed to distinguish the Unicorn by his horn.

They placed themselves close to where Hatta, the other Messenger, was standing watching the fight, with a cup of tea in one hand and a piece of bread-and-butter in the other.

'He's only just out of prison, and he hadn't finished his tea when he was sent in,' Haigha whispered to Alice: 'and they only give them oyster-shells in there—so you see he's very hungry and thirsty. How are you, dear child?' he went on, putting his arm affectionately round Hatta's neck.

Hatta looked round and nodded, and went on with his bread-and-butter.

'Were you happy in prison, dear child?' said Haigha.

Hatta looked round once more, and this time a tear or two trickled down his cheek; but not a word would he say.

'Speak, ca'n't you!' Haigha cried impatiently. But Hatta only munched away, and drank some more tea.

'Speak, won't you!' cried the King. 'How are they getting on with the fight?'

Hatta made a desperate effort, and swallowed a large piece of bread and butter. 'They're getting on very well,' he said in a choking voice: 'each of them has been down about eighty-seven times.'

'Then I suppose they'll soon bring the white bread and the brown?' Alice ventured to remark.

'It's waiting for 'em now,' said Hatta; 'this is a bit of it as I'm eating.'

There was a pause in the fight just then, and the Lion and Unicorn sat down, panting, while the King called out, 'Ten minutes allowed for refreshments!' Haigha and Hatta set to work at once, carrying round trays of white and brown bread. Alice took a piece to taste, but it was *very* dry.

'I don't think they'll fight any more today,' the King said to Hatta: 'go and order the drums to begin.' And Hatta went bounding away like a grasshopper.

For a minute or two Alice stood silent, watching him. Suddenly she brightened up. 'Look, look!' she cried, pointing eagerly. 'There's the White Queen running across the country! She came flying out of the wood over yonder— How fast those Queens *can* run!'

'There's some enemy after her, no doubt,' the King said, without even looking round. 'That wood's full of them.'

'But aren't you going to run and help her?' Alice asked, very much surprised at his taking it so quietly.

'No use, no use!' said the King. 'She runs so fearfully quick. You might as well try to catch a Bandersnatch! But I'll make a memorandum about her, if you like— She's a dear good creature,' he repeated softly to himself, as he opened his memorandum-book. 'Do you spell "creature" with a double "e"?'

At this moment the Unicorn sauntered by them, with his hands in his pockets. 'I had the best of it this time?' he said to the King, just glancing at him as he passed.

'A little—a little,' the King replied, rather nervously. 'You shouldn't have run him through with your horn, you know.'

'It didn't hurt him,' the Unicorn said carelessly, and he was going on, when his eye happened to fall upon

Alice: he turned round instantly, and stood for some time looking at her with an air of the deepest disgust.

'What—is—this?' he said at last.

'This is a child!' Haigha replied eagerly, coming in front of Alice to introduce her, and spreading out both his hands towards her in an Anglo-Saxon attitude. 'We only found it today. It's as large as life and twice as natural!'

'I always thought they were fabulous monsters!' said the Unicorn. 'Is it alive?'

'It can talk,' said Haigha solemnly.

The Unicorn looked dreamily at Alice, and said, 'Talk, child.'

Alice could not help her lips curling up into a smile as she began: 'Do you know, I always thought Unicorns were fabulous monsters, too? I never saw one alive before!'

'Well, now that we *have* seen each other,' said the Unicorn, 'if you'll believe in me, I'll believe in you. Is that a bargain?'

'Yes, if you like,' said Alice.

'Come, fetch out the plum-cake, old man!' the Unicorn went on, turning from her to the King. 'None of your brown bread for me!'

'Certainly—certainly!' the King muttered, and beckoned to Haigha. 'Open the bag!' he whispered. 'Quick! Not that one—that's full of hay!'

Haigha took a large cake out of the bag, and gave it to Alice to hold, while he got out a dish and carving-

knife. How they all came out of it Alice couldn't guess. It was just like a conjuring trick, she thought.

The Lion had joined them while this was going on: he looked very tired and sleepy, and his eyes were half shut. 'What's this!' he said, blinking lazily at Alice, and speaking in a deep hollow tone that sounded like the tolling of a great bell.

'Ah, what *is* it now?' the Unicorn cried eagerly. 'You'll never guess! *I* couldn't.'

The Lion looked at Alice wearily. 'Are you animal—or vegetable—or mineral?' he said, yawning at every other word.

'It's a fabulous monster!' the Unicorn cried out, before Alice could reply.

'Then hand round the plum-cake, Monster,' the Lion said, lying down and putting his chin on his paws. 'And sit down, both of you' (to the King and the Unicorn): 'fair play with the cake, you know!'

The King was evidently very uncomfortable at having to sit down between the two great creatures; but there was no other place for him.

'What a fight we might have for the crown, *now*!' the Unicorn said, looking slyly up at the crown, which the poor King was nearly shaking off his head, he trembled so much.

'I should win easy,' said the Lion.

'I'm not so sure of that,' said the Unicorn.

'Why, I beat you all round the town, you chicken!' the Lion replied angrily, half getting up as he spoke.

Here the King interrupted, to prevent the quarrel going on: he was very nervous, and his voice quite quivered. 'All round the town?' he said. 'That's a good long way. Did you go by the old bridge, or the market-place? You get the best view by the old bridge.'

'I'm sure I don't know,' the Lion growled out as he lay down again. 'There was too much dust to see anything. What a time the Monster is, cutting up that cake!'

Alice had seated herself on the bank of a little brook, with the great dish on her knees, and was sawing away diligently with the knife. 'It's very provoking!' she said, in reply to the Lion (she was getting quite used to being called "the Monster"). 'I've cut several slices already, but they always join on again!'

'You don't know how to manage Looking-glass cakes,' the Unicorn remarked. 'Hand it round first, and cut it afterwards.'

This sounded nonsense, but Alice very obediently got up, and carried the dish round, and the cake divided itself into three pieces as she did so. '*Now* cut it up,' said the Lion, as she returned to her place with the empty dish.

'I say, this isn't fair!' cried the Unicorn, as Alice sat with the knife in her hand, very much puzzled how to begin. 'The Monster has given the Lion twice as much as me!'

'She's kept none for herself, anyhow,' said the Lion. 'Do you like plum-cake, Monster!'

But before Alice could answer him, the drums began.

Where the noise came from, she couldn't make out: the air seemed full of it, and it rang through and through her head till she felt quite deafened. She started to her feet and sprang across the little brook in her terror, and had just time to see the Lion and the Unicorn rise to their feet, with angry looks at being interrupted in their feast, before she dropped to her knees, and put her hands over her ears, vainly trying to shut out the dreadful uproar.

'If *that* doesn't "drum them out of town,"' she thought to herself, 'nothing ever will!'

THE WIND ON THE MOON

Eric Linklater

Two sisters, Dinah and Dorinda, magically transformed into kangaroos, find themselves in the private zoo of Sir Lankester Lemon. Following the mysterious disappearance of both the Ostriches' egg and the girls' magic potion—without which they cannot return to human form—the animals combine to track down the thief...

Dinah took charge. She let Mr Parker have no time to argue, but gave him his instructions as calmly and clearly as if she had been her father issuing orders to his battalion. Mr Parker was full of admiration for her plan, but even more impressed when she admitted that she had a key which would open all the animals' cages, and he was positively awe-stricken when she divulged the name of the criminal who had been stealing Lady Lil's eggs.

'What put you on his trail?' he whispered. 'What was the final clue which enabled you to solve this baffling mystery?'

'There weren't any clues,' said Dinah. 'Someone told me who he was.'

'Ah, yes,' said Mr Parker wisely, 'that is often the way. A clue is a very good thing to have, and a lot of clues are still better, but an informer is best of all. The police are very fond of informers, because if they know the name of the criminal, and where he lives, they can solve the most difficult cases quite quickly and with perfect efficiency.'

'Look at that cloud,' said Dorinda. 'As soon as it blows a little more to the east, the moon will shine.'

'It is full tonight,' said Mr Parker.

'Then we have no time to lose,' said Dinah, 'for everybody should be in position before the moon comes out.'

Without another word she unlocked the door of their cage, let the Giraffe out of his, and went swiftly to the next block of cages, where Marie Louise the Llama, the Zebra, the Ant-eater, and the Kinkajous lived. She woke them all, opened all their doors, and leaving Mr Parker and Dorinda to explain what they had to do, she proceeded to call many other animals in their turn. Finally, she went to the prison cage where Bendigo the Grizzly Bear was confined. She had a long conversation with him. He was very ill-tempered about being wakened, but Dinah pacified him at last, and when he heard what was about to happen, and what she wanted him to do, he became very cheerful, and laughed in his throat with the sound of a little thunderstorm in a ravine.

By now the great dark cloud, the only one in the sky, which had covered the moon, had blown away to the east, obscuring a few thousand stars on its way but leaving the full moon shining bright and clear like a vast silver tray which had been polished by ten thousand housemaids for ten thousand years. The sky itself was a dark smooth blue, like the skin of a grape, and the park, towards which Dinah was now hurrying with long swift leap-after-leap, was flooded with milky light; but trees and shrubs cast inky shadows. Here and there in the shadow she could see the bright eyes of animals on guard.

Her plan had been to release all the animals who

could be trusted—but not the Puma, because many of the others were afraid of her—and post them like sentries round Lady Lil's nest. She had told Mr Parker that they must not go too near the nest, for Lady Lil should not be unnecessarily disturbed, but they had to be close enough to each other to prevent the thief from slipping through the ring unseen. He was strong and cunning: they must keep a good look-out.

She found the animals in position in a great circle surrounding the nest. They were all wide awake and eager to be the first to catch sight of the criminal. But a good many of them were rather frightened. They were all well concealed in the shadow of trees and bushes, and they stood perfectly still, as animals can.

Within the circle, and only about twenty yards from the nest where Lady Lil was calmly sleeping, there stood a group of lime-trees, and Mr Parker was standing between them with his long neck among the branches and his head looking over the topmost leaves. He stood so still that he was almost invisible, but Dinah could see that he had a good view of the nest, and he at least, she thought, was bound to see the thief if he came. 'If he doesn't fall asleep, that is,' she added, 'for he is leaning against a tree in a very comfortable-looking way, and he is shamefully fond of going to sleep.'

She hoped for the best, however, and after she had visited all the sentries, and encouraged them to be alert and brave, she went to look for Dorinda.

She had told Dorinda to wait for her on the far side of the sentry-ring. On the side farthest from the cages, that is, and nearest to the gate-keeper's cottage and the field where Mrs Grimble's bottle lay in a rabbit-hole. She had said nothing about the bottle to Mr Parker, of course, but she had told Dorinda, 'If the animals behave intelligently, and seem as though they can be trusted, then you and I will go and look for the rabbit-hole which the Falcon marked with the rabbit's tail. It should be easy to find in the moonlight, and we may be away for only a few minutes. Then we'll return and keep watch till morning if need be.'

So she and Dorinda waited for perhaps a quarter of an hour a little beyond the sentry-ring, and everything was quiet. The moonlight lay so thickly that Dorinda thought she could see it dripping off the leaves, and the moon, she said, was bulging out of the sky like the old mirror in the hall at home.

'After all,' said Dinah thoughtfully, 'he may not come tonight. The thief, I mean. Let's go and look for the bottle. But be careful! We must move as quietly as possible, for on a night like this the smallest sound will be heard—'

She was interrupted by a loud and fearful shriek that would have been heard in the midst of a winter gale.

'What's that?' cried Dorinda.

'Lady Lil!' said Dinah. 'Hurry, hurry!'

The nest, when they reached it, was already surrounded by some twenty or thirty feverishly excited animals, and Lady Lil, in a hoarse high voice, was weeping and bemoaning her loss. She was waving her head to and fro in agitated movement, and her eyes were sprinkling bright tears in the moonlight as though they had been watering-cans.

'It's gone, gone, gone!' she cried. 'My latest, loveliest, littlest egg is for ever gone.'

'It was quite a big egg when I saw it,' said Mr Parker suspiciously.

'What does that matter now,' screamed the Ostrich, 'when it's gone, gone, gone?'

'But how did it go?' asked the Cassowary. 'You have been sitting on it all night, and we have been watching you.'

'There was a pair of eyes,' said Lady Lil. 'I woke in a fright, and two great yellow eyes were staring at me. They were as yellow as, as . . .'

'As butter?' asked one of the Kinkajous.

'No, no!' said Lady Lil. 'They were hard and yellow, like, like . . .'

'Like cheese?' asked the young Baboon.

'*No!*' shouted Lady Lil. 'They were bright and hard and yellow . . .'

'Like a topaz,' said Marie Louise.

'Yes, like a topaz, and they glittered in the moonlight only a yard from mine. And then, I think, I fainted. I rose a little way from my nest, and fell again. And when I came to my senses, my egg was gone. My latest, loveliest egg, for ever gone. Ah me, I am the most miserable Ostrich that ever lived! Why, if this was to be my fate, did my poor mother sit so long and patiently to hatch me? In such a world as this, an Ostrich has no hope of happiness.'

'Mr Parker,' said Dinah in her most efficient voice, 'did you see this happen?'

'I saw nothing,' said Mr Parker. 'Absolutely nothing! I am completely baffled by this wholly unexpected development.'

'You were asleep,' said Dinah.

'I resent that,' said Mr Parker. 'I strongly resent it. I bitterly and deeply resent it. I resent it from the depths of my being. I am not unduly sensitive, but—'

'You were unduly sleepy,' said Dorinda unkindly.

'Anyway,' said Dinah, 'we are only wasting time standing here and talking. We should be looking for the thief. We all know who he is, and he has been too cunning for us. I believe that most of you were keeping a good look-out, but he has beaten you. He got through between two sentries and stole the egg. But he may not have eaten it yet, and perhaps he isn't far away. He may have gone towards home, but he won't get home very easily, for I've seen to that, and he is just as likely to be hiding somewhere quite near. So scatter and look for him. Some of you should go towards his cage, but all the others must hunt in every direction.'

'Admirable advice,' said Marie Louise. 'Scatter, my

friends, pray scatter! Two or three of you, however, may come with me.'

She spoke rather coldly, for she strongly disapproved of a young kangaroo like Dinah, who had so newly come to the zoo, setting herself up as a leader; but though Marie Louise was inclined to be jealous, she was also fair, and she knew that Dinah's plan was the proper one. So she offered a good example to the other animals, who quickly began to search for the criminal in all directions. But they were, by now, far too excited to keep quiet, as they had been while they stood sentry round the nest, so presently the moonlit air was trembling with the wild noises of the hunt, with baying and barking and crying and grunting and chattering and twittering and hissing and hollering and hip-hip-hurrahing and view-hulloing. But Lady Lil, entirely forgotten, sat alone upon her nest and wept.

Then Mr Parker, regarding the scene from his superior height, uttered a sudden tremendous shout and attracted nearly everyone's attention. 'Tally-ho, tally-ho!' shouted Mr Parker, with his forelegs stiffly braced and wide apart, his long neck stretching like the jib of a crane, and his great dark eyes ashine. The other animals looked in the direction to which he was pointing, and all were completely astonished. For there in the moonlight stood Sir Bobadil, and Sir Bobadil was obviously embarrassed. Sir Bobadil wore a guilty look, and midway between his beak and his breast, in the very middle of his neck, there was a sinister, suspicious bulge!

But Sir Bobadil was *not* the thief they had expected. It was not Sir Bobadil against whom they had been on guard and for whom they were now searching.

That, however, did not worry Mr Parker. Mr Parker forgot everything that Dinah had told him, and looking only at the bulge in Sir Bobadil's neck, exclaimed joyfully, 'A clue, a clue at last!'

'After him!' he shouted. 'Don't let him get away. Surround him, cut him off, capture him, there he goes!'

Mr Parker led the pursuit at a gallop, and Sir Bobadil might have been taken almost immediately if Mr Parker had looked where he was going. But in his excitement he tripped over the Ant-eater and fell heavily, which disorganized the chase. So Sir Bobadil got a good start and fled towards the wide lawn in front of Sir Lankester Lemon's mansion.

Now Sir Lankester had been wakened by the noise of the hunt, and was standing on the broad steps in front of the main door, wondering what it was all about. He was wearing a suit of yellow silk pyjamas with red braid on the jacket, a girdle with red tassels, and red Turkish slippers; and he carried a bolas and a boomerang.

Sir Bobadil the Ostrich ran frenziedly on to the lawn. Sir Lankester stepped forward, swung the bolas three times round his head, and let fly. His aim was sure. The iron-weighted rope wrapped itself round and round the base of Sir Bobadil's neck, who staggered, swayed, and fell.

At this very moment, however, the rest of the animals, a wild hunting pack led by Mr Parker, came charging across the lawn.

'Rebellion!' cried Sir Lankester. 'They have broken loose, we are attacked! Down, rebels, down! Virtus semper Viridis—Ma Foi et mon Droit—Du bleibst doch immer was Du bist!'

These foreign phrases were the mottoes of the Lemon family, and Sir Lankester used often to encourage himself by repeating them. They always made him feel even braver than before, so now he did not flinch from the charging animals, but instantly threw his boomerang at Mr Parker.

But this time his aim was not so good. The boomerang missed, by three yards at least, Mr

Parker's head, and began its return flight. It was not easy to see it in the moonlight, and Sir Lankester did not observe its approach. He was amazed when something struck him on the forehead. Or rather, he would have been amazed if he had had time to think about it. But he had no time, for immediately he fell to the soft turf, stunned.

Well in the van of the pursuing animals was Marie Louise the Llama, and when she saw her beloved master fall, she uttered a piercing scream and raced towards him. He made, indeed, a very handsome and pathetic sight as he lay in the moonlight in his yellow silk pyjamas, with their red braid and red tassels, and the red Turkish slippers, and a trickle of blood on his noble brow.

Marie Louise, kneeling beside him, laid her head on his chest and was convulsed with sobs. The young Baboon began to chafe his feet, the Kinkajous to rub his hands, while the Gnu blew gently on his face to give him air. He was surrounded by his animals, who all revealed, in various ways, the intensity of their grief and their utter devotion. Sir Bobadil was entirely forgotten.

There on the moonlit turf before his stately house lay Sir Lankester among the weeping animals, while a hundred yards away, on the open lawn, the poor silly Ostrich, choked by the bolas and gasping for air, felt sure he was about to die. Twice he struggled to his feet, and fell again. He tried a third time to get up, but rolled on to his back, kicking feebly with his long legs.

At this moment a kangaroo appeared on the edge of the lawn. It was Dorinda.

When Mr Parker set the animals off in pursuit of Sir Bobadil, Dinah and Dorinda with a Howler Monkey called Siren, who had a very loud voice, were already on their way to the main part of the zoo. There, they had thought, was the most important place to watch. But then, for a moment, they were undecided.

Perhaps it would be as well for one of them to join Mr
Parker's hunt, while the other kept to the original
plan? So Dorinda said that she would go with the
Giraffe, and as swiftly as she could she hurried after
the disappearing animals.

She arrived on the lawn too late to see the collapse of
Sir Lankester. The first thing she saw was Bobadil
waving his legs in the air.

'Who did this?' she asked, as she began to unwrap
the bolas from his neck.

'Urgk, urgk!' croaked Sir Bobadil, who could say no
more.

'And what's this?' she demanded, as she felt the
lump in his neck, which was about eighteen inches
higher up.

'Urgk!' said Sir Bobadil.

Dorinda felt it more carefully.

'I do believe,' she said, 'that it's something belong-
ing to me! And if it is, then you *are* a thief, as everyone
thought, because eating other people's property is
only another form of stealing, and it's greedy too. It
serves you right that it stuck in your throat, and
though you couldn't swallow it, you're going to
unswallow it, and unswallow it this minute, or I shan't
take this rope off your throat.'

'Urrurgk. Urrugagrurgk,' said Sir Bobadil.

'You mean you can't unswallow it unless I take the
rope off first?'

'Brurrugh.'

'But you promise you will?'

'Grurg.'

'All right then, I'll trust you. But if you don't—well,
something much worse than a bolas is going to hit
you!'

Then Dorinda unwrapped the rope that was wound
so tightly round Sir Bobadil's throat, and after some
wriggling, writhing, and coughing for a little while,
the Ostrich laid on the turf the bottle containing Mrs

Grimble's magic draught.

'Excuse me,' he said.

*

Bendigo the Bear lay in the shadow of a rock beside a group of cages, waiting. Here was where the thief lived, and Dinah, when she let Bendigo out of prison, had said: 'If the animals guarding the nest fail to capture him, he's almost certain to make for home. Then you will have to stop him. He'll be in a desperate mood, but you're very strong. Do you think you can do it?'

'Let me get my arms round him,' Bendigo had growled, 'and I'll crush him to death!'

During his imprisonment he had been, naturally enough, in a very bad temper, for he had no *Times* to read, and he was being punished for a crime which he had not committed. But now he had a chance to get rid of his anger upon the real thief. A glorious, honey-sweet revenge! With all his wrathful heart he hoped and prayed that the other animals would fail to find or hold the criminal, so that he, Bendigo, might have the exquisite pleasure of halting him, wrestling with him, and, if possible, breaking his abominable back.

That is what Bendigo promised himself as he waited in the shadow. 'I'll break his abominable back,' he growled, and grew impatient because the thief did not come at once.

In front of the cages, and in front of the rock beside which Bendigo lay, there was a narrow strip of grass, and before that a road about ten feet broad. Beyond the road there was more grass, with shrubs and bushes, and behind them could be seen a few trees, their leaves in the moonlight as still as the leaves on a Chinese scroll.

Suddenly Bendigo stiffened, and the coarse hair on his neck rose harsh and bristling. In the bushes beyond the road, only a few inches above the ground, he saw, like tiny yellow lamps, two palely glittering eyes. He lay perfectly still, and slowly, very slowly, the eyes came nearer. They left the darkness of the bushes, and drew close to the farther edge of the road. But only the eyes were visible. There seemed to be nothing else.

Then, with unbelievable speed, they were over the road, and behind them, with a fast-flowing movement, came a thick round body. Bendigo, with a roar, hurled himself upon it. It was the Python. The Python was the thief.

Now there began a fearful battle.

The Python was about twelve feet long, and first of all Bendigo seized it by the middle and tried to lift it off the ground. The middle came up in a great loop, but quickly the Python coiled its head-end round one of his legs, its tail-end round the other, and threw Bendigo off his feet. They rolled over and over on the road, the Bear tied up in the snake. Then the Python broke loose, and tried to escape into its house by a secret hole under the wall which it used, unknown to Mr Plum the keeper, for going in and out whenever it wanted. But Bendigo caught it by the tail, and there was a tug-of-war with Bendigo hauling and pulling in one direction, and the Python straining with all its length of mighty muscle to get away in the other.

Bendigo was unable to drag it away from the hole, but the Python couldn't get away from the Bear, so after three or four minutes of desperate pulling it suddenly turned, and its head, like a battering-ram, leapt straight at Bendigo's throat.

Just in time, Bendigo struck. His rough right paw hit the Python a dreadful blow on the side of the head, and the front end of the snake—some four or five feet of it—fell limply to the ground. But Bendigo, of course, had been obliged to let go the tail in order to hit the head, and before he could avoid it, the tail-end —some five or six feet of it—coiled itself round his waist and tried to squeeze him to death, while the head-end, recovering its breath, again struck at him like a battering-ram.

But again and again, now with his right paw and now with his left, Bendigo clouted the darting head, beating it to one side, then to the other, and at last the Python fell senseless to the ground, and its tail uncoiled from Bendigo's waist. Then Bendigo, picking up the loose body and holding it about three or four feet from the head-end, struck its skull against the wall of the nearest cage and killed it.

'Oh, well done, well done!' cried Dinah. 'Brave Bendigo!'

She had arrived, with Siren the Howler Monkey close beside her, in time to see most of the fight, and though she had been afraid, she had watched every blow and throw, every trick and turn of the struggle.

'Oh, brave Bendigo!' she repeated. 'How magnificently you fought! But I was terribly afraid for you. Every time that dreadful head struck at you, I felt sure

you were going to be killed. My heart almost stopped beating.'

'Nonsense,' said Bendigo, puffing and panting. 'It was just the sort of fight I like, and I feel all the better for it. Did you see that first punch I gave him?'

'It was wonderful,' said Dinah.

'You've got to know how to time your punches,' said Bendigo. 'Balance and timing—that's the secret of a good punch. I used to do a lot of boxing when I was a boy.'

'When were *you* a boy?' asked Dinah.

But Bendigo, in spite of the brave way in which he had been talking, was very tired. His last words had been no louder than a whisper, and now he was sitting on the grass with hanging head and shoulders relaxed, looking like the oldest and most weary bear in the world. He paid no attention to Dinah's question.

Siren the Howler had been examining the dead Python, and now he called softly to Dinah.

'Look!' he said, pointing to a round swelling in the snake's body. 'There's the egg, Lady Lil's egg. He swallowed it, but it doesn't seem to be broken.'

'But how can we get it out?'

'I don't know,' said Siren.

'If we had a knife,' said Dinah, 'we could do an operation and cut it out. Bendigo! Do you know where we can get a knife?'

'I've got a little one,' said Bendigo in a weary voice. 'I use it for cutting cigars. People sometimes give me a cigar on a Sunday afternoon.'

'I didn't know that bears could smoke cigars,' said Dinah.

'Didn't you?' asked Bendigo, and slowly, with a groan at every movement, he got up and shambled towards them.

He had a little knife on a chain round his neck. He opened it and made a long neat cut in the Python's hide. The egg was unharmed.

'You'd better take it back to Lady Lil while it's warm,' said Bendigo. 'I'm going to my bed. I'm just a trifle tired, I think. Don't forget to come and lock me in. And you'd better hurry up and get the others back to their cages, for it's nearly morning, and there'll be trouble if old Plum finds them out and about when he gets up.'

'But what are we going to do with *this*?' asked Dinah, pointing to the body of the Python.

'Let it lie,' said Bendigo. 'It isn't any good to any-one.' And limping and groaning, he went off to his cage.

'It seems very untidy to leave it lying there,' said Dinah, 'but what else can we do? Let's take the egg back to Lady Lil.'

The moon by now was low in the east, and its light was duller, as though it were dimly reflected from a silver tray that no one had cleaned for a long time. But already there was a little dawn-grey in the sky, and that made them hurry.

They found Lady Lil beside her nest. She was all alone, and with drooping head she looked at the empty place where the egg had lain. She was sobbing bitterly, and her long neck quivered, and now and then she touched with her beak the dry grass in the bed of the nest. Dinah herself could hardly keep from crying when she saw her, and quite forgot the little speech she had intended to make. She had meant to return the egg with a gracious gesture and a few polite words of congratulation, like Lady Lemon presenting Mrs Fullalove with the First Prize for Dahlias at the Midmeddlecum Flower Show, but all she could do was to hurry forward and exclaim, 'Stop crying! We've found your egg; here it is, stop crying *please*!'

For a moment Lady Lil stared at the egg as if she could not believe her eyes, but then she began to dance up and down with excitement, and asked twenty questions, and told Dinah what to do, and what not to

do, and laughed for pure joy, and cried for no reason at
all.

'Where did you find it?' she demanded. 'Who was
the thief?' Where has he gone? Put it down there. Oh,
be careful with it! No, not there, *there*. Is it all right? It's
quite warm. Why is it still warm? Oh, my egg, my
darling egg, where have you been? Oh, I'm so happy!
You're the cleverest kangaroo that ever lived! Darling
Kangaroo, where did you find it? No, don't tell me
now, I mustn't get excited. I must keep quiet and calm
for *its* sake. My dear, dear egg. . . .'

So they left her, and then Dinah said to Siren the
Monkey, 'Howl as loudly as you can, for it's time we all
got back to our cages.'

Then Siren opened his mouth and howled, and the
noise was heard far and wide, and all the animals
obeyed and went back to their cages. Marie Louise and
the others, who had gathered round Sir Lankester
when the boomerang hit him, were rather reluctant to
go, because Sir Lankester had by now recovered con-
sciousness, and was talking to them in the most
friendly way. He couldn't quite remember what had
happened, but the first thing he had seen when he
opened his eyes was the loving face of Marie Louise,
and then the other animals, all of whom, in one way or
another, were showing their affection for him. So he
sat up and told them what a happy man he was to have
so many good kind friends.

'There is only one recipe for happiness,' he said in
his most solemn voice, 'and that is to make others
happy. I have done my best, and I have every inten-
tion of doing more and more to give you pleasure and
promote your welfare.'

But what it was that he intended to do they could not
wait to hear, because at that moment they heard Siren
the Howler Monkey. And a few seconds later Sir
Lankester, in his yellow pyjamas, was left alone upon
the lawn. The rapid disappearance of the animals

bewildered him, and when he tried to think of all that had happened, and find a meaning for it, he grew still more bewildered. His head was aching, he was feeling cold, and there was no one to talk to. So he decided to go to bed.

Dinah was already hurrying from cage to cage and locking the doors. Bendigo was fast asleep, but she spoke a few words to all the other animals, praising them for what they had done, and telling the news that Lady Lil's egg had been safely restored and the Python was dead. She talked for several minutes to the Golden Puma, who had been anxiously awake all night, and she had to spend twice as long with Mr Parker before he could be made to understand what had happened.

Then she went to her own house, and there was Dorinda with Mrs Grimble's magic draught.

They were both far too happy to feel sleepy, so they lay talking till it was broad daylight. And then, without meaning to, they did go to sleep.

BY CALDRON POOL

C. S. Lewis

n the kingdom of Narnia, all is not well. King Tirian and the cruel Calormenes are preparing themselves for the final struggle between good and evil. And Shift the Ape has a plan . . .

In the last days of Narnia, far up to the west beyond Lantern Waste and close beside the great waterfall, there lived an Ape. He was so old that no one could remember when he had first come to live in those parts, and he was the cleverest, ugliest, most wrinkled Ape you can imagine. He had a little house, built of wood and thatched with leaves, up in the fork of a great tree, and his name was Shift. There were very few Talking Beasts or Men or Dwarfs, or people of any sort, in that part of the wood, but Shift had one friend and neighbour who was a donkey called Puzzle. At least they both said they were friends, but from the way things went on you might have thought Puzzle was more like Shift's servant than his friend. He did all the work. When they went together to the river, Shift filled the big skin bottles with water but it was Puzzle who carried them back. When they wanted anything from the towns further down the river it was Puzzle who went down with empty panniers on his back and came back with the panniers full and heavy. And all the nicest things that Puzzle brought back were eaten by Shift; for as Shift said, 'You see, Puzzle, I can't eat grass and thistles like you, so it's only fair I should make it up in other ways.' And Puzzle always said, 'Of course, Shift, of course. I see that.' Puzzle never complained, because he knew that Shift was far cleverer than himself and he thought it was very kind of Shift to be friends with him at all. And if ever Puzzle did try to argue about anything, Shift would always say, 'Now, Puzzle, I understand what needs to be done better than you. You know you're not clever, Puzzle.' And Puzzle always said, 'No, Shift. It's quite true. I'm *not* clever.' Then he would sigh and do whatever Shift had said.

One morning early in the year the pair of them were out walking along the shore of Caldron Pool. Caldron Pool is the big pool right under the cliffs at the western end of Narnia. The great waterfall pours down into it with a noise like everlasting thunder, and the River of Narnia flows out on the other side. The waterfall keeps the Pool always dancing and bubbling and churning round and round as if it were on the boil, and that of course is how it got its name of Caldron Pool. It is liveliest in the early spring when the waterfall is swollen with all the snow that has melted off the mountains from up beyond Narnia in the Western Wild from which the river comes. And as they looked at Caldron Pool Shift suddenly pointed with his dark, skinny finger and said,

'Look! What's that?'

'What's what?' said Puzzle.

'That yellow thing that's just come down the waterfall. Look! There it is again, it's floating. We must find out what it is.'

'Must we?' said Puzzle.

'Of course we must,' said Shift. 'It may be something useful. Just hop into the Pool like a good fellow and fish it out. Then we can have a proper look at it.'

'Hop into the Pool?' said Puzzle, twitching his long ears.

'Well how are we to get it if you don't?' said the Ape.

'But—but,' said Puzzle, 'wouldn't it be better if *you* went in? Because, you see, it's you who wants to know what it is, and I don't much. And you've got hands, you see. You're as good as a Man or a Dwarf when it comes to catching hold of things. I've only got hoofs.'

'Really, Puzzle,' said Shift, 'I didn't think you'd ever say a thing like that. I didn't think it of you, really.'

'Why, what have I said wrong?' said the Ass, speaking in rather a humble voice, for he saw that Shift was very deeply offended. 'All I meant was—'

'Wanting *me* to go into the water,' said the Ape. 'As if you didn't know perfectly well what weak chests Apes always have and how easily they catch cold! Very well. I *will* go in. I'm feeling cold enough already in this cruel wind. But I'll go in. I shall probably die. Then you'll be sorry.' And Shift's voice sounded as if he was just going to burst into tears.

'Please don't, please don't, please don't,' said Puzzle, half braying, and half talking. 'I never meant anything of the sort, Shift, really I didn't. You know how stupid I am and how I can't think of more than one thing at a time. I'd forgotten about your weak chest. Of course I'll go in. You mustn't think of doing it yourself. Promise me you won't, Shift.'

So Shift promised, and Puzzle went cloppety-clop on his four hoofs round the rocky edge of the Pool to find a place where he could get in. Quite apart from the cold it was no joke getting into that quivering and foaming water, and Puzzle had to stand and shiver for a whole minute before he made up his mind to do it. But then Shift called out from behind him and said: 'Perhaps I'd better do it after all, Puzzle.' And when Puzzle heard that he said, 'No, no. You promised. I'm in now,' and in he went.

A great mass of foam got him in the face and filled his mouth with water and blinded him. Then he went under altogether for a few seconds, and when he came up again he was in quite another part of the Pool. Then the swirl caught him and carried him round and round and faster and faster till it took him right under the waterfall itself, and the force of the water plunged him down, deep down, so that he thought he would never be able to hold his breath till he came up again. And when he had come up and when at last he got somewhere near the thing he was trying to catch, it sailed away from him till it too got under the fall and was forced down to the bottom. When it came up again it was further from him than ever. But at last, when he was almost tired to death, and bruised all over and numb with cold, he succeeded in gripping the thing with his teeth. And out he came carrying it in front of him and getting his front hoofs tangled up in it, for it was as big as a large hearthrug, and it was very heavy and cold and slimy.

He flung it down in front of Shift and stood dripping and shivering and trying to get his breath back. But the Ape never looked at him or asked him how he felt. The Ape was too busy going round and round the Thing and spreading it out and patting it and smelling it. Then a wicked gleam came into his eye and he said:

'It is a lion's skin.'

'Ee—auh—auh—oh, is it?' gasped Puzzle.

'Now I wonder . . . I wonder . . . I wonder,' said Shift to himself, for he was thinking very hard.

'I wonder who killed the poor lion,' said Puzzle presently. 'It ought to be buried. We must have a funeral.'

'Oh, it wasn't a Talking Lion,' said Shift. 'You needn't bother about *that*. There are no Talking Beasts up beyond the Falls, up in the Western Wild. This skin must have belonged to a dumb, wild lion.'

This, by the way, was true. A Hunter, a Man, had killed and skinned this lion somewhere up in the Western Wild several months before. But that doesn't come into this story.

'All the same, Shift,' said Puzzle, 'even if the skin only belonged to a dumb, wild lion, oughtn't we to give it a decent burial? I mean, aren't all lions rather—well, rather solemn? Because of you know Who. Don't you see?'

'Don't you start getting ideas into your head, Puzzle,' said Shift. 'Because, you know, thinking isn't your strong point. We'll make this skin into a fine warm winter coat for you.'

'Oh, I don't think I'd like that,' said the Donkey. 'It would look—I mean, the other Beasts might think—that is to say, I shouldn't feel—'

'What are you talking about?' said Shift, scratching himself the wrong way up as Apes do.

'I don't think it would be respectful to the Great Lion, to Aslan himself, if an ass like me went about dressed up in a lion-skin,' said Puzzle.

'Now don't stand arguing, please,' said Shift. 'What does an ass like you know about things of that sort?

You know you're no good at thinking, Puzzle, so why
don't you let me do your thinking for you? Why don't
you treat me as I treat you? *I* don't think I can do
everything. I know you're better at some things than I
am. That's why I let you go into the Pool; I knew you'd
do it better than me. But why can't I have my turn
when it comes to something I *can* do and you can't?
Am I never to be allowed to do anything? Do be fair.
Turn and turn about.'

'Oh, well, of course, if you put it that way,' said
Puzzle.

'I tell you what,' said Shift. 'You'd better take a good
brisk trot down river as far as Chippingford and see if
they have any oranges or bananas.'

'But I'm so tired, Shift,' pleaded Puzzle.

'Yes, but you are very cold and wet,' said the Ape.
'You want something to warm you up. A brisk trot
would be just the thing. Besides, it's market day at
Chippingford today.' And then of course Puzzle said
he would go.

As soon as he was alone Shift went shambling
along, sometimes on two paws and sometimes on
four, till he reached his own tree. Then he swung
himself up from branch to branch, chattering and
grinning all the time, and went into his little house. He
found needle and thread and a big pair of scissors
there; for. he was a clever Ape and the Dwarfs had
taught him how to sew. He put the ball of thread (it
was very thick stuff, more like cord than thread) into
his mouth so that his cheek bulged out as if he were
sucking a big bit of toffee. He held the needle between
his lips and took the scissors in his left paw. Then he
came down the tree and shambled across to the lion-
skin. He squatted down and got to work.

He saw at once that the body of the lion-skin would
be too long for Puzzle and its neck too short. So he cut
a good piece out of the body and used it to make a long
collar for Puzzle's long neck. Then he cut off the head

and sewed the collar in between the head and the shoulders. He put threads on both sides of the skin so that it would tie up under Puzzle's chest and stomach. Every now and then a bird would pass overhead and Shift would stop his work, looking anxiously up. He did not want anyone to see what he was doing. But none of the birds he saw were Talking Birds, so it didn't matter.

Late in the afternoon Puzzle came back. He was not trotting but only plodding patiently along, the way donkeys do.

'There weren't any oranges,' he said, 'and there weren't any bananas. And I'm very tired.' He lay down.

'Come and try on your beautiful new lion-skin coat,' said Shift.

'Oh bother that old skin,' said Puzzle, 'I'll try it on in the morning. I'm too tired tonight.'

'You *are* unkind, Puzzle,' said Shift. 'If *you're* tired what do you think *I* am? All day long, while you've been having a lovely refreshing walk down the valley, I've been working hard to make you a coat. My paws are so tired I can hardly hold these scissors. And now you won't say thank you—and you won't even look at the coat—and you don't care—and—and—'

'My dear Shift,' said Puzzle getting up at once, 'I am so sorry. I've been horrid. Of course I'd love to try it on. And it looks simply splendid. Do try it on me at once. Please do.'

'Well, stand still then,' said the Ape. The skin was very heavy for him to lift, but in the end, with a lot of pulling and pushing and puffing and blowing, he got it on to the donkey. He tied it underneath Puzzle's body and he tied the legs to Puzzle's legs and the tail to Puzzle's tail. A good deal of Puzzle's grey nose and face could be seen through the open mouth of the lion's head. No one who had ever seen a real lion would have been taken in for a moment. But if someone who had never seen a lion looked at Puzzle in his lion-skin he just might mistake him for a lion, if he didn't come too close, and if the light was not too good, and if Puzzle didn't let out a bray and didn't make any noise with his hoofs.

'You look wonderful, wonderful,' said the Ape. 'If anyone saw you now, they'd think you were Aslan, the Great Lion, himself.'

'That would be dreadful,' said Puzzle.

'No it wouldn't,' said Shift. 'Everyone would do whatever you told them.'

'But I don't want to tell them anything.'

'But you think of the good we could do!' said Shift. 'You'd have me to advise you, you know. I'd think of sensible orders for you to give. And everyone would have to obey us, even the King himself. We would set everything right in Narnia.'

'But isn't everything right already?' said Puzzle.

'What!' cried Shift. 'Everything right?—when there are no oranges or bananas?'

'Well, you know,' said Puzzle, 'there aren't many people—in fact, I don't think there's anyone but your-self—who wants those sort of things.'

'There's sugar too,' said Shift.

'H'm, yes,' said the Ass. 'It would be nice if there was more sugar.'

'Well then, that's settled,' said the Ape. 'You will pretend to be Aslan, and I'll tell you what to say.'

'No, no, no,' said Puzzle. 'Don't say such dreadful things. It would be wrong, Shift. I may be not very clever but I know that much. What would become of us if the real Aslan turned up?'

'I expect he'd be very pleased,' said Shift. 'Probably he sent us the lion-skin on purpose, so that we could set things to right. Anyway, he never *does* turn up, you know. Not nowadays.'

At that moment there came a great thunderclap right overhead and the ground trembled with a small

earthquake. Both the animals lost their balance and
were flung on their faces.

'There!' gasped Puzzle, as soon as he had breath to
speak. 'It's a sign, a warning. I knew we were doing
something dreadfully wicked. Take this wretched skin
off me at once.'

'No, no,' said the Ape (whose mind worked very
quickly). 'It's a sign the other way. I was just going to
say that if the real Aslan, as you call him, meant us to
go on with this, he would send us a thunderclap and
an earth-tremor. It was just on the tip of my tongue,
only the sign itself came before I could get the words
out. You've *got* to do it now, Puzzle. And please don't
let us have any more arguing. You know you don't
understand these things. What could a donkey know
about signs?'

*

About three weeks later the last of the Kings of Narnia
sat under the great oak which grew beside the door of
his little hunting lodge, where he often stayed for ten
days or so in the pleasant spring weather. It was a low,
thatched building not far from the Eastern end of
Lantern Waste and some way above the meeting of the
two rivers. He loved to live there simply and at ease,
away from the state and pomp of Cair Paravel, the
royal city. His name was King Tirian, and he was
between twenty and twenty-five years old; his
shoulders were already broad and strong and his limbs
full of hard muscle, but his beard was still scanty. He
had blue eyes and a fearless, honest face.

There was no one with him that spring morning
except his dearest friend, Jewel the Unicorn. They
loved each other like brothers and each had saved the
other's life in the wars. The lordly beast stood close
beside the King's chair, with its neck bent round
polishing its blue horn against the creamy whiteness
of its flank.

'I cannot set myself to any work or sport today,

Jewel,' said the King. 'I can think of nothing but this
wonderful news. Think you we shall hear any more of
it today?'

'They are the most wonderful tidings ever heard in
our days or our father's or our grandfathers' days,
Sire,' said Jewel, 'if they are true.'

'How can they choose but be true?' said the King. 'It
is more than a week ago that the first birds came flying
over us saying, Aslan is here, Aslan has come to
Narnia again. And after that it was the squirrels. They
had not seen him, but they said it was certain he was in
the woods. Then came the Stag. He said he had seen
him with his own eyes, a great way off, by moonlight,
in Lantern Waste. Then came that dark Man with the
beard, the merchant from Calormen. The Calormenes
care nothing for Aslan as we do; but the man spoke of
it as a thing beyond doubt. And there was the Badger
last night; he too had seen Aslan.'

'Indeed, Sire,' answered Jewel, 'I believe it all. If
I seem not to, it is only that my joy is too great to let
my belief settle itself. It is almost too beautiful to
believe.'

'Yes,' said the King with a great sigh, almost a
shiver, of delight. 'It is beyond all that I ever hoped for
in all my life.'

'Listen!' said Jewel, putting his head on one side and
cocking his ears forward.

'What is it?' asked the King.

'Hoofs, Sire,' said Jewel. 'A galloping horse. A very
heavy horse. It must be one of the Centaurs. And look,
there he is.'

A great, golden-bearded Centaur, with man's sweat
on his forehead and horse's sweat on his chestnut
flanks, dashed up to the King, stopped, and bowed
low. 'Hail, King,' it cried in a voice as deep as a bull's.

'Ho, there!' said the King, looking over his shoulder
towards the door of the hunting lodge. 'A bowl of wine
for the noble Centaur. Welcome, Roonwit. When you

have found your breath you shall tell us your errand.'

A page came out of the house carrying a great wooden bowl, curiously carved, and handed it to the Centaur. The Centaur raised the bowl and said,

'I drink first to Aslan and truth, Sire, and secondly to your Majesty.'

He finished the wine (enough for six strong men) at one draught and handed the empty bowl back to the page.

'Now, Roonwit,' said the King. 'Do you bring us more news of Aslan?'

Roonwit looked very grave, frowning a little.

'Sire,' he said. 'You know how long I have lived and studied the stars; for we Centaurs live longer than you Men, and even longer than your kind, Unicorn. Never in all my days have I seen such terrible things written in the skies as there have been nightly since this year began. The stars say nothing of the coming of Aslan, nor of peace, nor of joy. I know by my art that there have not been such disastrous conjunctions of the planets for five hundred years. It was already in my mind to come and warn your Majesty that some great evil hangs over Narnia. But last night the rumour reached me that Aslan is abroad in Narnia. Sire, do not believe this tale. It cannot be. The stars never lie, but Men and Beasts do. If Aslan were really coming to Narnia the sky would have foretold it. If he were really come, all the most gracious stars would be assembled in his honour. It is all a lie.'

'A lie!' said the King fiercely. 'What creature in Narnia or all the world would dare to lie on such a matter?' And, without knowing it, he laid his hand on his sword hilt.

'That I know not, Lord King,' said the Centaur. 'But I know there are liars on earth; there are none among the stars.'

'I wonder,' said Jewel, 'whether Aslan might not come though all the stars foretold otherwise. He is not the slave of the stars but their Maker. Is it not said in all the old stories that He is not a tame lion.'

'Well said, well said, Jewel,' cried the King. 'Those are the very words: *not a tame lion*. It comes in many tales.'

Roonwit had just raised his hand and was leaning forward to say something very earnestly to the King when all three of them turned their heads to listen to a wailing sound that was quickly drawing nearer. The wood was so thick to the West of them that they could not see the newcomer yet. But they could soon hear the words.

'Woe, woe, woe!' called the voice. 'Woe for my brothers and sisters! Woe for the holy trees! The woods are laid waste. The axe is loosed against us. We are being felled. Great trees are falling, falling, falling.'

With the last 'falling' the speaker came in sight. She was like a woman but so tall that her head was on a level with the Centaur's: yet she was like a tree too. It is hard to explain if you have never seen a Dryad but quite unmistakable once you have—something different in the colour, the voice, and the hair. King Tirian and the two Beasts knew at once that she was the nymph of a beech-tree.

'Justice, Lord King!' she cried. 'Come to our aid. Protect your people. They are felling us in Lantern Waste. Forty great trunks of my brothers and sisters are already on the ground.'

'What, Lady! Felling Lantern Waste? Murdering the talking trees?' cried the King leaping to his feet and drawing his sword. 'How dare they? And who dares it? Now by the Mane of Aslan—'

'A-a-a-h,' gasped the Dryad shuddering as if in pain—shuddering time after time as if under repeated blows. Then all at once she fell sideways as suddenly as if both her feet had been cut from under her. For a second they saw her lying dead on the grass and then she vanished. They knew what had happened. Her tree, miles away, had been cut down.

For a moment the King's grief and anger were so great that he could not speak. Then he said:

'Come, friends. We must go up river and find the villains who have done this, with all the speed we may. I will leave not one of them alive.'

'Sire, with a good will,' said Jewel.

But Roonwit said, 'Sire, be wary in your just wrath. There are strange doings on foot. If there should be rebels in arms further up the valley, we three are too few to meet them. If it would please you to wait while—'

'I will not wait the tenth part of a second,' said the King. 'But while Jewel and I go forward, do you gallop as hard as you may to Cair Paravel. Here is my ring for your token. Get me a score of men-at-arms, all well mounted, and a score of Talking Dogs, and ten Dwarfs (let them all be fell archers), and a Leopard or so, and Stonefoot the Giant. Bring all these after us as quickly as may be.'

'With a good will, Sire,' said Roonwit. And at once he turned and galloped Eastward down the valley.

The King strode on at a great pace, sometimes muttering to himself and sometimes clenching his fists. Jewel walked beside him, saying nothing; so there was no sound between them but the faint jingle of a rich gold chain that hung round the Unicorn's neck and the noise of two feet and four hoofs.

They soon reached the River and turned up it where

there was a grassy road: they had the water on their left and the forest on their right. Soon after that they came to the place where the ground grew rougher and thick wood came down to the water's edge. The road, what there was of it, now ran on the Southern bank and they had to ford the River to reach it. It was up to Tirian's arm-pits, but Jewel (who had four legs and was therefore steadier) kept on his right so as to break the force of the current, and Tirian put his strong arm round the Unicorn's strong neck and they both got safely over. The King was still so angry that he hardly noticed the cold of the water. But of course he dried his sword very carefully on the shoulder of his cloak, which was the only dry part of him, as soon as they came to shore.

They were now going Westward with the River on their right and Lantern Waste straight ahead of them. They had not gone more than a mile when they both stopped and both spoke at the same moment. The King said 'What have we here?' and Jewel said 'Look!'

'It is a raft,' said King Tirian.

And so it was. Half a dozen splendid tree-trunks, all newly cut and newly lopped of their branches, had been lashed together to make a raft, and were gliding swiftly down the river. On the front of the raft there was a water-rat with a pole to steer it.

'Hey! Water-Rat! What are you about?' cried the King.

'Taking logs down to sell to the Calormenes, Sire,'

said the Rat, touching his ear as he might have touched his cap if he had had one.

'Calormenes!' thundered Tirian. 'What do you mean? Who gave order for these trees to be felled?'

The River flows so swiftly at that time of the year that the raft had already glided past the King and Jewel. But the Water-Rat looked back over its shoulder and shouted out:

'The Lion's orders, Sire. Aslan himself.' He added something more but they couldn't hear it.

The King and the Unicorn stared at one another and both looked more frightened than they had ever been in any battle.

'Aslan,' said the King at last, in a very low voice. 'Aslan. Could it be true? *Could* he be felling the holy trees and murdering the Dryads?'

'Unless the Dryads have all done something dreadfully wrong—' murmured Jewel.

'But selling them to Calormenes!' said the King. 'Is it possible?'

'I don't know,' said Jewel miserably. 'He's not a *tame* lion.'

'Well,' said the King at last, 'we must go on and take the adventure that comes to us.'

'It is the only thing left for us to do, Sire,' said the Unicorn. He did not see at the moment how foolish it was for two of them to go on alone; nor did the King. They were too angry to think clearly. But much evil came of their rashness in the end.

Suddenly the King leaned hard on his friend's neck and bowed his head.

'Jewel,' he said, 'what lies before us? Horrible thoughts arise in my heart. If we had died before today we should have been happy.'

'Yes,' said Jewel. 'We have lived too long. The worst thing in the world has come upon us.' They stood like that for a minute or two and then went on.

Before long they could hear the hack-hack-hack of

axes falling on timber, though they could see nothing
yet because there was a rise of the ground in front of
them. When they had reached the top of it they could
see right into Lantern Waste itself. And the King's face
turned white when he saw it.

Right through the middle of that ancient
forest—that forest where the trees of gold and of silver
had once grown and where a child from our world had
once planted the Tree of Protection—a broad lane had
already been opened. It was a hideous lane like a raw
gash in the land, full of muddy ruts where felled trees
had been dragged down to the river. There was a great
crowd of people at work, and a cracking of whips, and
horses tugging and straining as they dragged at the
logs. The first thing that struck the King and the
Unicorn was that about half the people in the crowd
were not Talking Beasts but Men. The next thing was
that these men were not the fair-haired men of Narnia:
they were dark, bearded men from Calormen, that
great and cruel country that lies beyond Archenland
across the desert to the south. There was no reason, of
course, why one should not meet a Calormene or two
in Narnia—a merchant or an ambassador—for there
was peace between Narnia and Calormen in those
days. But Tirian could not understand why there were
so many of them: nor why they were cutting down a
Narnian forest. He grasped his sword tighter and
rolled his cloak round his left arm. They came quickly
down among the men.

Two Calormenes were driving a horse which was
harnessed to a log. Just as the King reached them the
log had got stuck in a bad muddy place.

'Get on, son of sloth! Pull, you lazy pig!' cried the
Calormenes, cracking their whips. The horse was
already straining himself as hard as he could; his eyes
were red and he was covered with foam.

'Work, lazy brute,' shouted one of the Calormenes:
and as he spoke he struck the horse savagely with his

whip. It was then that the really dreadful thing happened.

Up till now Tirian had taken it for granted that the horses which the Calormenes were driving were their own horses; dumb, witless animals like the horses of our own world. And though he hated to see even a dumb horse overdriven, he was of course thinking more about the murder of the Trees. It had never crossed his mind that anyone would dare to harness one of the free Talking Horses of Narnia, much less to use a whip on it. But as that savage blow fell the horse reared up and said, half screaming:

'Fool and tyrant! Do you not see I am doing all I can?'

When Tirian knew that the Horse was one of his own Narnians, there came over him and over Jewel such a rage that they did not know what they were doing. The King's sword went up, the Unicorn's horn went down. They rushed forward together. Next moment both the Calormenes lay dead, the one beheaded by Tirian's sword and the other gored through the heart by Jewel's horn.

A RING OF STONES

Alan Garner

hile staying on Gowther and Bess Mossock's farm in Cheshire, Colin and Susan are pursued by strange creatures on Alderley Edge. Saved by Cadellin the wizard, they learn of the band of knights sleeping beneath the hill who must one day awake to fight the evil Nastrond. But the knights are protected by a magic stone, and the stone has been lost...

Thursday at Highmost Redmanhey was always busy, for on top of the normal round of work Gowther had to make ready for the following day, when he would drive down to Alderley village to do the weekly shopping, and also to call on certain old friends and acquaintances whom he supplied with vegetables and eggs. So much of Thursday was taken up with selecting and cleaning the produce for Friday's marketing.

When all was done, Colin and Susan rode with Gowther to the wheelwright in the near-by township of Mottram St Andrew to have a new spoke fitted to the cart. This occupied them until teatime, and afterwards Gowther asked the children if they would like to go with him down to Nether Alderley to see whether they could find their next meal in Radnor mere.

They set off across the fields, and shortly came to a wood. Here the undergrowth was denser than on most of the Edge, and contained quite a lot of bramble. High rhododendron bushes grew wild everywhere. The wood seemed full of birds. They sang in the trees, rustled in the thicket, and swam in the many quiet pools.

'I've just realized something,' said Colin: 'I felt the Edge was unusual, and now I know why. It's the . . .'

'Birds,' said Gowther. 'Theer is none. Not worth speaking of, onyroad. Flies, yes; but birds, no. It's always been like that, to my knowledge, and I conner think why it should be. You'd think, with all them trees and such-like, you'd have as mony as you find here, but, considering the size of the place, theer's hardly a throstle to be found from Squirrel's Jump to Daniel Hill. Time's been when I've wandered round theer half the day, and seen nobbut a pair of jays, and that was in Clockhouse wood. No, it's very strange, when you come to weigh it up.'

Their way took them through a jungle of rhododendron. The ground was boggy and choked with dead wood, and they had to duck under low branches and climb over fallen trees: but, somehow, Gowther managed to carry his rod and line through it all without a snag, and he even seemed to know where he was going.

Susan thought how unpleasant it would be to have to move quickly through such country.

'Gowther,' she said, 'are there any mines near here?'

'No, none at all, we're almost on the plain now, and the mines are over the other side of the hill, behind us. Why do you ask?'

'Oh, I just wondered.'

The rhododendrons came to an end at the border of a mere, about half a mile long and a quarter wide.

'This is it,' said Gowther, sitting down on a fallen trunk which stretched out over the water. 'It's a trifle marshy, but we're not easy to reach here, as theer's some as might term this poaching. Now if you'll open yon basket and pass the tin with the bait in it, we can settle down and make ourselves comfortable.'

After going out as far as he could along the tree to cast his rod, Gowther sat with his back against the roots and lit his pipe. Colin and Susan lay full length on the wrinkled bark and gazed into the mere.

Within two hours they had three perch between them, so they gathered in their tackle and headed for home, arriving well before dusk.

The following morning in Alderley village Susan went with Bess to the shops while Colin stayed to help Gowther with the vegetables. They all met again for a meal at noon, and afterwards climbed into the cart and went with Gowther on his round.

It was a hot day, and by four o'clock Colin and Susan were very thirsty, so Bess said that they ought to drop off for an ice-cream and a lemonade.

'We've to go down Moss Lane,' she said, 'and we shanner be above half an hour; you stay and cool down a bit.'

The children were soon in the village café, with their drinks before them. Susan was toying with her bracelet, and idly trying to catch the light so that she could see the blue heart of her Tear.

'It's always difficult to find,' she said. 'I never know when it's going to come right . . . ah . . . wait a minute . . . yes . . . got it! You know, it reminds me of the light in Fundin. . . .'

She looked at Colin. He was staring at her, open mouthed. They both dropped their eyes to Susan's wrist where her Tear gleamed so innocently.

'But it *couldn't* be!' whispered Colin. 'Could it?'

'I don't . . . know. But how?'

But how?

'No, of course not!' said Colin. 'The wizard would have recognized it as soon as he saw it, wouldn't he?'

Susan flopped back in her chair, releasing her pent-up breath in a long sigh. But a second later she was bolt upright, inarticulate with excitement.

'He couldn't have seen it! I—I was wearing my mackintosh! Oh, *Colin* . . .!!'

Though just as shaken as his sister, Colin was not content to sit and gape. Obviously they had to find out, and quickly, whether Susan was wearing Firefrost, or just a piece of crystal. If it *should* be Firefrost, and had been recognized by the wrong people, their brush with the svarts would at last make sense. How the stone came to be on Susan's wrist was another matter.

'We must find Cadellin at once,' he said. 'Because if this *is* Firefrost, the sooner he has it the better it will be for us all.'

At that moment the cart drew up outside, and Gowther called that it was time to be going home.

The children tried hard to conceal their agitation, yet the leisurely pace Prince seemed to adopt on the 'front' hill, as it was called locally, had them almost bursting with impatience.

'Bess,' said Susan, 'are you sure you can't remember anything else about the Bridestone? I want to find out as much as I can about it.'

'Nay, lass, I've told you all as I know. My mother had it from her mother, and she always said as it had been passed down like that for I dunner know how mony years. And I believe theer was some story about how it should never be shown to onybody outside the family for fear of bringing seven years' bad luck, but my mother didner go in much for superstition and that sort of claptrap.'

'Have you always lived in Alderley?'

'Bless you, yes! I was born and bred in th'Hough' (she pronounced it 'thuff'), 'but my mother was a Goostrey woman, and I believe before that her family had connexions Mobberley way.'

'Oh?'

Colin and Susan could hardly contain themselves.

'Gowther,' said Colin, 'before we come home, Sue and I want to go to Stormy Point; which is the nearest way?'

'What! Before you've had your teas?' exclaimed Bess.

'Yes, I'm afraid so. You see, it's something very important and secret, and we *must* go.'

'You're not up to owt daft down the mines, are you?' said Gowther.

'Oh no,' said Colin; 'but, please, we must go. We'll be back early, and it doesn't matter about tea.'

'Eh well, it'll be your stomachs as'll be empty! But think on, we dunner want to come looking for you at midneet.

'Your best way'll be to get off at the gamekeeper's lodge, and follow the main path till it forks by the owd quarry: then take the left hond path, and it'll bring you straight to Stormy Point.'

They reached the top of the Edge, and after about quarter of a mile Gowther halted Prince before a cottage built of red sandstone and tucked in the fringe of the wood. Along the side of the cottage, at right angles to the road, a track disappeared among the trees in what Gowther said was the direction of Stormy Point.

The children jumped from the cart, and ran off along the track, while Gowther and Bess continued on their way, dwelling sentimentally on what it was to be young.

'Don't you think we'd better go by the path Cadellin told us to use? He said it was the only safe one, remember.'

'We haven't time to go all that way round,' said Colin; 'we must show him your Tear as soon as we can. And anyway, Gowther says this is the path to Stormy Point, and it's broad daylight, so I don't see that we can come to any harm.'

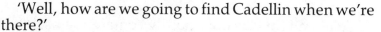

'Well, how are we going to find Cadellin when we're there?'

'We'll go straight to the iron gates and call him: being a wizard he's bound to hear . . . I hope. Still, we must try!'

They pressed deeper and deeper into the wood, and came to a level stretch of ground where the bracken thinned and gave place to rich turf, dappled with sunlight. And here, in the midst of so much beauty, they learnt too late that wizards' words are seldom idle, and traps well sprung hold hard their prey.

Out of the ground on all sides swirled tongues of thick white mist, which merged into a rolling fog about the children's knees: it paused, gathered itself, and leapt upwards, blotting out the sun and the world of life and light.

It was too much for Susan. Her nerve failed her. All that mattered was to escape from this chill cloud and what it must contain. She ran blindly, stumbled a score of paces, then tripped, and fell full length upon the grass.

She was not hurt, but the jolt brought her to her senses: the jolt—and something else.

In falling, she had thrown her arms out to protect herself, and as her head cleared she realized that there was no earth beneath her fingers, only emptiness. She lay there, not caring to move.

'Sue, where are you?' It was Colin's voice, calling softly. 'Are you all right?'

'I'm here. Be careful. I think I'm on the edge of a cliff, but I can't see.'

'Keep still, then: I'll feel my way to you.'

He crawled in the direction of Susan's voice, but even in that short distance he partly lost his bearing, and it was several minutes before he found his sister, and having done so, he wriggled cautiously alongside her.

The turf ended under his nose, and all beyond was a

sea of grey. Colin felt around for a pebble, and dropped it over the edge. Three seconds passed before he heard it land.

'Good job you tripped, Sue! It's a long way down. This must be the old quarry. Now keep quiet a minute, and listen.'

They strained their ears to catch the slightest sound, but there was nothing to be heard. They might have been the only living creatures on earth.

'We must go back to the path, Sue. And we've got to make as little noise as possible, because whatever it is that made this fog will be listening for us. If we don't find the path we may easily walk round in circles until nightfall, even supposing we're left alone as long as that.

'Let's get away from this quarry, for a start: there's no point in asking for trouble.'

They stood up, and holding each other's hand, walked slowly back towards the path.

As the minutes went by, Susan grew more and more uneasy.

'Colin,' she said at last, 'I hadn't run more than a dozen steps, I'm sure, when I tripped, and we've been walking for a good five minutes. Do you think we're going the right way?'

'No, I don't. And I don't know which *is* the right way, so we'll have to hope for the best. We'll try to walk in a straight line, and perhaps we'll leave this fog behind.'

But they did not. Either the mist had spread out over a wide area, or, as the children began to suspect, it was moving with them. They made very slow progress; every few paces they would stop and listen, but there was only the silence of the mist, and that was as unnerving as the sound of something moving would have been. Also, it was impossible to see for more than a couple of yards in any direction, and they were frightened of falling into a hidden shaft, or even the

quarry, for they had lost all sense of direction by now.

The path seemed to have vanished; but, in fact, they had crossed it some minutes earlier without knowing. As they approached, the mist had gathered thickly about their feet, hiding the ground until the path was behind them.

After quarter of an hour Colin and Susan were shivering uncontrollably as the dampness ate into their bones. Every so often the trunk of a pine tree would loom out of the mist, so that it seemed as though they were walking through a pillared hall that had no beginning, and no end.

'We must be moving in circles, Colin. Let's change direction instead of trying to keep in a straight line.'

'We couldn't be more lost than we are at present, so we may as well try it.'

They could not believe their luck. Within half a minute they came upon an oak, and beyond that another. The fog was as dense as ever, but they knew that they were breaking fresh ground, and that was encouraging.

'Oh, I wish Cadellin would come,' said Susan.

'That's an idea! Let's shout for help: he may hear us.'

'But we'll give our position away.'

'I don't think that matters any more. Let's try, anyway.'

'All right.'

'One, two, three. Ca-dell-in! Help! Ca-dell-in!!'

It was like shouting in a padded cell. Their voices, flat and dead, soaked into the grey blanket.

'That can't have carried far,' said Colin disgustedly. 'Try again. One, two, three. Help! Ca-dell-in! Help!!!'

'It's no use,' said Susan; 'he'll never hear us. We'll have to find our own way out.'

'And we'll do that if we keep going at our own pace,' said Colin. 'If whatever caused this had intended to attack us it would have done so by now, wouldn't it? No, it wants to frighten us into rushing over a precipice or something like that. As long as we carry on slowly we'll be safe enough.'

He was wrong, but they had no other plan.

For the next few minutes the children made their way in silence, Susan concentrating on the ground immediately in front, Colin alert for any sight or sound of danger.

All at once Susan halted.

'Hallo, what's this?'

At their feet lay two rough-hewn boulders and beyond them, on either side, could be seen the faint outline of others of a like size.

'What can they be? They look as though they've been put there deliberately, don't they?'

'Never mind,' said Colin; 'we mustn't waste time in standing around.'

And they passed between the stones, only to stop short a couple of paces later, with despair in their hearts, cold as the east wind.

Susan's question was answered. They were in the middle of a ring of stones, and the surrounding low, dim shapes rose on the limit of vision as though marking the boundary of the world.

Facing the children were two stones, far bigger than the rest, and on one of the stones sat a figure, and the sight of it would have daunted a brave man.

For three fatal seconds the children stared, unable to think or move. And as they faltered, the jaws of the trap closed about them; for, like a myriad snakes, the grass within the circle, alive with the magic of the place, writhed about their feet, shackling them in a net of blade and root, tight as a vice.

As if in some dark dream, Colin and Susan strained to tear themselves free, but they were held like wasps in honey.

Slowly the figure rose from its seat and came towards them. Of human shape it was, though like no mortal man, for it stood near eight feet high, and was covered from head to foot in a loose habit, dank and green, and ill concealing the terrible thinness and spider strength of the body beneath. A deep cowl hid the face, skin mittens were on the wasted hands, and the air was laden with the reek of foul waters.

The creature stopped in front of Susan and held out a hand: not a word was spoken.

'No!' gasped Susan. 'You shan't have it!' and she put her arm behind her back.

'Leave her alone!' yelled Colin. 'If you touch her Cadellin will *kill* you!'

The shrouded head turned slowly towards him, and he gazed into the cavern of the hood; courage melted from him, and his knees were water.

Then, suddenly, the figure stretched out its arms and seized both the children by the shoulder.

They had no chance to struggle or to defend themselves. With a speed that choked the cry of anguish in their throats, an icy numbness swept down from the grip of those hands into their bodies, and the children stood paralysed, unable to move a finger.

In a moment the bracelet was unfastened from Susan's wrist, and the grim shape turned on its heel and strode into the mist. And the mist gathered round it and formed a swirling cloud that moved swiftly away among the trees, and was lost to sight.

The sun shone upon the stone circle, and upon the figures standing motionless in the centre. The warm rays poured life and feeling into those wooden bodies, and they began to move. First an arm stirred jerkily, doll-like, then a head turned, a leg moved, and slowly the numbness drained from their limbs, the grass released its hold, and the children crumpled forward on to their hands and knees, shivering and gasping, the blood in their heads pounding like trip-hammers.

'Out—circle!' wheezed Colin.

They staggered sideways and almost fell down a small bank on to a path.

'Find Cadellin: perhaps . . . he . . . can stop it. I think
that may be . . . Stormy Point ahead.'

Their legs were stiff, and every bone ached, but they
hurried along as best they could, and a few minutes
later they cried out with relief, for the path did indeed
come out on Stormy Point.

Across the waste of stones they ran, and down to the
iron gates; and when they came to the rock they flung
themselves against it, beating with their fists, and calling the wizard's name. But bruised knuckles were all
they achieved: no gates appeared, no cavern opened.

Colin was in a frenzy of desperation. He prised a
stone out of the ground, almost as big as his head, and,
using both hands, began to pound the silent wall,
shouting, 'Open up! Open up! Open up!! Open up!!
Open up!!!'

'Now that is no way to come a-visiting wizards,' said
a voice above them.

*

Colin and Susan looked up, not knowing what to
expect: the voice sounded friendly, but was that any
guide now?

Over the top of the rock dangled a pair of feet, and
between these were two eyes, black as sloes, set in a
leathery face, bearded and bushy-browed.

'Rocks are old, stubborn souls; they were here before
we came, and they will be here when we are gone. They
have all the time there is, and will not be hurried.'

With this, the face disappeared, the legs swung out
of sight, there was a slithering noise, a bump, and
from behind the rock stepped a man four feet high. He
wore a belted tunic of grey, patterned with green spir-
als along the hem, pointed boots, and breeches bound
tight with leather thongs. His black hair reached to his
shoulders, and on his brow was a circlet of gold.

'Are—are you a dwarf?' said Susan.

'That am I.' He bowed low. 'By name, Fenodyree;
Wineskin, or Squabnose, to disrespectful friends.
Take your pick.'

He straightened up and looked keenly from one to
the other of the children. His face had the same qual-
ities of wisdom, of age without weakness, that they
had seen in Cadellin, but here there was more of
merriment, and a lighter heart.

'Oh please,' said Susan, 'take us to the wizard, if you
can. Something dreadful has happened, and he must
be told at once, in case it's not too late.'

'In case what is not too late?' said Fenodyree. 'Oh,
but there I go, wanting gossip, when all around is
turmoil and urgent deeds! Let us find Cadellin.'

He ran his hands down the rough stone, like a man
stroking the flanks of a favourite horse. The rock stirred ponderously and clove in two, and there were the
iron gates, and the blue light of Fundindelve.

'Now the gates,' said Fenodyree briskly. 'My father
made them, and so they hear me, though I have not
the power of wizards.'

He laid his hand upon the metal, and the gates
opened.

'Stay close, lest you lose the way,' called Fenodyree
over his shoulder.

He set off at a jog-trot down the swift-sloping tunnel. Colin and Susan hurried after him, the rock and
iron closed behind them, and they were again far from
the world of men.

Down they went into the Edge, and came at last, by
many zig-zag paths, to the cave where they had rested
after their first meeting with Cadellin. And there they
found him: he had been reading at the table, but had
risen at the sound of their approach.

'The day's greeting to you, Cadellin Silverbrow,'
said Fenodyree.

'And to you, Wineskin. Now what bad news do you
bring me, children. I have been expecting it, though I
know not what it may be.'

'Cadellin,' cried Susan, 'my Tear must be Firefrost,
and it's just been stolen!'

'What—tear is this?'

'*My* Tear! The one my mother gave me. She had it
from Bess Mossock.'

And out poured the whole story in a tumble of words.

The wizard grew older before their eyes. He sank
down upon his chair, his face lined and grey.

'It is the stone. It is the stone. No other has that heart
of fire. And it was by me, and I did not hear it call.'

He sat, his eyes clouded, a tired, world-weary, old
man.

Then wrath kindled in him, and spread like flame.
He sprang from his chair with all the vigour of youth,
and he seemed to grow in stature, and his presence
filled the cave.

'Grimnir!' he cried. 'Are you to be my ruin at the
end? Quick! We must take him in the open before he
gains the lake! I shall slay him, if I must.'

'Nay, Cadellin,' said Fenodyree. 'Hot blood has

banished cool thought! It is near an hour since the
hooded one strode swampwards; he will be far from
the light by now, and even you dare not follow there.
He would sit and mock you. Would you want that, old
friend?'

'Mock me! Why did he leave these children
unharmed, if not for that? It is not his way to show
mercy for mercy's sake! And how else could despair
have been brought to me so quickly? I am savouring
his triumph now, as he meant me to.

'But what you say is reason: for good or ill the stone
is with him. All we can do is guard, and wait, though I
fear it will be to no good purpose.'

He looked at the children, who were standing dejectedly in the middle of the cave.

'Colin, Susan; you have witnessed the writing of a
dark chapter in the book of the world, and what deeds
it will bring no man can tell: but you must in no way
blame yourselves for what has happened. The elf-road
would have been but short refuge from him who came
against you this day—Grimnir the hooded one.'

'But *what* is he?' said Susan, pale with the memory
of their meeting.

'He is, or was a man. Once he studied under the
wisest of the wise, and became a great lore-master: but
in his lust for knowledge he practised the forbidden
arts, and the black magic ravaged his heart, and made
a monster of him. He left the paths of day, and went to
live, like Grendel of old, beneath the waters of Llyn-
dhu, the Black Lake, growing mighty in evil, second
only to the ancient creatures of night that attend their
lord in Ragnarok. And it is he, arch-enemy of mine,
who came against you this day.'

'No one in memory has seen his face or heard his
voice,' added Fenodyree. 'Dwarf-legend speaks of a
great shame that he bears therein: a gad-fly of
remorse, reminding him of what he is, and of what he
might have been. But then that is only an old tale we

learnt at our mother's knee, and not one for this sad hour.'

'Nor have we time for folk-talk,' said Cadellin. 'We must do what we can, and that quickly. Now tell me, who can have seen the stone and recognized it?'

'Well, nobody . . .' said Colin.

'Selina Place!' cried Susan. 'Selina Place! My Tear went all misty! Don't you remember, Colin? She must have seen my Tear and stopped to make certain.'

'Ha,' laughed Fenodyree bitterly. 'Old Shape-shifter up to her tricks! We might have guessed the weight of the matter had we but known *she* was behind it!'

'Oh, why did you not tell me this when we first met?' the wizard shouted.

'I forgot all about it,' said Colin: 'it didn't seem important. I thought she was queer in the head.'

'Important? Queer? Hear him! Why, Selina Place, as she is known to you, is the chief witch of the morth-brood! Worse, she is the Morrigan, the Third Bane of Logris!'

For a moment it seemed as though he would erupt in anger, but instead, he sighed, and shook his head.

'No matter. It is done.'

Susan was almost in tears. She could not bear to see the old man so distraught, especially when she felt responsible for his plight.

'Is there nothing we can do?'

The wizard looked up at her, and a tired smile came to his lips.

'Do? My dear, I think there is little any of us can do now. Certainly, there will be no place for children in the struggle to come. It will be hard for you, I know, but you must go from here and forget all you have seen and done. Now that the stone is out of your care you will be safe.'

'But,' cried Colin, 'but you can't mean that! We want to help you!'

'I know you do. But you have no further part in this. High Magic and low cunning will be the weapons of the fray, and the valour of children would be lost in the struggle. You can help me best by freeing me from worry on your behalf.'

And, without giving the children further chance to argue, he took them by the hand, and out of the cave. They went in misery, and shortly stood above the swamp on the spot where they had first met the wizard, three nights ago.

'Must we *really* not see you again?' said Colin. He had never felt so wretched.

'Believe me, it must be so. It hurts me, too, to part from friends, and I can guess what it is to have the door of wonder and enchantment closed to you when you have glimpsed what lies beyond. But it is also a world of danger and shadows, as you have seen and ere long I fear I must pass into these shadows. I will not take you with me.

'Go back to your own world: you will be safer there. If we should fail, you will suffer no harm, for not in your time will Nastrond come.

'Now go. Fenodyree will keep with you to the road.'

So saying, he entered the tunnel. The rock echoed: he was gone.

Colin and Susan stared at the wall. They were very near to tears, and Fenodyree, weighed down with his own troubles, felt pity for them in their despondency.

'Do not think him curt or cruel,' he said gently. 'He has suffered a defeat that would have crushed a lesser man. He is going now to prepare himself to face death, and worse than death, for the stone's sake; and I and others shall stand by him, though I think we are for the dark. He has said farewell because he knows there may be no more meetings for him this side of Ragnarok.'

'But it was all our fault!' said Colin desperately. 'We *must* help him!'

'You will help him best by keeping out of danger, as he said; and that means staying well away from us and all we do.'

'Is that really the best way?' said Susan.

'It is.'

'Then I suppose we'll have to do it. But it will be very hard.'

'Is his task easier?' said Fenodyree.

They walked along a path that curved round the hillside, gradually rising till it ran along the crest of the Edge.

'You will be safe now,' said Fenodyree, 'but if you should have need of me, tell the owls in farmer Mossock's barn: they understand your speech, and will come to me, but remember that they are guardians for the night and fly like drunken elves by day.'

'Do you mean to say all those owls were sent by you?' said Colin.

'Ay, my people have ever been masters of bird lore. We treat them as brothers, and they help us where they can. Two nights since they brought word that evil things were closing on you. A bird that seemed no true bird (and scarce made off with its life) brought to the farm a strange presence that filled them with dread, though they could not see its form. I can guess now that it was the hooded one—and here is Castle Rock, from which we can see his lair.'

They had come to a flat outcrop that jutted starkly from the crest, so that it seemed almost a straight drop to the plain far below. There was a rough bench resting on stumps of rock, and here they sat. Behind them was a field, and beyond that the road, and the beginning of the steep 'front' hill.

'It is as I thought,' said Fenodyree. 'The black master is in his den. See, yonder is Llyn-dhu, garlanded with mosses and mean dwellings.'

Colin and Susan looked where Fenodyree was pointing, and some two or three miles out on the plain

they could see the glint of grey water through trees.

'Men thought to drain that land and live there, but the spirit of the place entered them, and their houses were built drab, and desolate, and without cheer; and all around the bog still sprawls, from out the drear lake come soulless thoughts and drift into the hearts of the people, and they are one with their surroundings.

'Ah! But there goes he who can tell us more about the stone.'

He pointed to a speck floating high over the plain, and whistled shrilly.

'Hi, Windhover! To me!'

The speck paused, then came swooping through the air like a black falling star, growing larger every second, and, with a hollow beating of wings, landed on Fenodyree's outstretched arm—a magnificent kestrel, fierce and proud, whose bright eyes glared at the children.

'Strange company for dwarfs, I know,' said Fenodyree, 'but they have been prey of the morthbrood, and so are older than their years.

'It is of Grimnir that we want news. He went by here: did he seek the lake?'

The kestrel switched to gaze to Fenodyree, and gave a series of sharp cries, which obviously meant more to the dwarf than they did to the children.

'Ay, it is as I thought,' he said when the bird fell silent. 'A mist crossed the plain a while since, as fast as

a horse can gallop, and sank into Llyn-dhu.

'Ah well, so be it. Now I must away back to Cadellin,
for we shall have much to talk over and plans to make.
Farewell now, my friends. Yonder is the road: take it.
Remember us, though Cadellin forbade you, and wish
us well.'

'Goodbye.'

Colin and Susan were too full to say more; it was an
effort to speak, for their throats were tight and dry
with anguish. They knew that Cadellin and Fenodyree
were not being deliberately unkind in their anxiety to
be rid of them, but the feeling of responsibility for
what had happened was as much as they could bear.

So it was with heavy hearts that the children turned
to the road: nor did they speak or look back until they
had reached it. Fenodyree, standing on the seat, legs
braced apart, with Windhover at his wrist, was outlined against the sky. His voice came to them through
the still air.

'Farewell, my friends!'

They waved to him in return, but could find no
words.

He stood there a moment longer before he jumped
down and vanished along the path to Fundindelve.
And it was as though a veil had been drawn across the
children's eyes.

PARTICLE GOES GREEN

Helen Cresswell

article's witchcraft book arrived two days before the Bensons were due to go on holiday. Eve was always the first to the door when the postman came because she was expecting any day to hear that she had won a cabin cruiser in a competition she had entered.

'What's this?' she pondered, examining the parcel. It bore a Sussex postmark. '"Richard Benson, Esq."—oh, it's that blessed Particle again. Now what?'

She took the book up to her younger brother's bedroom. She had to pick her way over brilliantly splashed sheets of newspaper where he had been action-painting the night before.

'Come on, Particle,' she said. 'Wake up.'

He might, of course, already be awake. It was difficult to see through the mosquito net. He had been sleeping under it for three weeks now, despite the fact that Number 14 Sanders Close rarely saw a bluebottle, let alone a mosquito.

'I am awake,' came his voice. 'Has the post come?'

Eve pulled aside the net. Particle, already wearing his spectacles, was sitting up in bed making clothespegs. He had met a gypsy a few days before, camping in a field beyond the town. Particle had presented him with one of Bill's sports jackets, and in return the gypsy had shown him how to make clothes-pegs.

'Really, Particle! Look at all those shavings!'

'I've made fourteen since I woke up,' Particle informed her, in his high, serious voice. 'It's just a question of practice. That, and a bit of knack thrown in. I don't expect I shall ever be quite up to gypsy standard. Peg-making's inborn in them, over generations.'

Eve, despite herself, regarded him fondly.

'He's so refreshing,' she was always telling her friends. 'Honestly, when you think what nine-year-old boys can be like . . . I mean, he's just like a dear little old man, sometimes.'

'Is that for me?' inquired Particle. 'The parcel?'

She handed it over. He gave a couple of expert twists with his jack-knife and the book was in his hands.

'I shan't get up this morning,' he told her. 'I shall stay in bed and read this.'

'What on earth is it? It's not even a new one. It's years old, if you ask me. How much did you pay for it?'

'Binding Spells.' He held the book up.

'Binding what?'

'Spells.'

'I've never heard of it. Who by?'

'A witch, I expect,' he said. He turned the flyleaf. 'Look at this—f's instead of s's! It's old, all right!' He was gleeful. 'By Allifon Grofs. The Witch of Northumberland.'

'Oh, Particle. You really are the limit. What on earth possessed you to send for that? And where's it from?'

'An antiquarian bookseller. I wrote to him. I asked him for a book on the subject of witchcraft of the greatest possible antiquity. This is it.'

'How much?' asked Eve. 'We're going on holiday the day after tomorrow, you know. You needn't come borrowing from me if you run out of money halfway through.'

Particle shook the book and a letter fell out. He read it.

'Not all that expensive,' he told her. 'Not considering its antiquity.'

'Well, I should get up, if I were you,' Eve said. 'Bill and Fay aren't going to like this a bit. In fact I expect you've done it on purpose, just to annoy them.'

'Not at all,' said Particle. He really did look like a little old man, propped up against his pillows in his too-large pyjamas and too-large spectacles. 'They should both be very pleased. Witchcraft is an art and a science.'

'I just hope so, that's all,' Eve threw over her shoulder as she went. She paused by her parents' bedroom door. She could hear Bill's voice—they were evidently awake.

'Want a cup of tea?' she called. 'Postman's been.'

'Oh, bless you, darling,' came Fay's voice, and the door opened. Eve kissed her mother and handed her the three letters.

'Nothing for you, dear?'

Eve shook her head.

'Never mind. You know what these competitions are. I'm sure you'll hear soon. That marvellous slogan! I'll be down myself in a minute. I told Bill he could have a lie-in this morning while I scurry round packing, and things.'

Eve nodded and went on down. It was a morning just like any other morning. Even the book on witchcraft didn't mark it as anything special—not at the time. The sunlight fell in pools on the golden oak floor and lit the copper bowl of roses on the chest.

Stepping into the kitchen first thing in the morning was always something of a jolt. It was not really so much a kitchen, Eve thought for the thousandth time, as a laboratory. Apart from that, it came as such a shock after the rest of the house. Whenever people remarked on it, Fay always said:

'Ah, well, of course, the kitchen's Bill's. The rest of the house is pure me, but I gave him free rein in the kitchen. After all, a kitchen's one place where you must be scientific, mustn't you?'

She would make one of her lovely vague gestures, press a knob, and watch a tin opener glide from a concealed socket in the wall, or a waste disposal bin rise from the tiles. The guests would crowd in, enchanted, and Fay would run through the whole performance, igniting cookers, boiling water, making mayonnaise, all by remote control. As her final piece she would always get them to look through the window and then close the front gates under their very eyes. Back in the drawing-room with its oak beams, inglenook, and Dresden china, the guests would wonder if they had dreamed it all.

'I'm so thankful I married a scientist,' Fay would coo, drifting in with a tray of sandwiches that had been cut, buttered, and filled by Bill's latest recruit to the army of kitchen robots. 'It's so relaxing.'

Eve herself was never so sure. Bill and Fay were both marvellous in their own ways, she appreciated that. It was just that sometimes she felt as if her own personality were being split in two by them, and she herself was a strange hybrid of half-scientist, half-actress. It was so confusing.

Even Particle seemed to suffer from it. The ideas he had, all the outrageous schemes, were straight from Fay. But the precision, the deadly earnestness with which he pursued each one to its logical (or even illogical) conclusion, was unmistakably the same as the passion that drove Bill to pursue electrons into the early hours of the morning, and invent devices so secret that they had to install a concealed safe behind the nineteenth-century print of skaters in the dining-room.

Not that Bill was usually anxious to claim Particle as his own. From the time when Particle had begun to

have ideas of his own and put them forward in his high, reedy voice, Bill had been frowning and cross-questioning and finally exploding.

'There isn't a particle of sense in a word you're saying! Not a particle!'

Eve sighed as she regulated the dial for the toast. The holiday began tomorrow—in fact it had as good as started already, since Bill was staying at home—and holidays always seemed to point the problem more sharply. One of these days, she thought, I really shall have to make my mind up. Which am I? Bill or Fay? It occurred to her that even the reason why she and Particle called their parents by their Christian names was not clearcut. Bill believed in it because he thought that 'mummy' and 'daddy' were unscientific, senti-mental and probably unhygienic. Fay simply thought that it was modern and rather fun.

When Fay flounced in now, wearing one of her frilled housecoats and the lipstick without which she vowed she couldn't face the milkman, Eve wondered whether it might not be wise to mention the book on witchcraft. She realized that it was bound to produce one of the situations in which the cleft between science and art in the family would yawn into one of its periodic chasms. Fay was already producing from the wall the gadget that was to make her fresh lemon juice. Then the telephone rang and Fay cried:

'Heavens, the 'phone!' and made a swirling exit.

Eve arranged the neat, popped-up toast, ready curled butter, and home (machine) made marmalade on her father's tray. The egg (timed for three minutes twenty seconds precisely) was placed in its stainless-steel heat-retaining egg-cup with its bread (cut to three-eighths of an inch) and ready-spread butter (set at Number 3—medium heavy spreading).

Satisfied, she picked up the tray, went to the door, trod on the door-operating switch, and went into the hall where the newspapers, as if also operated by a timing device, were just appearing through the letter box.

Bill was already up, doing his three minutes' deep breathing by the window. Eve knew better than to interrupt. She laid the tray on the bedside table, blew a kiss towards his intent, reddened face, and withdrew. She went back to Particle's room. He was still in bed.

'Come on,' said Eve. 'Get up. Fay'll never let you stop in bed. There's too much to do.'

From behind the mosquito net came a low, muffled chant. Particle had not even heard her.

'Oh, for heaven's sake!' cried Eve. 'You're not chanting spells, I hope!'

She pulled back the mosquito net. Particle was still propped against his pillows, the book resting on his knees. He broke off, startled. Eve stared at him. She stared so hard that she could feel herself staring, her eyes fixed and bulging. He blinked at her, struck by her expression.

'What's the matter?' he demanded. 'Your eyes are all—'

Then she screamed. She heard herself, too. When the scream, a long, high, frantic one, was out, she ran.

She collided with Fay in the hall.

'Eve! Whatever—?'

Eve faced her mother. For a moment she was speechless. What she had to say was after all, impossible, it must be.

'That scream! And you're white as a ghost. Whatever is it, darling?'

'It's Particle,' Eve heard herself saying. 'He's gone green.' Fay gasped.

'Oh, Eve! Not one of his bilious attacks! Not at a time like this. He can't, he just can't!'

'You don't understand,' cried Eve. 'He's gone green actually!'

'I know it does sometimes seem like it,' agreed Fay.

'You'd better take him up some of his usual mixture, and if he stays in bed—'

'Green! Green!' Eve's voice was rising to a scream again.

'I'll go up and have a look,' said Fay. Eve, watching her go up the stairs, had a sudden wild hope that in a moment she would be down again, rummaging round for Particle's tummy mixture and grumbling all the while under her breath, and everything would be miraculously all right again.

Fay's scream was even louder than Eve's. Even Bill heard it—or perhaps by now he had finished his deep breathing anyway. Eve ran up the stairs to find them locked in collision by Particle's door.

'Green!' moaned Fay. 'Oh Bill, I must be going mad!'

'Green?' repeated Bill. 'What's green? Now come along, Fay, pull yourself together. And what's all this screaming?'

'Particle's green!' shrieked Fay. She stepped back and pointed a dramatic finger. 'Look! Go on! Look!'

Bill went into the bedroom. Eve and Fay stared at each other, waiting. Bill came out.

'He is green,' he admitted.

'Pea green!' shrieked Fay. 'Do something, Bill!'

In the silence that followed, Eve was aware of the patter of light footsteps over the bedroom carpet, and for the first time thought of Particle, alone in there, green as grass and probably scared half out of his wits. She pushed past her parents and ran in to find him settling himself against the pillows and pulling up the blankets. His eyes behind the too-large spectacles looked enormous and she fancied that the green was a shade paler now—on his face, at least.

'Oh, Particle,' she said, 'what have you done?'

'I got up,' he said in his high voice, 'and had a look in the mirror . . . I think I had better stay in bed, after all.'

He looked down at his hands, just visible below the cuffs of his tangerine pyjamas. They clashed horribly.

Despite herself, Eve could not help noticing with interest that the actual fingernails were still pinkish. Particle, too, was studying them intently, frowning a little.

'Is it—I mean—are you—all over?' asked Eve in a lowered voice.

Without speaking Particle drew a leg from under the bedclothes and waved a skinny, dragonish foot in the air. Eve let out another little scream and Particle looked at her reproachfully.

'I'm sorry, Particle,' she said. 'It's just the shock, you know.'

Particle put his leg back under the blankets. As he did so, the book on witchcraft slid to the floor. Eve seized it.

'It's this!' she cried. 'Isn't it? It's a spell!'

Particle nodded slowly.

'It must be,' he said.

'Which one? Which?' Eve began to thumb feverishly through the pages. She seemed to remember that in all the fairy tales every spell had had an anti-spell, to undo it. That was usually where the good fairy had come in.

'It's no good doing that, you know,' Particle told her. She looked up.

'Why not?'

'This is just Volume 1, Spells and Charms,' he said. 'You need Volume 2 to lift them.'

Eve dropped the book on to the bed. She looked again at Particle with his rumpled hair and calm, perfectly green face and had a sudden wild desire to burst into laughter. Downstairs she could hear the milk bottles being clattered on to the step, and beyond that her parents' high, excited voices. Hearing them reminded her. They did not know about the witchcraft. She made for the door, then turned.

'Wait here,' she ordered. 'Don't move. And don't dare read one other single spell. Don't dare!'

Fay was on the telephone. Eve opened her mouth but Bill held up a warning finger.

'Doctor!' he whispered loudly.

'No . . . no . . .' Fay was saying. 'I mean really green, Doctor. Yes . . . yes . . ., he's got plenty of the medicine you gave him last time. No . . . yes . . . but Doctor, I mean actually green. Green!'

Her voice was rising to a shriek again. There was a small pause. 'Yes, yes . . .' her voice trailed off. She put the receiver down.

Eve and Bill looked inquiringly at her.

'He says he'll call tomorrow morning if he's no better,' she said blankly. 'Tomorrow! Oh, Bill! My poor little Particle!'

Bill looked definitely worried.

'Must be some bug or other,' he said. 'Has he got a temperature?'

'How do I know if he's got a temperature?' wailed Fay.

'We'll find out,' said Bill. 'Yes, that's the first thing. It should give us a pointer.'

'I've heard of yellow fever,' moaned Fay, 'but this is green! There's no such thing! There's yellow fever and scarlet fever and I'm not sure there isn't a black fever, but I've never in all my life—'

'Now listen,' said Bill, 'you go and make some strong black coffee. There's some perfectly logical explanation for all this, and we'll find it in no time. Some kind of disturbance in pigmentation, perhaps, or faulty diet, or—I'll go and get that thermometer.'

He went out. Eve could see that now he was more interested than worried. He was going to do some research. Just as if poor little Particle were some specimen in a bottle, she thought disgustedly. To Fay she said:

'He needn't bother. There's nothing the matter with Particle—not in that way. It's a spell.'

Fay looked at her. She seemed not to have heard.

'Catching . . .' she murmured. 'What if it's catching?'

'It's witchcraft,' Eve went on. 'Particle sent for a book about it, it came this morning. When I went up just now he was chanting one of the spells. He must have picked the wrong one, or got it mixed up, or something, and—'

She broke off at the expression on Fay's face.

'Witchcraft?' Fay whispered. 'Did you say witch-craft?'

Her face was an alarming, chalky white. It occurred fleetingly to Eve that she didn't seem astonished or even surprised, simply—stunned.

'The Witch of Northumberland, or something,' said Eve. Bill came back with the thermometer.

'Normal,' he said. 'Not even a point in it. The little chap seems to be taking it all quite calmly. "There's bound to be a remedy," he says, cool as a cucumber. Quite scientific about the whole thing. A chip off the old block, after all.'

Eve saw her mother's face change from white to red in an instant.

'Nonsense!' she said sharply.

Bill stared at her.

'All right,' he said, 'no need to be huffy. I merely said that in his whole approach to the thing—'

'I know what you said,' Fay said.

Bill cleared his throat.

'I'll run him down to the surgery,' he said. 'See what Jenkins has to say. No, on second thoughts—the hospital. They've got the equipment there, and so on. This'll be right outside Jenkins's experience.'

'No,' said Fay.

They looked at her.

'Leave him alone,' she said.

'But we're going on holiday the day after tomorrow,' exploded Bill. 'You're not proposing to take a pea-green child to the Royal, I hope. There was enough fuss last year about his marine specimens floating round in the wash basins, and if they once see him—'

'He'll be all right by then,' said Fay.

Bill snorted.

'You mean you hope he'll be all right. If only you could learn the elementary lesson of distinguishing between personal wishes and scientific facts, you'd—'

'He will,' said Fay. She rarely let Bill finish a sentence.

'Fay, can I have my breakfast now?'

It was Particle, in his dressing gown and slippers, looking more than ever like a pantomime hobgoblin, and so obviously impossible among the chintzy chairs and sporting prints that all further discussion was suddenly pointless.

'Of course, darling!' Fay rushed over and hugged him, something she often did, and usually to his annoyance, but this morning he seemed grateful, and even patted a thin green hand on her arm in return.

'Come and have it in the kitchen. Luckily it isn't one

of Mrs D's days for coming in, so—' she broke off. 'Oh I'm sorry, darling!'

'It's all right,' said Particle. 'I don't blame you. I do look pretty horrible green.'

'Oh, you don't!' cried Fay, struck with remorse. 'Does he, Eve? You look absolutely sweet, once the first shock of it wears off. Rather like a dear little . . . dear little . . . well, sweet anyway. It's just that Mrs D's such a dreadful gossip, and you can't possibly expect her to understand a thing like this. Now you—'

The door of the kitchen slid across and cut off her voice. Eve looked at Bill. He did not seem anxious to meet her eyes.

'Bound to be some scientific explanation,' he said.

'Not this time,' said Eve. It was out at last.

'What do you mean?'

'I mean,' she said, 'that Particle's gone green because there's a spell on him. It's witchcraft.'

Bill stared at her for a moment, then roared with laughter. Eve watched him. Gradually his laughter tailed off rather uneasily under her serious gaze.

'That's rich, that is,' he said.

'Yes, it is,' agreed Eve. 'I thought you'd see the funny side of it.'

'What on earth gave you that idea, anyway?' Bill asked. 'Lord, I've just remembered. My breakfast! I haven't even touched it.'

'It's in your room,' Eve told him. 'And if I were you, I should just take a look at that book on Particle's bed.'

He looked startled, nodded, and went upstairs. Eve settled down to make a list for packing. After a while she became fidgety. Fay and Particle were still in the kitchen. It was not long before she began to wonder if she had imagined the whole thing. Out of sight, a green Particle was even more impossible than when he was actually visible. Eve began to feel that she must have another look, or burst.

She went in. There was no doubt about it. Particle, green as ever, was eating his cornflakes while Fay was fiddling with the toaster. From the way they both looked at her Eve felt certain that they had been in the middle of a very interesting conversation.

'We've decided that the most sensible thing to do is just to carry on exactly as if nothing had happened,' Fay began.

'Oh?' said Eve. She felt nettled by the indefinable atmosphere of conspiracy that excluded herself. 'Particle's going for his swimming lesson at eleven as usual, is he? That'll be interesting.'

'Almost exactly as if nothing had happened,' Fay amended. 'Obviously Particle's not going parading about outside, but there's nothing to stop the rest of us carrying on as normal. There's plenty for Particle to do about the house. There's all his packing, for a start.'

'Will we be going, then?' Eve asked.

'Yes, we shall,' said Fay firmly.

'But Bill said—'

'Never mind what Bill said. He's far too scientific to have the least inkling of what's happening. And while we're on the subject, Particle and I have decided that it would be best not to mention anything about witchcraft to your father.'

'It's too late,' said Eve. 'I've already told him.'

'What did he say?' gasped Fay.

'He laughed.'

Her mother seemed relieved.

'I'll go up and have a word with him,' she said.

Eve watched her go. All things considered, she seemed to be taking the whole thing very calmly. She turned her attention back to Particle. For someone who was a rich and unbecoming pea-green from head to toe and with no immediate prospect of ever being anything else, he too seemed irritatingly unconcerned.

'You know, later on,' he said, 'do you think you could possibly take a colour photo of me? Just for the records?'

'Honestly, Particle,' she cried. 'Fancy thinking of a thing like that at a time like this!'

'If we don't,' said Particle, 'no one's ever going to believe us. In fact about ten years from now we shan't even believe it ourselves.'

Eve shuddered.

'I certainly hope I've forgotten about it long before then,' she told him. Then, rather unkindly, 'If, of course, you're not still green.'

She immediately regretted saying it, but he munched imperturbably and seemed not to have noticed.

'It's all my own fault, of course,' he said.

'Of course it is,' said Eve. 'Who else's?'

'No, I mean for not believing. It said as clear as anything that the spell was for turning people green. I just didn't believe it.'

'I should think not!' cried Eve. 'As if anyone believes in spells and things in this day and age.'

She stopped abruptly. There, set square among the glittering host of electronic gadgets, was the indisputable work of witchcraft. Wherever she looked she could see faint greenish reflections of it in the aluminium and stainless steel. She shivered.

Bill and Fay came in.

'It's all settled,' said Fay almost gaily. 'No hospital and no fuss. Now what does everyone want for lunch?'

It was a queer sort of day all the same. It was not just the frenzied scuffles and panics every time the doorbell rang, nor even the sight of Particle himself, more impossible-looking than ever in his faded blue jeans and tee shirt. It was an extraordinary feeling of unreality that intensified as the day went on.

Eve went shopping in the afternoon, and walking

down the street felt an almost irresistible urge to greet everyone she met with:

'Have you heard? My brother's gone green! Green as grass from top to toe!'

By the time she reached home her head was aching with the effort of not telling.

Oddly enough the one who was taking it hardest was Bill. At lunchtime Fay and Particle were making silly jokes about his eating up all his greens, and Eve noticed then that Bill was the only one who was not laughing. By teatime he was thoroughly on edge. He sat darting restless, miserable looks at the serenely emerald Particle, and finally burst out:

'Right! That's enough of this whole farce. Get your things on, Particle.'

Particle, halfway through a slice of chocolate cake, blinked inquiringly.

'We're going to the hospital.'

'No,' said Fay.

'If you think I'm going to sit here and watch a son of mine suffering from some obscure and horrible disease without—'

'Nonsense,' said Fay calmly. 'There's not a thing the matter with him.'

'Not a thing the what?' roared Bill. 'Look at him! Just look! We all sit round drinking tea and passing the sugar as if green people grew on trees! I won't have it! I won't have my son that impossible colour. It's impossible! It's beyond all reason!'

They all looked at him.

'It's witchcraft,' said Eve at last.

'Don't keep saying that!' shouted Bill. He lowered his voice. 'I'm sorry. I don't mean to shout. But you must stop all this medieval mumbo-jumbo about witchcraft. We are in the twentieth century. We have electric light. The atom has been split. There is no such thing as witchcraft.'

'I didn't believe it, either,' said Particle.

Bill glared at him, breathing heavily.

'All right!' he said. 'We'll see!'

He stormed out.

'Oh dear,' said Fay. She turned over a cup, the hot tea ran on to Eve's leg, Eve screamed and in the ensuing commotion it was not surprising that no one heard the front doorbell ring, or Bill's voice as he spoke to the visitor. They had just settled themselves when the door opened and Bill came in, saying:

'If you'd just like to wait here a moment, Constable, I'll—' His voice tailed away.

There was an enormous, welling, blinding silence. Particle, his chocolate cake poised halfway to his lips, stared at the constable. The constable, his face a mixture of horror and disbelief, stared back. The silence went on and on. It took possession. Isn't anyone going to say anything, thought Eve. Ever?

The policeman gave his head a violent shake, as if to clear his brain or vision. It evidently worked, because he turned his gaze away from Particle and over the others as if looking for clues on their blank faces.

'Good evening, Constable,' said Fay firmly. 'Will you have some tea?' He shook his head.

'No? Perhaps you'd like to sit down a moment while my husband—was it your licence and insurance he wanted to see, dear?'

'I'll get them,' said Bill and vanished.

The constable sat suddenly. Eve looked at him with interest. She had never actually seen a policeman, complete with helmet, sitting in a chair before.

'Won't you take your hat off?' inquired Fay. 'Are you sure you won't have some tea? Particle, fetch another cup and saucer, will you, darling?'

She's taking it too far, thought Eve. This is one thing she won't talk her way out of.

Particle got up and obediently padded into the kitchen. He was barefoot, as he usually was in the house. The policeman's eyes followed his dragonish feet. Slowly he got to his feet. He cleared his throat.

'That—er—boy . . .' He nodded towards the door.

'Particle?' cried Fay. 'Oh, take no notice of him, Constable. He's always—'

'He's green,' said the constable accusingly.

'Well, yes,' admitted Fay. 'But only temporarily. You see—'

'All over, from what I could see,' he went on. 'From head to foot.'

'Here we are!' It was Bill. 'All in order, I think you'll find.'

The policeman took the documents, examined them with irritating slowness, and handed them back.

'Quite in order, sir. Sorry to have troubled you, but it's all part—'

'I know. Quite so. Perhaps I can see you out, if there's nothing else . . .?'

'There's just this other little matter that's arisen, sir.' The constable stood his ground. 'I'd just like to ask one or two questions, sir, if you don't mind. About the green child, sir.'

'Well?' said Bill.

'Well,' said the policeman. 'What about it, sir? I mean, why is the child green?'

'The child is green entirely by his own choice,' said Bill. 'He chooses to be green.'

'Temporarily,' put in Fay.

'I don't like it, sir,' said the policeman flatly. He looked about the room. Eve could tell that he was

already beginning to wonder if he was dreaming the whole thing, now that Particle had disappeared.

'As far as I know,' said Bill, 'there's no actual law about people being green. Is there?'

'Well, sir—'

'Or any other colour, as far as I know,' went on Bill. 'As far as I know, a citizen is entitled to adopt any colour he chooses, as long as in so doing he does not constitute a public nuisance. If, for instance, I were to turn bright blue and then go dancing in my bathing trunks on Waterloo Bridge, thereby creating a disturbance and bringing traffic to a halt, that, in my view, would constitute an offence. But as to going green, blue, ginger, or buff in the privacy of one's own home, then that's a very different matter indeed, Constable.'

It was at moments like this that Eve could see the advantages of having a scientific mind. The policeman looked distinctly shaken. Then he rallied.

'That's a matter that will have to be gone into, sir,' he said stiffly.

Then Particle returned with the cup and saucer. He grinned, and the flash of white teeth in his green face set the law again into a helpless boggle. Once or twice he opened his mouth as if he were going to say something to Particle, but was uncertain how to go about it, never having addressed a green person before.

'Will you have some tea, Sergeant?' inquired Fay sweetly.

'I shall not stop, thank you, madam,' said the policeman. He rose. 'I'll get along back to the station and make my report.'

'I should think the Inspector will enjoy that,' commented Bill.

'The Inspector will doubtless be calling himself, sir,' said the policeman. 'And the N.S.P.C.C. will have to be informed as well, I'm afraid.'

'The N.S.P.—' Bill stared. Then he and Fay broke into uncontrollable mirth.

'Oh dear!' gasped Fay, her eyes watering.

The constable, with a final outraged glare at their helplessly heaving shoulders, went out. Fay, wiping her eyes, hurried after him, but too late. The front door banged. The laughter stopped abruptly.

'That's done it,' said Bill. 'We shall have Particle's picture plastered over every colour supplement in England now.'

'You don't really think he'll come back, do you?' gurgled Fay. 'Oh, it was so comical. Did you—'

'Comical?' Bill was shouting again. 'Don't you realize what's happened? Don't you care? And what about Particle? Are you mad? Yes, you are!'

'There's no need to shout,' said Fay. 'If you hadn't let him in without warning us first this would never have happened. And now we shall have to do something I didn't want to do at all. Come along, Particle.'

'Oh, Fay,' said Particle. 'I've hardly even got used to the idea yet. Just let me—'

'Come along,' said Fay. He came. Bill and Eve were left staring after them.

'Now what?' muttered Bill. 'I'll go and get the car out.'

'What for?'

'To get Particle away. They'll probably take him away.'

'But why? Particle's just the same as he's always

been. He's just green, that's all. I think he's even beginning to enjoy it.'

'So do I,' said Bill grimly. 'I'll get the car.'

Then Fay and Particle came in. Particle was no longer green. The shock was stunning. He looked exactly the same as he always had and yet, for an instant, was a stranger. In that moment Eve felt a curious sense of flatness and disappointment. The vital touch of magic was gone. The room seemed to shrink and settle into itself again. Everything was back to normal. She shivered.

'And what happened?' inquired Bill finally.

'I took the spell away,' said Fay. 'I'm a witch myself, you know. Not a real witch, but descended from witches.'

'Witch?' croaked Bill.

'I know you don't believe in them,' Fay said, 'and if you like we'll forget all about what's happened and not mention it again. I wouldn't have told you if it hadn't been for the policeman. You see all those spells were twenty-four-hour ones—all the Northumberland Witch's are. Particle would have been as right as rain in the morning.'

Particle was over by the mirror examining his face as if looking for any stray patches of green that might have been left. When he turned away Eve could see that he, too, was disappointed.

'We never even took those colour photos,' he said.

'You could try again, some time,' said Eve.

'It's no good. Fay said that was a chance in a million. You're supposed to be a seventh child of a seventh child, and I'm only the second. Fay says that the law of heredity—'

'Ah!' Bill's face brightened. 'Heredity. Now as I see it, what happened was this, Fay herself, being the seventh child of a—'

'Sixth,' said Fay.

'Pardon?'

'Sixth child of a seventh child,' said Fay. 'I told you, I'm not a real witch, any more than Particle is. We just have our moments.'

She and Particle exchanged smug glances. Bill said, 'I'm going to make some more tea.'

They all followed him into the kitchen.

'Aaah!' Bill let out a long breath and looked around him with relief. He was on home territory. He fiddled with his dials for a long time, grateful for something that he could understand.

'You know,' he said then, 'it's obvious now what happened today.'

'Oh?' said Fay.

'Yes. Mass hysteria. It's a well known phenomenon. You see, Eve, knowing that Particle had a book on witchcraft, subconsciously—'

The front doorbell rang.

'I think that this,' said Fay, 'will be the police. And the N.S.P.C.C. And the reporters.'

Then Bill said, 'I think Particle had better answer the door, don't you?'

The Bensons looked at each other with sudden glee. Eve thought fleetingly, 'Particle said witchcraft was an art and a science', and then they were all crowding into the hall to see the fun. Because tomorrow it was going to be difficult to believe that any of this had happened at all, and the day after, harder still . . .

ESCAPE TO THE EMERALD CITY

L. Frank Baum

ip's creation, Jack Pumpkinhead, has been brought to life by the wicked witch Mombi. Now, no longer in need of Tip's help, Mombi has threatened to turn him into a marble statue . . .

Tip reflected.

'It's a hard thing to be a marble statue,' he thought rebelliously, 'and I'm not going to stand it. For years I've been a bother to her, she says; so she's going to get rid of me. Well, there's an easier way than to become a statue. No boy could have any fun forever standing in the middle of a flower garden! I'll run away, that's what I'll do—and I may as well go before she makes me drink that nasty stuff in the kettle.'

He waited until the snores of the old witch announced she was fast asleep, and then he arose softly and went to the cupboard to find something to eat.

'No use starting on a journey without food,' he decided, searching upon the narrow shelves.

He found some crusts of bread, but he had to look into Mombi's basket to find the cheese she had brought from the village. While turning over the contents of the basket he came upon the pepper-box which contained the Powder of Life.

'I may as well take this with me,' he thought, 'or Mombi'll be using it to make more mischief with.' So he put the box in his pocket, together with the bread and cheese.

Then he cautiously left the house and latched the door behind him. Outside both moon and stars shone brightly, and the night seemed peaceful and inviting after the close and ill-smelling kitchen.

'I'll be glad to get away,' said Tip softly, 'for I never did like that old woman. I wonder how I ever came to live with her.'

He was walking slowly towards the road when a thought made him pause.

'I don't like to leave Jack Pumpkinhead to the tender mercies of old Mombi,' he muttered. 'And Jack belongs to me, for I made him—even if the old witch did bring him to life.'

He retraced his steps to the cow-stable and opened the door of the stall where the pumpkin-headed man had been left.

Jack was standing in the middle of the stall, and by the moonlight Tip could see he was smiling just as jovially as ever.

'Come on!' said the boy, beckoning.

'Where to?' asked Jack.

'You'll know as soon as I do,' answered Tip, smiling sympathetically into the pumpkin face. 'All we've got to do now is to tramp.'

'Very well,' returned Jack, and walked awkwardly out of the stable and into the moonlight.

Tip turned towards the road and the man followed him. Jack walked with a sort of limp, and occasionally one of the joints of his legs would turn backwards, instead of frontwise, almost causing him to tumble. But the Pumpkinhead was quick to notice this, and began to take more pains to step carefully, so that he met with few accidents.

Tip led him along the path without stopping an instant. They could not go very fast, but they walked steadily; and by the time the moon sank away and the sun peeped over the hills they had travelled so great a distance that the boy had no reason to fear pursuit from the old witch. Moreover he had turned first into one path, and then into another, so that should any-one follow them it would prove very difficult to guess which way they had gone, or where to seek them.

Fairly satisfied that he had escaped—for a time, at least—being turned into a marble statue, the boy stopped his companion and seated himself upon a rock by the roadside.

'Let's have some breakfast,' he said.

Jack Pumpkinhead watched Tip curiously, but refused to join in the repast.

'I don't seem to be made the same way you are,' he said.

'I know you are not,' returned Tip; 'for I made you.'

'Oh! Did you?' asked Jack.

'Certainly. And put you together. And carved your eyes and nose and ears and mouth,' said Tip proudly. 'And dressed you.'

Jack looked at his body and limbs critically.

'It strikes me you made a very good job of it,' he remarked.

'Just so-so,' replied Tip modestly, for he began to see certain defects in the construction of his man. 'If I'd known we were going to travel together I might have been a little more particular.'

'Why, then,' said the Pumpkinhead, in a tone that expressed surprise, 'you must be my creator—my parent—my father!'

'Or your inventor,' replied the boy with a laugh. 'Yes, my son; I really believe I am!'

'Then I owe you obedience,' continued the man, 'and you owe me—support.'

'That's it exactly,' declared Tip, jumping up. 'So let us be off.'

'Where are we going?' asked Jack when they had resumed their journey.

'I'm not exactly sure,' said the boy; 'but I believe we are headed South, and that will bring us, sooner or later, to the Emerald City.'

'What city is that?' inquired the Pumpkinhead.

'Why, it's the centre of the Land of Oz, and the biggest town in all the country. I've never been there myself, but I've heard all about its history. It was built by a mighty and wonderful wizard named Oz, and everything there is of a green colour—just as everything in this Country of the Gillikins is of a purple colour.'

'Is everything here purple?' asked Jack.

'Of course it is. Can't you see?' returned the boy.

'I believe I must be colour-blind,' said the Pumpkinhead, after staring about him.

'Well, the grass is purple, and the trees are purple, and the houses and fences are purple,' explained Tip. 'Even the mud in the roads is purple. But in the Emerald City everything is green that is purple here. And in the Country of the Munchkins, over at the East, everything is blue; and in the South country of the Quadlings everything is red; and in the West country of the Winkies, where the Tin Woodman rules, everything is yellow.'

'Oh!' said Jack. Then, after a pause, he asked: 'Did you say a Tin Woodman rules the Winkies?'

'Yes; he was one of those who helped Dorothy to destroy the Wicked Witch of the West, and the Winkies were so grateful that they invited him to become their ruler—just as the people of the Emerald City invited the Scarecrow to rule them.'

'Dear me!' said Jack. 'I'm getting confused with all this history. Who is the Scarecrow?'

'Another friend of Dorothy's,' replied Tip.

'And who is Dorothy?'

'She was a girl that came here from Kansas, a place in the big, outside World. She got blown to the Land of Oz by a cyclone, and while she was here the Scarecrow and the Tin Woodman accompanied her on her travels.'

'And where is she now?' inquired the Pumpkinhead.

'Glinda the Good, who rules the Quadlings, sent her home again,' said the boy.

'Oh. And what became of the Scarecrow?'

'I told you. He rules the Emerald City,' answered Tip.

'I thought you said it was ruled by a wonderful wizard,' objected Jack, seeming more and more confused.

'Well, so I did. Now, pay attention, and I'll explain it,' said Tip, speaking slowly and looking the smiling Pumpkinhead squarely in the eye. 'Dorothy went to the Emerald City to ask the Wizard to send her back to Kansas; and the Scarecrow and the Tin Woodman went with her. But the Wizard couldn't send her back, because he wasn't so much of a wizard as he might have been. And then they got angry at the Wizard, and threatened to expose him; so the Wizard made a big balloon and escaped in it, and no one has ever seen him since.'

'Now, that is very interesting history,' said Jack, well pleased; 'and I understand it perfectly—all but the explanation.'

'I'm glad you do,' responded Tip. 'After the Wizard was gone, the people of the Emerald City made His Majesty, the Scarecrow, their King; and I have heard that he became a very popular ruler.'

'Are we going to see this queer King?' asked Jack, with interest.

'I think we may as well,' replied the boy, 'unless you have something better to do.'

'Oh no, dear father,' said the Pumpkinhead. 'I am quite willing to go wherever you please.'

*

The boy, small and rather delicate in appearance,

seemed somewhat embarrassed at being called 'father' by the tall, awkward, pumpkin-headed man, but to deny the relationship would involve another long and tedious explanation; so he changed the subject by asking, abruptly:

'Are you tired?'

'Of course not!' replied the other. 'But,' he continued, after a pause, 'it is quite certain I shall wear out my wooden joints if I keep on walking.'

Tip reflected, as they journeyed on, that this was true. He began to regret that he had not constructed the wooden limbs more carefully and substantially. Yet how could he ever have guessed that the man he had made merely to scare old Mombi with would be brought to life by means of a magical powder contained in an old pepper-box?

So he ceased to reproach himself, and began to think how he might yet remedy the deficiencies of Jack's weak joints.

While thus engaged they came to the edge of a wood, and the boy sat down to rest upon an old saw-horse that some woodcutter had left there.

'Why don't you sit down?' he asked the Pumpkin-head.

'Won't it strain my joints?' inquired the other.

'Of course not. It'll rest them,' declared the boy.

So Jack tried to sit down, but as soon as he bent his joints farther than usual they gave way altogether, and he came clattering to the ground with such a crash that Tip feared he was entirely ruined.

He rushed to the man, lifted him to his feet, straightened his arms and legs, and felt his head to see if by chance it had become cracked. But Jack seemed to be in pretty good shape, after all, and Tip said to him:

'I guess you'd better remain standing hereafter. It seems the safest way.'

'Very well, dear father, just as you say,' replied the

smiling Jack, who had been in no wise confused by his tumble.

Tip sat down again. Presently the Pumpkinhead asked: 'What is that thing you are sitting on?'

'Oh, this is a horse,' replied the boy, carelessly.

'What is a horse?' demanded Jack.

'A horse? Why, there are two kinds of horses,' returned Tip, slightly puzzled how to explain. 'One kind of horse is alive, and has four legs and a head and a tail. And people ride upon its back.'

'I understand,' said Jack, cheerfully. 'That's the kind of horse you are now sitting on.'

'No it isn't,' answered Tip promptly.

'Why not? That one has four legs and a head and a tail.'

Tip looked at the saw-horse more carefully, and found that the Pumpkinhead was right. The body had been formed from a tree trunk, and a branch had been left sticking up at one end that looked very much like a tail. In the other end were two big knots that resembled eyes, and a place had been chopped away that might easily be mistaken for the horse's mouth. As for the legs, they were four straight limbs cut from trees and stuck fast into the body, being spread wide apart so that the saw-horse would stand firmly when a log was laid across it to be sawed.

'This thing resembles a real horse more than I imagined,' said Tip, trying to explain. 'But a real horse is alive, and trots and prances and eats oats, while this is nothing more than a dead horse, made of wood, and used to saw logs upon.'

'If it were alive, wouldn't it trot, and prance, and eat oats?' inquired the Pumpkinhead.

'It would trot and prance, perhaps; but it wouldn't eat oats,' replied the boy, laughing at the idea. 'And of course it can't ever be alive, because it is made of wood.'

'So am I,' answered the man.

Tip looked at him in surprise.

'Why, so you are!' he exclaimed. 'And the magic powder that brought you to life is here in my pocket.'

He brought out the pepper-box, and eyed it curiously.

'I wonder,' said he musingly, 'if it would bring the saw-horse to life.'

'If it would,' returned Jack calmly—for nothing seemed to surprise him—'I could ride on its back, and that would save my joints from wearing out.'

'I'll try it!' cried the boy, jumping up. 'But I wonder if I can remember the words old Mombi said, and the way she held her hands up.'

He thought it over for a minute, and as he had watched carefully from the hedge every motion of the old witch, and listened to her words, he believed he could repeat exactly what she had said and done.

So he began by sprinkling some of the magic Powder of Life from the pepper-box upon the body of the saw-horse. Then he lifted his left hand, with the little finger pointing upwards, and said: 'Weaugh!'

'What does that mean, dear father?' asked Jack, curiously.

'I don't know,' answered Tip. Then he lifted his right hand, with the thumb pointing upwards, and said: 'Teaugh!'

'What's that, dear father?' inquired Jack.

'It means you must keep quiet!' replied the boy, provoked at being interrupted at so important a moment.

'How fast I am learning!' remarked the Pumpkin-head, with his eternal smile.

Tip now lifted both hands above his head, with all the fingers and thumbs spread out, and cried in a loud voice: 'Peaugh!'

Immediately the saw-horse moved, stretched its legs, yawned with its chopped-out mouth, and shook a few grains of the powder off its back. The rest of the powder seemed to have vanished into the body of the horse.

'Good!' called Jack, while the boy looked on in astonishment. 'You are a very clever sorcerer, dear father!'

*

The Saw-Horse, finding himself alive, seemed even more astonished than Tip. He rolled his knotty eyes from side to side, taking a first wondering view of the world in which he had now so important an existence. Then he tried to look at himself; but he had, indeed, no neck to turn, so that in the endeavour to see his body he kept circling around and around without catching even a glimpse of it. His legs were stiff and awkward, for there were no knee-joints in them; so that presently he bumped against Jack Pumpkinhead and sent that personage tumbling upon the moss that lined the roadside.

Tip became alarmed at this accident, as well as at the

persistence of the Saw-Horse in prancing around in a
circle; so he called out:

'Whoa! Whoa, there!'

The Saw-Horse paid no attention whatever to this
command, and the next instant brought one of his
wooden legs down upon Tip's foot so forcibly that the
boy danced away in pain to a safer distance, from
where he again yelled:

'Whoa! Whoa, I say!'

Jack had now managed to raise himself to a sitting
position, and he looked at the Saw-Horse with much
interest.

'I don't believe the animal can hear you,' he
remarked.

'I shout loud enough, don't I?' answered Tip
angrily.

'Yes, but the horse has no ears,' said the smiling
Pumpkinhead.

'Sure enough!' exclaimed Tip, noting the fact for the
first time. 'How, then, am I going to stop him?'

But at that instant the Saw-Horse stopped himself,
having concluded it was impossible to see his own
body. He saw Tip, however, and came close to the boy
to observe him more fully.

It was really comical to see the creature walk; for it
moved the legs on its right side together, and those on
its left side together, as a pacing horse does; and that
made its body rock sidewise, like a cradle.

Tip patted it upon the head, and said, 'Good boy!
Good boy!' in a coaxing tone; and the Saw-Horse
pranced away to examine with its bulging eyes the
form of Jack Pumpkinhead.

'I must find a halter for him,' said Tip; and having
made a search in his pocket he produced a roll of
strong cord. Unwinding this, he approached the
Saw-Horse and tied the cord around its neck, afterwards fastening the other end to a large tree. The
Saw-Horse, not understanding the action, stepped

backwards and snapped the string easily; but it made no attempt to run away.

'He's stronger than I thought,' said the boy, 'and rather obstinate too.'

'Why don't you make him some ears?' asked Jack. 'Then you can tell him what to do.'

'That's a splendid idea!' said Tip. 'How did you happen to think of it?'

'Why, I didn't think of it,' answered the Pumpkin-head; 'I didn't need to, for it's the simplest and easiest thing to do.'

So Tip got out his knife and fashioned some ears out of the bark of a small tree.

'I mustn't make them too big,' he said as he whittled, 'or our horse would become a donkey.'

'How is that?' inquired Jack from the roadside.

'Why, a horse has bigger ears than a man; and a donkey has bigger ears than a horse,' explained Tip.

'Then, if my ears were longer, would I be a horse?' asked Jack.

'My friend,' said Tip gravely, 'you'll never be anything but a Pumpkinhead, no matter how big your ears are.'

'Oh,' returned Jack, nodding; 'I think I understand.'

'If you do, you're a wonder,' remarked the boy, 'but there's no harm in *thinking* you understand. I guess these ears are ready now. Will you hold the horse while I stick them on?'

'Certainly, if you'll help me up,' said Jack.

So Tip raised him to his feet, and the Pumpkinhead went to the horse and held its head while the boy bored two holes in it with his knife-blade and inserted the ears.

'They make him look very handsome,' said Jack admiringly.

But those words, spoken close to the Saw-Horse, and being the first sounds he had ever heard, so

startled the animal that he made a bound forward and tumbled Tip on one side and Jack on the other. Then he continued to rush forward as if frightened by the clatter of his own footsteps.

'Whoa!' shouted Tip, picking himself up. 'Whoa! you idiot—whoa!'

The Saw-Horse would probably have paid no attention to this, but just then it stepped a leg into a gopher-hole and stumbled head over heels to the ground, where it lay upon its back frantically waving its four legs in the air.

Tip ran up to it.

'You're a nice sort of a horse, I must say!' he exclaimed. 'Why didn't you stop when I yelled "whoa"?'

'Does "whoa" mean to stop?' asked the Saw-Horse in a surprised voice as it rolled its eyes upwards to look at the boy.

'Of course it does,' answered Tip.

'And a hole in the ground means to stop also, doesn't it?' continued the horse.

'To be sure; unless you step over it,' said Tip.

'What a strange place this is,' the creature exclaimed as if amazed. 'What am I doing here, anyway?'

'Why, I've brought you to life,' answered the boy, 'but it won't hurt you if you mind me and do as I tell you.'

'Then I will do as you tell me,' replied the Saw-Horse humbly. 'But what happened to me a moment ago? I don't seem to be just right, someway.'

'You're upside-down,' explained Tip. 'But just keep those legs still a minute and I'll set you right side up again.'

'How many sides have I?' asked the creature wonderingly.

'Several,' said Tip briefly. 'But do keep those legs still.'

The Saw-Horse now became quiet, and held its legs

rigid, so that Tip, after several efforts, was able to roll him over and set him upright.

'Ah, I seem all right now,' said the queer animal with a sigh.

'One of your ears is broken,' Tip announced after a careful examination. 'I'll have to make a new one.'

Then he led the Saw-Horse back to where Jack was vainly struggling to regain his feet, and after assisting the Pumpkinhead to stand upright Tip whittled out a new ear and fastened it to the horse's head.

'Now,' said he, addressing his steed, 'pay attention to what I'm going to tell you. "Whoa!" means to stop; "Get-up!" means to walk forward; "Trot!" means to go as fast as you can. Understand?'

'I believe I do,' returned the horse.

'Very good. We are all going on a journey to the Emerald City to see His Majesty, the Scarecrow; and Jack Pumpkinhead is going to ride on your back, so he won't wear out his joints.'

'I don't mind,' said the Saw-Horse. 'Anything that suits you suits me.'

Then Tip assisted Jack to get upon the horse.

'Hold on tight,' he cautioned, 'or you may fall off and crack your pumpkin head.'

'That would be horrible!' said Jack with a shudder. 'What shall I hold on to?'

'Why, hold on to his ears,' replied Tip after a moment's hesitation.

'Don't do that!' remonstrated the Saw-Horse; 'for then I can't hear.'

That seemed reasonable, so Tip tried to think of something else.

'I'll fix it!' said he, at length. He went into the wood and cut a short length of limb from a young, stout tree. One end of this he sharpened to a point, and then he dug a hole in the back of the Saw-Horse, just behind its head. Next he brought a piece of rock from the road and hammered the post firmly into the animal's back.

'Stop! Stop!' shouted the horse. 'You're jarring me terribly.'

'Does it hurt?' asked the boy.

'Not exactly hurt,' answered the animal; 'but it makes me quite nervous to be jarred.'

'Well, it's all over now,' said Tip encouragingly. 'Now, Jack, be sure to hold fast to this post, and then you can't fall off and get smashed.'

So Jack held on tight, and Tip said to the horse: 'Get-up.'

The obedient creature at once walked forward, rocking from side to side as he raised his feet from the ground.

Tip walked beside the Saw-Horse, quite content with this addition to their party. Presently he began to whistle.

'What does that sound mean?' asked the horse.

'Don't pay any attention to it,' said Tip. 'I'm just whistling, and that only means I'm pretty well satisfied.'

'I'd whistle myself, if I could push my lips together,' remarked Jack. 'I fear, dear father, that in some respects I am sadly lacking.'

After journeying on for some distance the narrow path they were following turned into a broad roadway, paved with yellow brick. By the side of the road Tip noticed a sign-post that read:

NINE MILES TO THE EMERALD CITY

But it was now growing dark, so he decided to camp for the night by the roadside and to resume the journey next morning at daybreak. He led the Saw-Horse to a grassy mound upon which grew several bushy trees, and carefully assisted the Pumpkinhead to alight.

'I think I'll lay you upon the ground overnight,' said the boy. 'You will be safer that way.'

'How about me?' asked the Saw-Horse.

'It won't hurt you to stand,' replied Tip; 'and as you can't sleep, you may as well watch out and see that no one comes near to disturb us.'

Then the boy stretched himself upon the grass beside the Pumpkinhead, and being greatly wearied by the journey was soon fast asleep.

ACKNOWLEDGEMENTS

The publishers would like to extend their grateful thanks to the following authors, publishers and others for kindly granting permission to reproduce the extracts and stories included in this anthology:

THE TRUTH ABOUT PYECRAFT by H. G. Wells from *The Complete Short Stories of H. G. Wells*. Reprinted by permission of The Executors of the Estate of H. G. Wells.

WARRIORS IN THE MIST from *A Wizard of Earthsea* by Ursula Le Guin. Copyright © 1968 by Ursula K. Le Guin. Reprinted by permission of Houghton Mifflin Company.

DOCTOR DOLITTLE'S REWARD from *The Story of Doctor Dolittle* by Hugh Lofting. Copyright © Hugh Lofting, 1922.

THE WHITE-HAIRED CHILDREN from *The Phantom Cyclist and Other Stories* (1971) by Ruth Ainsworth. Copyright © 1971 by Ruth Ainsworth. Reprinted by permission of André Deutsch Ltd.

HARRIET'S HAIRLOOM from *A Small Pinch of Weather* by Joan Aiken. Copyright © 1959, 1962, 1964, 1966, 1968, 1969 by Joan Aiken. Reprinted by permission of Jonathan Cape Ltd and Brandt & Brandt Literary Agents, Inc.

THE WAY OUT from *The Borrowers Afloat* by Mary Norton. Copyright © Mary Norton, 1959. Reprinted by permission of J. M. Dent & Sons Ltd and Harcourt Brace Jovanovich, Inc.

RIDDLES IN THE DARK from *The Hobbit* by J. R. R. Tolkien. Reprinted by permission of George Allen & Unwin and Houghton Mifflin Company.

THE PHANTOM TOLLBOOTH from *The Phantom Tollbooth* by Norton Juster. Copyright © 1961 by Norton Juster. Reprinted by permission of Collins Publishers and Random House, Inc.

THE WIND ON THE MOON from *The Wind on the Moon* by Eric Linklater. Reprinted by permission of A. D. Peters & Co Ltd.